"How can you defend the man who murdered my wife?"

"Michael, you never told me the name of the person who caused the accident. I never knew…"

"Claire, I—" Michael hesitated, then turned to look at her. "I love you. I think I could handle anything you wanted to do, support you in any venture, but not this. Do you know that after two years I'm still running an ad in the paper looking for witnesses to help me put Senator Beske behind bars?"

Claire stood very still. "I love you, too, Michael," she said. "But when I became a lawyer I took an oath to represent my clients to the best of my ability. I like to think of myself as an honest person, a person with self-respect, and I've given my word to Senator Beske."

"Then I think you'd better ask someone else to supervise you on this case." Although he hadn't raised his voice, his anger was so real, Claire imagined she could feel it on her skin. "And I want you to keep your distance. Unless it's necessary for firm business, I don't want to see you anymore…

"Ever!"

ABOUT THE AUTHOR

Firm Commitment, Linda Markowiak's second Superromance novel, was a real labor of love. The author enjoyed incorporating aspects of her husband's Polish-American culture. "I'm always moved by stories of immigrants," says Linda. "People of energy and courage and dreams who give up everything familiar to come to a new land."

Linda and her husband, Jim, operate a commercial greenhouse on their farm in Michigan. In addition to writing romance novels, Linda is a part-time lawyer and a full-time mother to eight-year-old Stephen.

Books by Linda Markowiak

HARLEQUIN SUPERROMANCE
629—COURTING VALERIE

Linda Markowiak
FIRM COMMITMENT

Harlequin Books

TORONTO • NEW YORK • LONDON
AMSTERDAM • PARIS • SYDNEY • HAMBURG
STOCKHOLM • ATHENS • TOKYO • MILAN
MADRID • WARSAW • BUDAPEST • AUCKLAND

ISBN 0-373-70717-7

FIRM COMMITMENT

This edition published by arrangement with Harlequin Books S.A.

® and TM are trademarks of the publisher. Trademarks indicated with
® are registered in the United States Patent and Trademark Office, the
Canadian Trade Marks Office and in other countries.

Printed in U.S.A.

For Buzzie, Lori and Tony, critique partners and
friends—you guys are great.
And for Zilla, who told me to just keep writing...
and not look back.

PROLOGUE

April 1994

MICHAEL CHALINSKI'S throat was dust-dry. It felt so thick and closed that even swallowing was difficult. This, he was learning, was one of the symptoms of anguish. He reached for his eleven-year-old daughter's hand.

His wife's casket—hurriedly chosen—was closed and rested on the damp ground.

Father John intoned a prayer, and Michael tried to concentrate on the words. The prayer was in English. Mary Jo had never liked the English mass; both she and Michael had been raised on the Latin. And he had tried so hard to make everything perfect—his second-to-last act for his beloved wife. How could he have forgotten to ask Father John to say the prayer in Latin?

By his side, Angela pulled her hand from his and gazed forward.

Michael looked down at the top of her wheat-blond head, then out over the large group of mourners. As a public defender, he was acquainted with a lot of people, and they had come to show their support. He saw that five feet away his father wept a little, and his mother's mouth was drawn in a tight line. Mary Jo's two brothers were somewhere over there, to his left, standing ramrod-straight. Michael smelled the pungency that a recent rain had left in the earth, earth that would soon take his wife.

He'd known Mary Jo since they had sat next to each other in the second grade at Saint Stephen's Parochial, and she'd been his wife for almost thirteen years.

Now his life was utterly changed, all because of a drunk driver, and one of those accidents you read about that you are secretly, smugly convinced would never happen to you or your family—not to you who had a promising career, and a wife you loved, who had given you a daughter and who, in a few months, would give you another child.

Michael bit the inside of his cheek, hard, and stared across the cemetery beyond the casket, beyond the thirty-three candy-pink roses that adorned it, one for each year Mary Jo had lived. He stared beyond the priest, beyond the first tier of mourners, until his eye caught that of Rex Caspar.

Look at me, Michael silently commanded. *Look at me and tell me again that you won't prosecute the son of a bitch who killed my wife.*

"There's nothing I can do." Rex's voice had been weary over the phone, low-pitched. "The cops never even gave him the breath test."

"Ryan West thinks he might have smelled alcohol on Beske's breath, and Ryan is a cop. His testimony would be good. And half the south side knows Beske drinks." Lawyer to the core, Michael's instincts had taken over for the moment. He knew how to set up a case. As deputy prosecuting attorney, Rex knew how, too. And Rex had been more than a colleague these last five years. He'd been a friend.

"He's a state senator, and a popular one at that. He's a big supporter of the police," Rex had said. "You know how it goes, Michael. I'm truly sorry about what happened to Mary Jo. It's a tragedy." Rex had let out his breath on a long sigh. "But the cops didn't do anything at the scene. The evidence would all be circumstantial. My chief won't take it. Believe me, I went to bat for you." There was a pause. "It wouldn't bring her back anyway, would it, Michael?"

"Find some eyewitnesses," Michael had snapped.

"There weren't any."

"Find some. Put together a case. It's your job!"

There had been silence on the other end of the line, and now, today at the cemetery, Rex looked away. This wasn't the end, Michael thought. Not by any means.

Michael's last conversation with Mary Jo had been his promise to bring Senator Beske to justice. He'd held his wife's hand and made a solemn vow to bring him to trial, and Mary Jo had whispered, "You do, that, Mikush. You do that." Today, Michael's classified ad would start running in the *Chicago Tribune:*

Reward. To anyone who witnessed the accident at Cavendish and Petrove on April 3rd, reward for your testimony. Call . . .

And Michael would keep pressing. He'd go to Rex's boss, go to the state attorney general if he had to. There would be justice for Mary Jo. He'd believed in justice all his life, tried to carry it out at the public defender's office. Now he needed some for Mary Jo, and for his daughter, and for the child who'd never had a chance to live. And for anyone else who might be driving in the path of Senator Beske.

He looked down at Angela, then oblivious to the other mourners, oblivious to the protocol of the traditional service, he squatted. "Come here, Angel," he whispered. She let him put his arm around her, but she remained stiff, unyielding in his embrace. "I want...Mom," she whispered. "I'm scared, and I want my mom."

"So do I, baby, so do I." His voice was thick. It was hard to breathe, much less whisper. Angela smelled of Tinkerbell soap, a little-girl scent that reminded him that he and Angela were on their own now. For the thousandth time since his wife was killed five days ago, Michael wished he knew his daughter better.

Mary Jo had loved being a wife and mother. She'd done all the housework, cooking and child care. She'd loved to decorate, and plan little family celebrations. These parties were all her doing, executed with perfection, any of Michael's suggestions sweetly rebuffed. With Angela, too, from babyhood, Mary Jo had just seemed to know exactly what to do, how to soothe their daughter's colic, how to dress her, what would be good educational experiences. He'd appreciated Mary Jo's efforts, admired her ability to run a home so efficiently, loved her for her tenderness with Angela. But sometimes he would have liked to help plan a party, even clean up afterward as they talked things over. Sometimes he would have liked to tend Angela when she was sick, help pick out a preschool. There were so many times he had felt...superfluous. Sometimes he would have sworn Mary Jo resented his trying to spend time with Angela—

His mind turned abruptly from the thought.

He was wrong to think that. Mary Jo had been a wonderful mother and a good wife. No matter how long he lived, no matter how many years she was gone, he'd still love her.

The last prayer had been read, and the service was over. Father John handed the prayer book to Michael. "I've marked the passages I read today. There'll be long days ahead, and it might bring you comfort."

Michael took the book.

"Angela will want it someday." His father's voice was next to his ear, a deep baritone with the hard consonants of his native Polish.

"They're the words of God," his mother added. His mother had loved Mary Jo, but her eyes were dry. Sophie Chalinski did her mourning in private. "This is hard to understand, Michael. But the will of God sometimes is."

His parents stood beside him, silent now, but their presence was welcome. For them, he would always be grateful. Mary Jo was gone, but he still had his mother and father, people who had guided him, who believed in him and loved him.

His father reached out, putting a steady hand on Michael's arm. "You'll get Beske, Michael. This is America. You'll get justice for Mary Jo."

How like his father, Michael thought. Not only did Mike Chalinski have a deep, unwavering faith in the American system of justice, he also had a way of knowing exactly what Michael was thinking. Of all the people who had gathered on this day, he felt truly understood by only one of them—his immigrant father, the man who had fought the Nazis and the Communists and had fought for a place for his family in America.

"I made a promise to myself, Dad. I swore that there would be justice." Michael truly believed that someday Beske would go to jail. He had to believe it. He had to believe in something.

He must go on, not be paralyzed by grief. Angela needed him. He squatted again, searching for the right words. He used the finger of one hand to stroke his daughter's cheek. She didn't recoil, but she didn't respond, either. Michael held out his arms, but she didn't come into them.

"Angel, I'm going to make you a promise. I'm going to be a good dad to you, the best father in the whole world. I know I don't know much about what you like to do, and I've never played with Barbie, but—"

"I don't play with dolls anymore." Her lower lip trembled.

Michael paused. "Okay. We'll find new things to do together. It's going to take some time, but we'll be fine. We'll love each other."

She came into his arms, then, and he closed them around her. "I love you, Daddy."

"I love you, too, Angel. I love you, too."

CHAPTER ONE

October 1995

MICHAEL PROPPED the pizza box between his chest and the hallway wall of his high-rise condominium. He'd had to set down the giant-size bottle of Pepsi on the floor as he rummaged in his pocket for his keys. Angela loved Pepsi, so over the last year or so he'd gotten used to it himself.

When he finally managed to get the key in the lock, he opened the door to find the living room empty. As he stepped inside, the odor of burned cabbage hit him. Angela's "surprise" dinner for him had burned, thanks to his being late. The smell was like a kick in the teeth.

There were a lot of reasons he'd left the public defender's office for a position at the huge law firm of Haynes, Haynes, Collingwood and Crofts. But the bottom line was that he hadn't been able to stay on as a public defender after Mary Jo's death. He couldn't stand the wheeling and dealing with prosecutors anymore, the same prosecutors who hadn't had the courage to bring his wife's killer to justice. Unfortunately, ever since he'd made the move, he arrived home late more nights than not. Damn George Fanal, and his endless, pointless meetings, he thought with a spurt of resentment. He knew it was a privilege to attend George's meetings—a sure sign that Michael was on the fast track to partner. But just now he would have given anything to have not attended tonight's.

"Angel?" he called. There was no answer. He set the cardboard box on the French provincial table in the dining alcove and headed down the hall, tugging at his tie as he went.

"Angel? Are you home?"

The door to her bedroom was closed. Of course. She could be found in her bedroom—with the door closed—just about all the time these days. Angel still mourned her mother. They both did, but nowadays it seemed as if sorrow was their only bond. For a while, he'd thought he was getting to know his daughter, but these last few months had been like living with a new person. Angela had just turned thirteen. He'd heard teenagers were difficult, but was it supposed to be this hard, this soon? He knocked.

"What do you want?" The voice that had been tearful when he'd taken her call at the office a short while ago, now sounded defiant. "I'm talking on the phone in here, Dad."

"Tell Sabrina you'll call her back." Michael didn't have to ask who she was on the telephone with. His daughter and Sabrina talked for hours every day. Michael thought Sabrina was too sophisticated, and condescending toward Angela. But Angela had had difficulty making friends in the private school she attended, now that her old parish school had closed. "I want to talk to you, Angel."

"Now? You mean, right now?"

"It won't take long."

Through the closed door, he could hear Angela on the phone. "I'll call you back in a minute. It's just my dad, and he wants to say he's sorry, like always."

Michael balled his hands into fists. She was right—he was sorry, he was "always sorry." Couldn't she cut him a little slack, though? He hadn't wanted to go to the meeting; it was a command performance, and it was his job.

She threw open the door and stood there, glaring at him. Her school clothes were rumpled, the ruffle around her neck mashed down on one side. She'd undone the braid that usually hung down her back. Her curly hair was in wild disarray around her face. Behind her, Michael saw that her stuffed animals were strewn over the floor. The tops of the white wicker furniture Mary Jo had purchased the year before her death were full of school papers, books, fluorescent-colored markers and CDs. The room was a mess, as usual.

"I brought dinner, Angel."

"I *made* dinner. *Golombki* with sour cream. Your favorite."

Michael felt a fresh stab of guilt. She'd been on the telephone in hushed conference with his mother several times this week, discussing the recipe for stuffed cabbage. Michael had pretended he didn't know what she was making, and he'd promised her to be home early tonight. "I tried to be home on time," he told her. "I thought I'd show my face at the meeting, then slip out. But my partner had me do a rundown on the cases. I went as fast as I could, Angel."

"Not fast enough."

She gave no quarter, this daughter of his, and although in her younger years she had reminded him of Mary Jo, with her soft, feminine ways, now she displayed herself as very much Michael Chalinski's daughter.

"What do you want me to say, honey? You're always telling me you're not a little girl anymore. So, I'm trying to treat you as an adult, and explain. You know my job is important. I've told you this year is critical. If I make partner, I'll have better hours and financial security. It's not just you I worry about, it's your *busia,* and *dzia dzia,* too, now that he's had his stroke—" Michael stopped. It wasn't fair to burden Angela with his worries, he realized, but he would like a smidgen of understanding from her.

He could see he wasn't going to get it, not tonight. Her blue eyes shifted, and she half turned. Michael imagined she was looking longingly at her precious telephone, a gift from Michael on her thirteenth birthday.

He couldn't think of much more to say. He never knew what to say. Finally, he gave up. "Come on and eat. I've got Pepsi."

"Diet?"

He shook his head.

"I'm so fat, Dad. How could you have brought home *regular* Pepsi?"

"Angel, you're slender, just like your mom was. And I'm not sure a thirteen-year-old girl should diet." Her expression was mutinous. He'd managed to make her even more angry. He made one last try. "Okay, we won't talk about work, or your dieting. Just come on out and eat." He was dead-tired. All he wanted was to put on his sweats, sit down with his daughter to dinner and act like a family.

"I've got to call Sabrina back."

"Well, come out when you're done with your phone call. I'll put the pizza in the oven to keep warm."

Her eyes narrowed, and too late, Michael remembered the burned *golombki.* Before he could correct his mistake, she slammed the door in his face.

Michael had had enough. Angela talked on the telephone instead of to him. Her room was a wreck, and she had just slammed the door. She did that at least twice a week. His hand was on the knob, his mouth open to demand she come out. He might have been the one in the wrong tonight, initially, but he didn't appreciate her lack of respect. He'd never have been disrespectful with his own parents. They would never have let him say the kinds of things Angela got away with.

"Daddy?" His daughter's voice had softened, lowered. "Are you there?"

His hand stilled. "Yes."

"I just wanted to say... Happy birthday, Daddy."

His throat thickened. "Thank you, Angel."

If he'd hoped that the softening he heard in her voice was in preparation to her coming out of her room, he was wrong. Michael waited for a moment more, until he heard the beeps signaling she was using the telephone, then he headed back down the hall.

Happy Birthday. Happy thirty-fifth birthday. He hadn't been happy for a year and a half. These days, he wasn't even aiming for "happy." Now he wanted only three things out of life: to be a real father to Angela, to make partner at Haynes, Haynes, Collingwood and Crofts and to see Senator Beske go to jail.

In the kitchen, he poured himself a glass of Pepsi, hoping the sugar would give him some energy. He put a slice of pizza on a paper plate and stuck the rest of the pizza into the oven on low. Given the lingering smell of cabbage, he half expected to see the pan of burned *golombki* still in the oven, but Angela must have got rid of it.

A couple of minutes later, he carried his plate, Pepsi and pizza to the living room. Then he settled himself into

the only comfortable chair in the house, his worn recliner, and hit the remote to start the compact disc player.
The sound of soft jazz filled the room.

God, what a day. There was Angela and the burned
birthday dinner. At work today, he'd had no end of
problems, including a crisis on a case that was set for trial
in three days. And just as he was leaving to come home,
he'd also had a run-in with—of all people—Claire Logan.

ACROSS TOWN in her own apartment, Claire Logan sank
lower into the warmth of her bubble bath, rehashing the
day's events. Earlier, she had stood in the coffee area of
the Real Estate Department of Haynes, Haynes, Collingwood and Crofts, and told herself that she could handle
gossip. After all, gossip was part of life as a big-firm lawyer, and by now she should be used to it.

But it hurt. Mostly because transferring to the Litigation Department, headed by Michael Chalinski, had been
her dream for some time now.

Her first months at Haynes, Haynes, Collingwood and
Crofts had been rough, before she'd won that victory for
Edward Halmeyer, a small-businessman who had been
denied a building permit, against the whole Chicago
housing bureaucracy. And it had been especially rough
because nothing about her small-town life, or even her
work for a federal judge, had prepared her for the hassles
of the city or the work schedule of an associate at a huge
law firm. That schedule didn't leave much time for making new friends.

The only real friend she'd made in Chicago was Michael Chalinski. Correction. He was the friend she had
thought she'd made. One night, the first of many she'd
spent in the firm's library searching for a way to **win the**

Halmeyer case, she'd recognized Michael as a senior in Litigation, and introduced herself. Then she'd asked him whether he knew anything about the Chicago housing bureaucracy.

He'd closed his book and questioned her about her case. Claire outlined the facts, then said, "Halmeyer never even got a hearing. Nobody thinks I can win this case, but I'm going to."

She braced herself for a cynical comment. Most of the lawyers at the firm thought she was a fool to work so hard on a case that her own senior, Larry Oliver, had declared was unwinnable. But Michael's hazel eyes had lit with a wry, almost reluctant amusement that didn't feel like a put-down. "An attitude like that can be a help."

"An attitude is all I've got right now," she admitted. "I've been going through the whole city legal code. Somewhere in all those laws, I ought to come up with something. Actually, I'm not sure exactly what I *am* looking for."

"There are several thousand pages to the code," he reminded her.

"Have you got a better idea?"

Michael frowned. "Not really. I've found the best way to deal with bureaucrats is to find some of their own law to turn back on them. They love regulations, so if you can quote some, you've got it made."

The next night, she was back in the library, and so was he.

"Here, I'll help you," he'd said. Next to her, he reached out and plucked a thick book from the shelves. The glaring fluorescent lights lit his dark blond hair, highlighted his cheekbones, picked out the barest stubble of golden beard.

Lord, he was so good-looking. Tonight, his nearness seemed to make her heart pump harder than normal. And it warmed her to know he'd taken an interest in her case.

For several nights, he helped her with the Halmeyer case. When they'd discuss it, even argue about it, Claire found herself energized by his intellect. He challenged her to defend her theories. After two weeks, when she thought she might have to end her search—and her chance to be with Michael—she'd thanked him for all the time he'd spent with her. "Now I know why all your associates give you that heroworship."

To her surprise, he'd colored a little at the remark. Michael was not shy. So why...?

Could it be, Claire had wondered, that he spent so much time with her because he was as attracted to her as she was to him. Sometimes, she caught him looking at her, studying her with an intensity that left her breathless. At those times, when her gaze met his, he looked away immediately.

On the sixteenth night, she found what she was looking for. An obscure subsection that showed the housing authorities had forgotten to give her client a particular document.

Claire won the case. Halmeyer would get his building permit.

"We won!" Michael had been late coming to the library the night she'd found out. She stood to emphasize her words.

"Congratulations, Claire." Next to her, he shrugged out of his suit coat and plunked down his briefcase. He was so close, she could see the little flecks of green in his eyes. The man had sinfully beautiful eyes, whether he was concentrating intensely, as he was most of the time, or whether he had the sad, wistful expression she sometimes noticed. His words of congratulation were quieter than her own. Michael was quieter than she was. Heck, most people were. But she was so sure she saw admiration in his gaze, and maybe something more, something that sent a swift rise of heat to her cheeks.

"You've helped me so much, Michael. Will you let me buy you dinner?"

As soon as the words were out of her mouth, his whole face closed. The light went out of his eyes. "You don't owe me a thing. I helped you because..." There was a pause. "Because you asked me to. That's all."

Claire persisted. "Well, if not dinner, then how about coffee? There's that place on State Street. Their amaretto cream is delicious. We could go on Friday or Saturday night, whenever you don't have to work late."

Michael's jaw was firm, his body tense. He was obviously uncomfortable. He seemed remote, nothing like the man she'd thought she was coming to know. As long as they'd talked about law, he'd been friendly, animated. She'd obviously misread the signals, she decided. Claire had lousy instincts when it came to men, but with Michael she had really hoped she'd recognized genuine personal interest.

Although she was embarrassed, Claire looked straight at him. He avoided her gaze. "Claire, I'm sorry if I gave you the wrong impression. You're an interesting person. But I don't date."

"Oh, I see." Her cheeks flamed again. She hadn't asked a man out in years; only winning the Halmeyer case had propelled her to take the chance with Michael. Did he really not date, or didn't he want to date *her?* She knew he was a widower, but the gossip mill around the firm had always concentrated more on Michael's chances for partnership than on his love life.

There was an awkward pause, then he spoke again. "Look, I just stopped by to tell you I can't stay tonight." Michael picked up his coat jacket and shrugged back into it. "Congratulations again. You did great." He smiled, a small half smile. "Don't let that bastard Oliver or anyone else tell you differently."

Without a goodbye, he was gone.

The next night, he hadn't been in the library, nor the next. After three days, Claire knew for sure he'd found somewhere else to do his research. She felt . . . bereft. The depth of her reaction to Michael's absence was unsettling. She had fallen for the man, hard.

Then today, four months later, the sixth person to let her know that Michael didn't want her in Litigation had added a new, infuriating twist to the gossip. Claire could barely resist the urge to throw her coffee in Russ Mallory's smug face.

Russ was slowly adding cream to his own coffee and continuing, "So, the old man told Michael he'd have to take you, no matter what. Whether he liked it or not. I heard Michael tried to out and out refuse, and really ticked old George off."

"And you came down four floors from Litigation to tell me that?" she said tightly. "Or was your coffee area out of cream?" She brushed by him to empty the contents of her cup into the sink, glad to have something to do so that Russ wouldn't see the sudden, hot prick of tears in her eyes. Michael might not want to supervise her, but to go to his boss about it . . . that was way too much!

Her clinky bracelet with its rows of oversize charms caught on the buttonhole of her blazer, and she jerked it free.

"I thought you'd want to know, that's all," Russ said. "I was just thinking of you."

Oh, right, Claire thought. One of the seniors who loved to bait the newer lawyers, he'd told her because he wanted to see her reaction. If she wasn't careful, she'd be giving him exactly what he wanted. Instead, she forced a sweet smile. "You know, I've always thought highly of your work, Russ. If Michael doesn't want to supervise me, how about asking for me yourself? I wouldn't mind requesting a switch to you. And I'd be useful." Her mouth curled even farther, until she hoped her smile was brilliant. "Believe me, I can do research twelve hours a day."

"I'd ask for you, Claire, I really would, and I'm flattered that you'd want to come over to my half of Litigation." Russ pasted on a smile as false as her own must look. "But I've already got fifteen associates to supervise, plus my own caseload, and, well, I just wouldn't have time."

He left quickly. Claire's small sense of satisfaction vanished with his departure. Russ might have deliberately tried to get a rise out of her, with his smarmy smile and false concern for her feelings, but it was Michael Chalinski who deserved her anger. It was Michael who was responsible for the snag near the buttonhole of her new suit and the too-hot feel of her cheeks.

She went back to her office but there she continued to stew. As a junior associate, being poorly treated was a rite of passage in a big law firm, but Larry Oliver had been brutal. He'd dumped "emergency" work on her most Sunday mornings, and twice Oliver had criticized her work in front of a client. There wasn't a thing she could do about it, because to complain meant you weren't a good sport, a loyal colleague and an eager junior associate.

Larry Oliver had given her the Halmeyer case because no one thought there was a chance of victory. But when she'd won it, she'd gotten noticed, and Larry had been less than pleased when one of the partners, George Fanal, had sent her a pot of ivy. She'd been able to use his approval to engineer a transfer.

And now Michael didn't want her in Litigation, and the whole damn firm was making sure she knew it. Putting down her pen, she decided it was time to get something straight. She wasn't the starry-eyed new associate she'd been less than a year ago, fresh from the scholarly atmosphere of the federal court. Claire took the elevator up four floors to Litigation and marched down the hall.

His office door was open. Inside, Michael was stuffing papers into a briefcase.

"I hear you don't want me to work in Litigation. Why is that?" she asked without a greeting, without even clearing her throat so that he'd know she was in the doorway.

Michael looked up, and a split second of surprise was quickly masked. His face was strong-featured, his wide cheekbones hinting at a Slavic origin. His elegant dark suit played up the pure gold highlights in his hair.

Claire liked how he looked. She had *always* liked how he looked. That she still found him attractive, despite the fact that he had spurned her friendship only heightened her indignation.

The silence lasted a beat or two more. "I've heard it from six different people, so it must be true, ' she said. She remained by the door. And she had the sensation that he was deliberately not replying in order for her words to hang in the air.

"Is that how you judge the quality of gossip around here?" he asked. He glanced at a sheaf of papers in his hand, then stuffed them into his briefcase. "By the number of people who tell it to you?"

She put her hands on her hips. "Is it true?"

Finally, he had the good grace to look a little uncomfortable. Heck, he looked *very* uncomfortable. Then, straight out, he said, "Yes, it's true."

Claire hadn't realized until that second that she had come to his office hoping that he'd deny it. Well, he had been blunt, hurtfully so, but now she knew for sure where she stood.

"I see," she said tightly. "Let's get this all out in the open. You didn't want me, and Fanal told you that you have to take me." She kept her voice soft; she meant what she was about to say. "Well, Counselor, you got the best bargain of your life. I know a lot about law and I've had to learn to be tough. You should be glad I've decided on Litigation."

"Oh, hell." The words were quiet, sounding more self-reproachful than anything else. "Look, it's not your fault. But it *is* after hours, Claire, at least technically. And we're not going to talk about it tonight." He looked away quickly, raking a frustrated hand through his hair. "It's after seven, and I've been trying to get out of here for two hours."

"Only the partners get to keep reasonable hours," Claire noted. "And I know for a fact that you stay late."

She hadn't meant to evoke memories of those late-night talks in the library. He glanced at her again, with the oddest expression on his face. If she hadn't known better, she would have thought it was something like... longing. That was ridiculous. Even if he *was* remembering, he had made it clear he wasn't interested in her. And the way she'd embarrassed herself then certainly didn't help how she felt now. "I want you to tell me why you're trying to keep me from this transfer, Michael." She remained by the door. "You owe me that."

"I've got sixteen associates to supervise."

"Everybody works hard around here."

"Why don't you give it a rest, Claire? We're not going to talk about it right now." It was as if that brief, intense glance had never been. He snapped his briefcase shut and reached for his camel-hair topcoat. He was visibly wired. That was a switch. The Michael Chalinski she knew was always in control. When she'd first come up here, she'd been too intent on her mission to notice his agitation. Realizing it now took some of the sting from his words.

"Hey, are you okay?" she asked.

The telephone rang before he could respond. He pulled on his coat at the same time he stabbed at a button on the phone.

"It's all burned." A disembodied voice floated into the room. Michael must have pushed the speaker button. The voice was young, adolescent-sounding, and Claire heard a sob. "I kept it in the oven too long. You promised."

The hard lines of Michael's face immediately softened. Wearily, he ran a hand over his forehead. "Oh, God, I'm so sorry, Angel." He clicked off the speaker phone, then put the receiver to his ear. He turned his back to Claire.

She felt a quick jab of guilt. She had been so intent on having this discussion, she'd ignored his obvious need to leave. It sounded as if he'd had a legitimate reason to put her off.

Quietly, she turned to go.

Michael's voice was gentle, persuasive. "I'll bring home a pizza, with extra cheese and pepperoni. You can try making *golombki* some other time."

There was a pause. Then he said, "Well, maybe not tomorrow night. I've got a meeting at five-thirty."

Claire had reached the door, when she heard him say, "I love you, Angel. It's the thought that counts."

Claire slipped out the door. There had been an ache in Michael's voice, a deep, husky sound, and Claire had no doubt he loved Angel, whoever she was. His daughter? She hadn't known he had a family. And Michael had sounded...tender. In all those late-night talks about law, she had never seen him tender.

The feel of ice-cold water on her skin brought Claire back to the present. She wanted this transfer. She hated corporate politics, but she'd played them to transfer to a position where she could do trial work. Her personal feelings, or Michael's, would not affect the way she did her job, she decided as she climbed out of the tub. She was going to be working with the man now, and he could teach her a lot about law.

MICHAEL FINISHED his pizza and downed the last of the Pepsi, irritated with himself because he was still thinking about Claire.

Vibrant, vivid, vehement Claire Logan. He always managed to come up with all those V words when he thought of her. He'd hurt her feelings today. He'd been too anxious to get home, to explain why he'd resisted her transfer to Litigation.

Well, Claire was coming to work in the department, whether he wanted her or not. He'd have to talk to her about what had happened. As her new supervisor, he was responsible for making sure bad feelings didn't linger. He'd just tell her that the extra work was too much, when he was trying to find time to be with Angela.

That was the truth. Part of it, anyway. The part he wouldn't tell her, the part he shied away from, himself, had something to do with the glossy dark hair she pulled into a seal-sleek, no-nonsense ponytail, and that crazy jewelry she always wore, and the way her eyes lit when she was arguing her point. The part he wouldn't tell her had something to do with all those V words, too.

The telephone rang. Michael knew darned well Angela wouldn't answer what she now called *his* phone, so he headed out to the kitchen to pick up the portable.

"Mikush, it's Mom. Happy birthday. How's your day been?"

No one but his mother called him Mikush anymore, the *ush* a Polish endearment reserved for family and close friends. The truth almost spilled out, then he stopped himself. She had more than enough to deal with, herself.

"Fine, Mom."

"How did my Angel do with the *golombki?*"

"Ah, good, I think." He paused. "That is, it would have been good, if I hadn't been late."

"It was ruined?"

"Yes." He sighed. "Angela's mad, and I feel rotten about that."

"Mikush, you've got to do better. Angela wanted to please you, and you're all she has. She misses her mother."

Mary Jo was my wife. And I miss her, too, sometimes more than I can stand, Michael thought. "I know, Mom," was all he said.

"Dad and I want to see you both. It's been a while since you came for dinner, Mikush. I thought you and Angela might come over on Sunday, and we could have a birthday cake for you."

Michael knew she was trying to help, but he had a hard time getting through these family celebrations anymore. Too much had changed. Mary Jo was gone, and Angela made a great show of hating family get-togethers. Ever since his father's stroke six months before, Michael had found it hard to go home. He loved his father, and knew how much his dad must hate being trapped by the effects of the stroke—unable to speak, confined to a wheelchair. But dinner was the worst. Watching his formerly tough, take-charge father drooling, struggling to chew a morsel of food, was almost more than Michael could bear sometimes.

"I'll probably bring home a mountain of work this weekend. I've got a trial set to go on Monday." For his mother's sake, as well as his own, Michael allowed himself the small lie. "But I really wish I could, Mom."

"Just for a while, Mikush. I could show Angela that skirt I'm making for her, and you and Dad could watch the Bears on television." At the carefully banked plea in her voice, Michael felt a rush of affection. His mother just kept going, with a quiet acceptance of whatever life dealt.

"Sure, we'll be there," he said.

"We'll eat early. I think the Bears are playing at three. I'll check in the newspaper."

"That sounds good. And I'll bring some wine, Mom."

"Oh, no, we don't need wine," she protested. "It's so expensive. We'll do fine without it."

"I'm bringing wine," he said firmly. His mother always refused more substantial financial help—it was an old argument between them—but this sort of thing she usually let him provide.

He crooked the telephone into his neck. "How is everything over there, Mom? How are you, and how's Dad?"

"Dad's fine," she said immediately, not answering Michael's question about herself. "He had a good nap this afternoon and he seems cheerful tonight. He got excited about something that was on the news."

"How's the new nurse working out?"

His mother sighed. "All right, I guess. I wish I could manage on my own and just—"

"You can't, it's too much for you," he cut in quickly. This argument was six months old. His mother had never understood why she couldn't handle all the care of a large man who couldn't eat, dress or perform nearly any of the tasks of ordinary life for himself. She allowed a nurse to come in for an hour in the mornings to help his father get out of bed and bathe, and once again at night to settle him for sleep. That was it. For nearly every other minute of every day, she took care of him herself.

"I know I can't do it all," she agreed quietly, and readily enough, considering that she usually disputed the point. "Now, do you want to talk to Dad?"

Please, no, he thought. "Yes," he said.

There was the sound of the telephone being put down. Michael could hear his mother's voice, saying, "Dad? Dad. Come on, now, it's Mikush, on the telephone, and he wants to talk to you." A pause. Then, "There, you've got it now," as his mother presumably helped put the telephone against his father's ear and mouth. "Talk, Mikush."

For a second, Michael couldn't think of a word to say, and the momentary tightness in his throat wouldn't allow any words past anyway. Finally, he said, "Mom said you had a good day. She said something on the news was interesting."

He waited, and finally there was a small noise that must be agreement from his father. "I didn't get a chance to watch the news, Dad, or we could talk about it." Once, his father had argued with ardor about current events; he'd been a voracious reader and always concerned with happenings in his native Poland. It hurt Michael to listen to his father, who had been so articulate, struggle to get out a single sound.

"A lot of things are going on in Europe now," Michael went on. He waited, but there was no answering sound from the other end.

"I wonder if there's anything new on the diplomatic front. I read in the *Tribune* last Sunday that there's a commission studying manufacturing in the old Iron Curtain countries. Mom read it to you, I suppose."

Silence.

"It was interesting, Dad..."

And so it went, this stumbling, one-sided, excruciating conversation, and Michael had no choice but to keep talking on and on. He couldn't even ask his dad to hand the phone back to his mom so that Michael could tell her they were done with the conversation.

Finally, she picked up the receiver. "Mikush. Thank you, dear. Your dad was real pleased to hear from you. Now, don't forget the time Sunday. One-thirty. Dad's looking forward to it, I know."

A few minutes later, Michael clicked off the telephone and hung it up. How different things were. In the old days, his parents would have been over to help him celebrate his birthday. Mary Jo would have bought him something expensive, wrapped it elaborately. How she would have loved his new job, the money he was making now, and his cushy office. They'd talked about such things as kids, dreamed of the time when he'd be a lawyer.

But those days were gone forever. Now it looked as if, birthday or no, Angela would be holed up in her room for the duration of the evening. He might as well get started on the work he had brought home.

Michael opened the briefcase. His papers had been shoved in haphazardly, and he cursed softly. He was tired, and he didn't feel like sorting through this mess tonight. But he knew he'd do it, anyway.

That night Michael dreamed the kind of dream he had when he was exhausted. It was as if his subconscious knew when he'd had enough, when he ached inside and out, and then his mind brought back a detailed image of Mary Jo.

In his dream, it was dark, and he couldn't see her face. But as she rolled against him under the comforter, he knew she was naked. Mary Jo always wore a nightgown, and it was so different and exciting to feel soft, bare skin. He was hard in an instant. After all, it had been so long since they'd made love. Almost a year and a half too long...

His arms heavy with need, and with that peculiar heaviness of sleep, he drew her close and waited to smell the scent of lavender that clung to her skin. In his dreams, it was always more potent than it had been in real life.

But tonight, instead of the lavender scent he would forever associate with Mary Jo, she was wearing something fresher, sharper. Citrusy and tropical. It was lovely, a real turn-on, actually. But confusing.

He reached out a hand, cupping her breast. Her nipple stiffened instantly against his palm. He sighed in pleasure, then froze as he realized the breast he held was full, lush. Mary Jo had been slender and small-boned. As the surprise registered, his arm brushed something else: a huge, silver-and-amber pendant, an outsize, fanciful piece.

Oh, my God. Claire Logan.

Instantly, he was awake—sweating, hard as a rock, so hard that for a moment he was afraid to move.

Once before he'd dreamed of her, the night she'd asked him out for dinner.

He didn't want to dream of Claire Logan. His dreams of Mary Jo were a comfort, a gift.

He was carving out a new life for himself, a life that included Angela, and taking care of his parents, anticipating the financial security and power a partnership would give him. He had never given up on his plan to see Beske prosecuted, even though he'd hit one dead end after another.

Michael didn't want a woman. He didn't even want to think about a woman, much less Claire. She was nothing like his wife had been. Claire was too pushy, too talkative. His wife had been quiet, shy. He was used to that. He had loved her, and no woman could ever mean as much to him as Mary Jo.

CHAPTER TWO

AFTER CHANGING into her sneakers, Claire headed down to State Street for her late-afternoon walk. She'd skip lunch if she had to. In fact, she did most days, but she hardly ever missed the chance for a walk to break up her very long days. Moving just fast enough to feel winded, she did her usual two miles and then, refreshed, slowed down for a quick fifteen minutes of window-shopping before heading back to work. The exercise was necessary, but the small waste of precious time on window-shopping was pure luxury.

In the window of a large department store on Michigan was a gorgeous purple suit, just her style. She sighed, knowing there was no way she could wear something like that at the firm. The partners had such rigid ideas about everything.

Claire had wanted to be a lawyer nearly all her life, ever since seventh grade when she figured out that lawyers read a lot of books and got paid to talk. Law school, then her stint clerking for a federal judge, had brought considerably more reality into her dreams, but neither had prepared her for Haynes, Haynes, Collingwood and Crofts. For one thing—she knew it was petty—the dress code grated on her nerves. She didn't see why attorneys had to wear so much gray. The lawyers at the firm might take themselves a tad less seriously if they wore, say, purple to work. She also resented the firm's insistence that everything in her life revolve around Haynes, Haynes, Collingwood and Crofts.

Clare cast a last, regretful look at the brilliant fabric, then checked her watch and headed back to the office. She had an appointment with Michael at five o'clock to talk over her caseload. Wondering what he'd think of her in royal purple, she felt a surge of anticipation that had nothing to do with the case they were scheduled to discuss.

The anticipation was inappropriate, of course. In the month since she'd transferred to Litigation, Michael had never once given her any indication that he viewed her as anything but a colleague. She knew exactly where she stood with him. She hadn't had to graduate third in her class at Harvard Law to figure out that he wasn't interested in her as a woman. His respect and professional attention were all she had a right to expect, she told herself. Both were more than she'd ever gotten before at the firm.

After a quick stop to get her files, she was at Michael's office door promptly at five.

"Hi," she said with a bright smile.

He looked up with a more restrained smile of his own. "Hi, yourself, Claire."

For a second, she enjoyed just watching him. In response to official quitting time, Michael had loosened his tie and opened his shirt a couple of buttons. She had a tiny glimpse of gleaming golden hair in the V of his neck. It was just like the hair that dusted his strong, square hands.

After a moment, she crossed the room and sat in the chair opposite his desk. As he always did with the associates he supervised, he left his desk to take the seat beside her. An odd, constrained friendship of sorts had developed between them this last month. Always within the confines of his office or hers, they talked about law and lawyers. Michael politely and skillfully rebuffed any attempts on Claire's part to make the discussion more personal.

Claire put her files on the low table between them and immediately launched into her case and her plans for it.

He listened carefully, nodding at intervals, offering a suggestion or two.

Claire was finishing. "So, anyway, I was figuring I wouldn't let on we'd tracked down that witness. We should spring it on them at the trial." She made a note with her pen. "You know, bring the witness into the courtroom while Rolland is actually on the stand. I'll step out of his line of vision at the right moment and let him see her for the first time while I'm doing my cross-examination."

A wry smile stole across his lips. "We might be a litigation department, but the partners hate theatrics. They want us to leave the stunts to the guys who chase ambulances."

"But you know it might work," Claire argued. She hated being reined in. Larry Oliver had done it every day of the week.

"Fanal won't like it."

"Fanal is the partner who sent me the ivy that's on my desk."

"Fanal can also fire you, if you blow the Rolland case after your transfer over here."

"Look, I'm not saying I won't do my homework, prepare this case as well as I can. You know I do that, Michael. You saw me do it with the Halmeyer case. Pulling a stunt isn't inconsistent with good trial work, and if our insurance clients are a bit starchy, they still ought not to dictate— What?"

The wry little half smile had become a full-fledged grin.

"Wonderful. Now you think it's funny." Claire kept her words sharp. There was no way she'd let Michael see what that smile did to her insides.

He wiped the smile off his face. "I think your idea might work. Maybe it won't shake your witness, but the jury will love it. In a long trial, keeping a jury awake is half the battle."

"So, why were you smiling?"

Abruptly, Michael rose, went to the small window behind his desk and gazed through it. The window was important. In a place where every perk was totted up and gossiped over, an office with a window, however small, was a status symbol. Claire noticed how the office lights picked out the gold in his hair. Those same lights emphasized his broad shoulders, perfectly encased in a dark suit. Michael made no attempt to answer her question, and there was an awkward silence.

There was no reason for awkwardness, no reason for her to be thinking about her long-ago efforts to deepen their relationship. They were getting to be friends, and Claire hadn't made many friends since she'd come to Chicago. Although she wasn't sure what had triggered Michael's sudden silence, she tried to lighten things a bit. "You know, Michael, I like Litigation. You do things more as a team here, and everyone has accepted me as an associate. For the first time, I feel like a lawyer, plotting strategy, interviewing witnesses. One of the team. Just one of the guys."

He turned, finally. "You'll never be one of the guys, Claire."

There was no amusement in his voice now, nor in his gaze. He was intent. He meant what he'd said. Claire lifted her eyes to his and there was a brightness to his hazel gaze, a warmth that shimmered from him to her. She was jolted to her toes by that warmth; it spread throughout her body. She was excited, but confused. He kept giving her glimpses of something, some deeply buried feeling, and then pulling away. But if Michael Chalinski desired her, he certainly had never acted upon it.

Careful, she cautioned herself. *Guys don't go for you, and this man keeps giving you the brush-off. And he's your boss.*

"Well, no, I guess not," she finally said. Picking up her pen again, she noticed that her palms had grown damp. "I never have fit in anywhere, so it's not a big surprise that I'm different here, too."

There was no arguing with the fact that her fit at the firm was not a natural one, and Michael didn't try. Instead, he went to his credenza and surveyed the two neat stacks of paper that represented the work he'd scheduled for this evening. Using the pretense of opening a file, Michael's gaze slid covertly to Claire. She was writing notes in the inner cover of her file. Today, she was wearing a charcoal-gray suit, but tied around her simple dark ponytail was a yard-long silk scarf in vivid tomato-red.

The scarf bobbed and shimmered when she walked. He'd already noticed that in the hallway today; it seemed to call attention to the sway of her hips, punctuate the husky laugh he'd heard her exchange with one of the associates. The firm had an unwritten dress code, heavy on neutral colors and finely made wool or linen. Claire managed to both comply with and defy the code at the same time.

Take yesterday. Yesterday, her small defiance had been a pair of dangling earrings, huge gold hoops so absurdly gypsy-like that they'd brought a smile to his lips. The day before that it had been a pin, a silver cat with a tiny hinged tail that moved when she did— Lord, he thought in sudden, genuine irritation, how ridiculous was it to be thinking about Claire's wardrobe? He was thinking about Claire Logan way too much these days.

Quickly sorting the papers, he looked for his notes on the settlement entry he intended to write that night. For some reason, his notes weren't in either pile. Already impatient, he ground his teeth in frustration at the thought of having to go through all the files again to find them.

"Something the matter, Michael?"

He looked over to see that Claire had packed her files into her heavy briefcase and was watching him.

"I need my notes on the Cooper settlement," he explained, careful not to sound abrupt. "If I can't find them, I can't do the entry."

"Let me help," Claire offered. Joining him at the credenza, she began shuffling through the papers of one stack while he went through the other. They were quiet for a few moments.

"They aren't here," she finally announced.

"Well, that's just great." There were other things he could do tonight, but he'd planned to finish the Cooper entry. And having Claire right next to him was distracting him again, because every time she moved or bent to search through a file, he could smell her tropical flowers-and-citrus scent. Her red scarf had fallen over her shoulder and hung over her breasts. He had a crazy, quickly suppressed wish to lift it, glide his fingers over her breast and smooth the red silk into place along her neck.

Hard on the heels of that wish was another one, equally inexplicable. Quite simply, he wished he didn't have to work tonight. In fact, he wasn't sure he could make himself sit at that desk again today.

For a long moment, Michael surveyed the mess the two of them had made of his paperwork and then swore softly.

"You know, Claire, for some reason, tonight I just don't feel like working."

Claire nodded in understanding. "Gets to a person sometimes, doesn't it?"

He shook his head. "Not really. Not usually. Sometimes, I think if I hadn't had my work, these past months—" He bit back the words, substituting more neutral ones. "But tonight, for some reason..."

He ran his fingers through his hair. "It's Friday night, and my daughter, Angela, always sleeps over at her friend Sabrina's on Friday nights. It's my evening to play catchup, to make sure I've got at least Sunday free for her."

Claire wondered about his love life. His words meant he wasn't reserving his Friday nights for another woman. In a way, she'd hoped there was someone he dated, so that when he rebuffed her attempts to get to know him, she could tell herself it wasn't personal. She studied him. Despite his obvious fatigue, he was going to work tonight so that he could spend time with his daughter. She was impressed by that. And she could sympathize with him having to struggle with the unreasonable workload that the firm expected of its lawyers. "You could surely take one Friday night off. The work will be here next week, Michael."

He was sorting papers now, piling them into three uneven stacks. "Not if I want to make partner in two or three years."

"Come on, Michael, one Friday night isn't going to screw up your plans. And is making partner so important?"

"Yes, it is."

His grim tone suddenly struck Claire as faintly challenging. "You could always play hooky."

"Hooky?" He looked up, seeming nonplussed at the suggestion.

"Hooky. As in, you blow off the evening's work. It'll be waiting for you next week."

His voice was dry. "Well, if I did, it would hardly be hooky. It's seven o'clock. Technically, the office closed over an hour ago."

"My point exactly." She gestured with her hand. "In fact, I rest my case."

That wry smile was back; his shoulders relaxed. "You don't know when to quit, do you?"

People had said that to her before. Sometimes the words had stung. But the way Michael said them, it almost sounded as if he admired her.

She took a deep breath. "Play hooky," she said again. "Go ahead, be bad."

And then Michael Chalinski did something extraordinary, something she'd never seen him do. He laughed.

"All right, we're going," he said suddenly, and strode purposefully to the closet for his topcoat.

A few months ago, he'd turned down a date with her. An hour ago, he'd been all-business. She wasn't sure how she'd actually pulled it off, but a thrill of anticipation shot through her as she realized she was spending the evening with Michael, playing hooky.

ON THE STREET, it was windy, the air cold, in that crisp way of late autumn, when everything was frozen but it had yet to snow for the first time. The streets were brightly lit, and crowded. A few people carried briefcases, heading home to a late dinner, but most were in the city for shopping or a show.

"So, exactly how do we play hooky?" Michael asked her, taking her briefcase from her. Now that they were actually on the street, he seemed somewhat at a loss.

Keep it light, she told herself. She still wasn't sure why he'd agreed to spend the evening with her. "Well, the first thing you do is go down to the creek with a pack of cigarettes, and smoke and cough while you sit on a warm rock. You keep an eye out for snakes and dangle your toes in the water. You also bring a can of beer to pass among your friends, if you think your mom won't notice that one's missing."

"You've done this before." Michael chuckled, and his genuine amusement did something to his face, lightened the lines and planes until he was the most gorgeous man she'd ever seen. The breath went out of her lungs.

But she kept her tone light. "Well, I wasn't too bad, but my sister, well, that's where I got my lessons in hooky."

"Let's see," he said thoughtfully. "Lake Michigan would be pretty chilly for toe-dunking tonight, but I'll buy you a beer. Will that do?"

"I knew you could get the hang of this," she said.

Michael took her to an old firehouse that had been converted into a combination restaurant and bar. When they walked through the door, the heat and noise hit them like a wall. "Ever been here before?" Michael asked, having to practically shout in her ear.

She shook her head. "It looks like fun," she shouted back.

Michael appeared doubtful, but guided her to a table in the cavernous space, as far from the noisy bar as possible. There was no sign of a waitress, so he headed for the bar.

Claire studied her surroundings while she waited. Whoever had remodeled the restaurant had left the place looking a bit like a real firehouse. Hoses, ladders and other fire-fighting paraphernalia lined the walls and were hung around the bar. In the center of the room, the firemen poles were still there, now thickly swirled with red lights. Claire loved it. But she couldn't imagine Michael choosing such a place.

Michael returned with menus and two steins of dark beer.

Claire took a sip of hers. It was heavy, richly brown, with a bouquet so complex it reminded her of wine. The foam on top was thick and creamy.

"Is this a favorite haunt of yours?" She had to raise her voice.

He shook his head. "Are you kidding? I've never been here before. I remembered it because some of the guys at work said they liked it."

Claire opened a menu to find that most of the items featured were blackened or charred and had names like Smoldering Seven-Layer Burrito and Four-Alarm Jalapeño Burger. The names suddenly struck her as extremely funny. A giggle rose from her throat, which became a laugh, which quickly became a bigger laugh. Tears formed in the corners of her eyes.

Michael watched her solemnly. "What's so funny?"

"This." She gestured at the ceiling, on which revolving orange-and-red bands of light simulated a fire. "This." She waved her menu as another spurt of laughter overcame her and she gasped for breath. "You, of all people, bringing me to a place that features . . . Burning Basement . . . Bottomless Chili."

That reluctant smile tugged at this mouth. "Ah, Claire," was all he said.

A waitress came up finally, and, with effort, Claire calmed herself. Claire asked Michael to go ahead and order while she scanned the menu again. He chose a plain rib-eye steak, and passed on the char-grilled onion topping.

"Spoilsport," she chided, before ordering Smoke-Damage Smoked Salmon Salad for herself.

The music switched to something quieter. "That's a relief, anyway," Michael said. "What do you think of your beer?"

"It's great."

He nodded. "It's a Rathdenburg, which is a tiny local brewery. When I was a kid, that's the only beer my dad would drink. They don't bottle the stuff anymore. You have to get it on tap."

"You know, it's the kind of thing I came to Chicago for. To try new things, go to places like this."

He was incredulous. "Places like *this*?"

"Yes, Michael, to places like this." She took another sip of her beer. "Let me tell you about Hespin, Nebraska. There are about six hundred people there. Well, five hundred and ninety-nine, now." She smiled a little. "There's one wide main street on the flattest part of the prairie, and the town only exists because of the grain elevator where the farmers store their wheat. In summer, the grass on the prairie and the lawns in town turns the same shade of brown, and the heat hits you like a wave every time you open the door, and there's dust on everything. When we were kids, we'd go down the street after dark and use our fingers to wipe messages on car hoods, something silly or dirty, for their owners to find in the morning. That was all there was to do."

He nodded in understanding. "You didn't like it there, I take it."

"Oh, yes, I did. At least when I was really young. When I was thirteen—" She cut herself off.

"Something happened when you were thirteen?" he prompted. His eyes searched her face as if he really wanted to hear her answer.

"Oh, you know. Lots of people get divorced nowadays."

"Your parents divorced?"

"Yes." Even now, it hurt. It shouldn't, but it did. She took a deep breath. "My father fell in love with the minister's wife. You can't imagine the scandal, in a little town. People talked about it for years. Everywhere we went, my mom, my sister, or me, we felt that people were gossiping about us. Finally, my dad and Betsy moved to Lincoln."

"I'm sorry," Michael said quietly.

"I didn't see him much after that. He and Betsy had a baby, and I went to see them, but . . ." Her voice trailed away.

"He didn't have time for you anymore."

That wasn't it at all. Her father had asked her to visit several times, but each time she'd gone, he'd been filled with sharp criticism. Claire talked too much. She should learn to be quiet, sweet, not like her mom. Like Betsy. Men liked a woman like that, and soon Claire would want boys to like her. Even then, Claire knew she couldn't be like Betsy, pretty and blond and gazing with adoration at her husband. So, after a while, she pretended she was too busy with her friends to make the long trip to Lincoln. Now that she was an adult, she and her father had an uneasy relationship. But she was never quite able to forgive him for his criticism.

No way was she going to tell Michael how awkward she sometimes felt about men and the mysteries of sexual attraction, even if he was watching her with what she could have sworn was sympathy.

"I know something about loss," he said quietly.

"I know you lost your wife."

"A year and seven months ago. Her name was Mary Jo."

Claire was stunned. She had known Michael's wife was dead, but she had assumed he had been widowed years ago. "I'm so sorry, Michael. What was she like?"

He paused a long moment, his features shadowed. "She was perfect," he finally said quietly.

There was a small silence. It was clear he didn't intend to elaborate on Mary Jo's perfection, and Claire was grateful for that. She knew it was wrong of her to be jealous of a woman who was dead, but Michael had virtually admitted he was still in love with his wife.

"Would you like to leave?" she asked at the same time he said, "Would you like another beer?"

She shook her head. Michael turned abruptly. "Where the hell is that waitress? I could use a beer." With that, he was up and headed toward the bar again.

Claire watched him go. She was sure she hadn't pushed too hard. Well, pretty sure. She hadn't asked him too many questions, had she?

He was gone a long time, long enough for Claire to wonder if he intended to join her again. Finally, he was back, but instead of the expected beer, he held two bright red mugs of coffee.

"Look, I'm sorry," he said immediately. "I have trouble talking about Mary Jo, that's all."

"That's okay." That damn awkwardness was there again between them, Claire struggled to fill the silence with conversation. "Why don't you tell me what your neighborhood was like when you were growing up?"

His obvious relief tugged at her heart. She knew for once she'd said exactly the right thing.

He spoke quickly. "There are neighborhoods in Chicago that are like small towns. Then there are places like this." He lifted a hand to indicate the garish firehouse.

"Did you grow up in one of those old neighborhoods?"

"Oh, yeah, it was like a little Poland. My parents still live there, actually. I was their only kid, and they were always disappointed I didn't stay around, that I wanted to live downtown."

"Did you like it?" It was her turn to ask the question.

He sipped his coffee for a moment, thinking, and his shoulders started to relax. "Sure, when I was little. We played softball in the street and raced model cars at Czychinski's Raceway and ate pierogies at each other's houses. I was an altar boy at Saint Stephen's for six years. I never really fit in, though."

She heard the tinge of sadness in his voice. She knew how it felt to be different. "I never fit in, either. One summer I was fascinated by politics, so I'd go to the public library and read the *New York Times*. Nobody would even talk to me about it. If the subject didn't have something to do with cattle or wheat or the Hespin Raiders, no one was interested. One boy I really liked said to me once, 'You're too smart, you know. Guys don't like a girl who's smarter than them.'"

As soon as the words were out of her mouth, Claire wished she hadn't added that last part. The words still stung, even years after she'd decided to be herself, even after she'd become a lawyer, a good lawyer, and been rewarded precisely because she was smart. And what she'd just said reminded her too forcefully of Michael and the fact that he was a man, another man she was attracted to who showed no romantic interest in her.

"Well, surely by this time you've found men who like smart women."

Claire tried to smile. "Well, in law school, I dated a bit. But the firm doesn't give me lots of time to socialize. And let's face it, Michael. I talk too much, and I don't know how to flirt or anything. I'm no femme fatale."

He shook his head. "You're too hard on yourself. I always think of you as..."

Her breath caught as she waited. There was a long pause during which he looked very uncomfortable. "As vivid," he finally said.

Vivid? What on earth was that supposed to mean? "Vivid," she repeated.

"Yeah." His voice was utterly devoid of emotion, but he was watching her for her reaction. "Vivid."

"Oh." In the worst way, she wanted to ask him if that was good or bad, if he liked "vivid" women. On any other subject, she would have forged ahead. But on this one, she couldn't.

There was no personal subject, it seemed, that was easy. No wonder, Claire thought, they talked about law all the time. So she ate, he ate, and Claire finally gave up any attempt at conversation. The music was hard rock, and the bass beat reverberated through the large space.

It was a relief to be finally out on the street again, even though the air had grown colder. Claire wanted to return to the camaraderie they'd shared earlier.

"Why don't we go shopping?" Claire suggested.

Michael glanced at this watch. "Well, it's getting late—"

"Oh, no, Michael. You're not going back to work, are you?" She read his expression perfectly, knew now that the way to keep Michael from bolting was to keep things light and easy. "This is hooky. We're going shopping. I've got my Christmas list to start," she said. "You can look for your Christmas gifts, too."

"It's not even Thanksgiving yet." Last year, Michael had let his mother choose Angela's new clothes. Then he'd gone down his daughter's Christmas list, getting whatever she had on it. Then, as always, he'd let the Marshall Field shopping assistant pick out the gifts he gave at work. He hadn't known what to buy for his parents; Mary Jo had always selected their gift. So, at the last minute, he'd sent a giant fruit basket and potted poinsettia. This year, if he could order Angela's stuff by phone and get it delivered, his holiday shopping could be done in an hour.

With Claire, shopping was different. She touched everything, for one thing, running supple, feminine fingers over one item after another. First, a lamb's-wool muffler she was considering for her mother, then an emerald-green silk kimono she was thinking of buying her sister.

"Do you think this kimono is too much, Michael? I'm making more money than I ever dreamed, but I don't want to rub it in. Amy and Dave do all right, but their kids cost them a lot."

"It's pretty." It *was* pretty, if a little bright. As to whether it was "too much," Michael didn't have a clue. Actually, he was too busy trying to bury the treacherous thought that the emerald silk would contrast nicely with Claire's dark hair.

"I'll take it," she decided impulsively, and then was disappointed that the store didn't have its Christmas gift-wrap service available yet.

Before he knew it, they were again on the street, and Claire was wandering from store window to store window. She seemed to have an opinion, positive or negative, about everything. "Boring," she said about a man's subtly striped tie that Michael rather liked. "Terrific" was her pronouncement over a woman's red sweater with a black-and-gold Scottish terrier appliquéd on the front, complete with a big brass button for an eye and fringed yarn whiskers. The sweater was so ugly Michael couldn't believe it, yet he had an absurd wish to buy it for her, to see her wearing it.

His thoughts were careening out of control again. He tried to think of something to distract himself. "I guess I might try picking out my daughter's clothes this Christmas. She didn't care for the stuff her grandmother bought last year."

"What's her style?" Claire asked immediately, her voice bright with interest.

"Her style?"

"Yes, what colors and styles does she like?"

He frowned. "I don't know. Angela's just thirteen, so she wouldn't have a style. I do know she doesn't like pink." Angela had had a fit over the rose-checked skirt his mother had just made her. She'd thanked her *busia* nicely, then later exploded in the car going home. "I hate pink! Everything I've got is pink. Ruffly, ugly, rotten *pink!*" Taken aback by her reaction, Michael had said something about Mary Jo liking pink. Then Angela had burst into tears, and at home, she'd slammed her bedroom door. Again. "I don't know much about Angela these days."

"Well, if you want, I could help her pick some things out, sometime." Her voice softened. "Thirteen's a hard age for a girl, Michael. Any woman can remember how hard it was. I could help you."

"No, thanks. I want to be the one Angela turns to." He hoped she understood, didn't think he was being rude. But he'd worked too hard getting **to kn**ow Angela this last year and a half to lose her as she became a teenager. "We'll work it out. We're a family."

Stopping to look in each store window, picking their way over grates in the walk that sent up clouds of misty vapor, they finally arrived at the garage where their cars were parked. Michael found he was reluctant to see the evening end, realizing with a shock that he hadn't thought about work since they'd finished dinner in that bizarre restaurant.

He walked her to her car on the sixth floor, handed her the heavy briefcase he'd hauled for blocks and waited until she'd found her keys and settled in the driver's seat.

She rolled down her window. "This was fun, Michael," she said. In the harsh light of the parking garage, her dark eyes sparkled, and her wind-chilled lips were red and slightly swollen. The office seemed a long way away, a world away. Maybe that was why he had another absurd wish—this time more compelling—to lean into the car and put his mouth to hers ...

Before he knew it, his hands were gripping the edge of the open window, and he was starting to lean forward. Fortunately, some sense returned, and he straightened immediately.

"Thank you, Claire," he said, and he meant it. For the first time in ages, he felt loose. Energized. *Alive.*

"I knew we could be friends." Claire's voice held a deep sense of satisfaction.

Friends. The word washed over him. Friends. It seemed a safe word, much safer than some of the words he'd been imagining.

But Michael Chalinski and Claire Logan could not be friends. If he didn't need the evidence of two heated dreams to be convinced, he could look at tonight. He'd taken a woman out to dinner. Not just any woman.

Claire. And he'd been focused on her; only once or twice did he think of Mary Jo, and then he'd firmly pushed down the thought. And Mary Jo had been gone less than two years.

Was this how unfaithful husbands did it, just made themselves not think of their wives, when they were captivated by a woman and bent on seduction?

He didn't know. Michael had never slept with another woman, ever. Hell, he'd loved Mary Jo for so many years, he'd hardly *looked* at another woman. And Claire was so different from Mary Jo. Was wanting to touch a woman like Claire some sort of betrayal of his wife, of her values, of everything she had meant to him?

Suddenly Michael knew he could never spend another evening like this with Claire. He gazed into her expectant face. "Claire, I don't know how to say this without hurting your feelings, but I think it's best if we have a professional relationship. Just a professional relationship." Her face crumpled for a split second, then she immediately regained her composure, even though two bright spots of color appeared on her already flushed cheeks. "Look," he said, "I know I may have misled you tonight. It was my fault. I've been kind of lonely, but I know that doesn't excuse anything."

She shook her head, and her chin went up. "I asked for friendship, remember? Nothing more. And I don't want you to put yourself out." She inserted her key in the ignition. "Now, you'll have to excuse me. It's very late."

Her window went up. He stepped aside and let her back her car out of its space. Then he stood for several moments, listening as the sound of her engine faded away. He had never felt more alone.

CHAPTER THREE

SOPHIE CHALINSKI kissed her husband on his warm, dry cheek. Mike's better eye flickered. With obvious effort, one-half of his mouth worked until he made the sound that Sophie knew meant goodbye. Then he and his wheelchair were loaded into the special van that would take him to one of his twice-weekly therapy sessions. Sophie watched it drive away. It was hard to let Mike out of her sight, even for a little while.

She heard a door slam. Turning, Sophie saw that her next-door neighbor, Theresa Panski, had come out onto her porch with her small, brown terrier. The dog trotted down the steps and sniffed at the frozen grass.

"Hello, Theresa, how are you?" she called in Polish. Even though they saw each other nearly every day, Sophie was always glad to see Theresa.

Theresa smiled. "Pretty good, for an old *busia*. Going shopping?"

Sophie nodded as Theresa took a few slow steps down onto the lawn proper, following the dog. "Just to get milk and bread and a few other things at Domeniak's," Sophie explained.

Theresa squatted, found a stick and threw it a few feet for the dog to fetch. She straightened slowly. Theresa's back must be bothering her again, Sophie thought. She'd have to make a coffee cake or something, and send it over to cheer her neighbor up.

Theresa moved closer to the fence. "There's some bad news, Sophie. I was over at Domeniak's yesterday. He's not carrying milk anymore. He says he can't sell enough of it before it goes bad."

Theresa's calm words belied the importance of the news. Because if Pete Domeniak didn't carry milk anymore, how on earth was Sophie going to buy any? Domeniak's was the only grocery store left in the neighborhood. The supermarkets were at least five miles away; it was too far to walk, and it was even too far to catch a bus and be sure of making it back before Mike got home from his therapy session. "We've got to have milk, Theresa," Sophie said, a touch of desperation in her tone. "Dad likes his milk."

In the course of her seventy years, Sophie had known hardship and sadness, and she'd faced both without complaint. She'd left her homeland to live with an aunt she'd never met, in a city that seemed bigger than all of Poland. She'd learned to speak English, practically on her own, and worked as a maid, cooking and cleaning.

Then she had married Mike, and found out that after Michael, she couldn't have more children, children she wanted more than anything else in the world. Seven months ago, she'd accepted the news that her husband had had a massive stroke and would never walk or speak normally again, and she had tried to be cheerful, for Mike's sake, as he'd wrestled with the therapy that seemed to do so little good. Before that, Sophie had stood by as Michael buried his wife—a woman Sophie had loved, the mother of her beloved Angela. It had been hard to watch Michael then, stiff with agony, and she worried about him now, wondered if her only child could ever be happy again. And if Sophie Chalinski cried about those things, late at night, well, no one but God needed to know about it.

In comparison to everything else life had given Sophie to bear, the fact that Pete Domeniak wasn't selling milk anymore was a small thing. But she felt it, in the deepest, most private part of her, and knew that this night she would be crying because she couldn't buy milk in her neighborhood anymore.

"What will I do?" she asked. For the first time in years, she felt helpless.

"I can get it for you when Stanley drives me to the supermarket on Tuesday mornings," Theresa offered. "But that won't really take care of the problem. Pete's old, Sophie. Pretty soon he's going to have to close the grocery store. You need to find a way to get to a store where you can really shop. Maybe Michael—"

"Not Michael," Sophie said quickly. "Michael's too busy with his practice. He's got an important job, people who depend on him." Too late, she saw that in her maternal pride she'd hurt her friend. Theresa's son Stanley had a job in the stamping plant. He had four little ones, but, according to Theresa, he always had time for his mother. "I know Stanley's busy, too," she said immediately.

Theresa turned away to call her dog, her thick legs moving stiffly. "Let me know what you want me to do about the milk, Sophie." Sophie could see that her hasty attempt to compliment Stanley hadn't been quite enough to soothe her friend's ruffled feathers. And it had been wrong of her to show so much pride in her only child. Pride was a sin.

Sophie adjusted her scarf so that it protected her hairdo more securely and called goodbye to her neighbor. She began to walk toward the little grocery, but it was without her usual brisk sense of purpose.

She was unsettled. Late at night, Sophie had had thoughts even more sinful than the one of pride, thoughts that bothered her greatly. Her sin was sometimes wishing Michael had been a different kind of boy. One who'd grown up to take a job in the stamping plant, too. For a time, Sophie had been in awe of her own son, at what he knew and how many important people he'd met. But now...

His father had understood him. The two had argued about subjects Sophie didn't begin to comprehend. Naturally, Mikush had to be a lawyer. His intelligence was a gift from the good Lord. All the nuns at Saint Stephen's Parochial had told her how smart he was from the moment he started school. And this was America, where the son of a maid and a factory sweeper from Polaski Street could be a lawyer. When Michael passed the bar, there had been a hundred people in Sophie's tiny backyard, celebrating the tremendous success of one of their own.

But Michael's being a lawyer wasn't going to put milk on the table!

Picking up her pace, Sophie crossed the street and headed up Koblek. She was wasting precious time. If she didn't hurry, no one would be home to help the van driver with Mike and his wheelchair. At least for now, Pete Domeniak still stocked fresh bread.

A block down on Koblek, she passed a house that was burned and partially gutted. She'd heard from one of the neighbors that they sold drugs in what was left of that house. She hurried past it, half-afraid to look at it. A few blocks farther, the neighborhood changed some, got better again. There were no burned-out hulks and no graffiti. The small lawns were kept up and the windows washed. Sometimes, she saw young families, a mother and father, out raking or sweeping.

One of those young mothers stood at the curb now, unloading a toddler from his car seat as Sophie passed. She stopped for a minute to admire the little boy. "He's so cute. I remember when my Michael was like this. It doesn't seem so long ago."

"Thank you. Kenny's our first." The mother smiled, chatted a little, but, like Sophie, she had to hurry. She'd just got home from work and needed to start dinner.

Sophie's spirits rose. The young woman hadn't looked Polish, but Sophie no longer cared. The older people were mostly gone. Her own neighborhood was going downhill, but on this block some younger families had moved in. They were kind of poor, but they kept the old places up, though not like the Polish people had. Mikush said that the cost of housing in Chicago was making this neighborhood "viable" again. She'd looked up the word in the dictionary. It was a good word.

Mikush was after her to move out of her house. He didn't think it was safe, and he kept telling her she could have a modern kitchen in a condominium he'd buy, that all she had to do was pick it out. Sophie didn't want a modern kitchen. She liked the neighborhood; it was home. And Michael might be rich beyond her wildest hopes for her boy, but nobody wanted their son to have to buy them a place to live.

She had gone the remaining block to where she was to make the final turn to Domeniak's. All of a sudden, there they were—two boys, big boys, roughly dressed and mean-looking. "Hey, lady, you got an extra dollar on you?"

She didn't, not really, but they were crowding her so. Quickly, she looked around. There was nobody else within sight. The cars on the street were whizzing by too fast to notice her.

"Well, yes, I think I've got a bit extra," she finally said, deciding it might be best to give them what they wanted. Slowly, she opened her purse.

One of them laughed, and it was the ugliest sound Sophie had ever heard. Then he snatched for her purse, pulling until the strap broke against her arm.

"No," she cried. Suddenly, she was hot all over, and furious. She lapsed into Polish. "No, no, *no!* I won't let you have my money!"

They were so startled at her fury, that when she grabbed the purse, they actually let go. Clutching her purse to her stomach, Sophie started to run. She hadn't run in thirty years, but she was moving.

But those boys were right behind her, and it was no contest. They pushed her down, and Sophie felt a snapping pain shoot up her leg as she hit the ice-cold pavement. The concrete grazed her cheek. One of the boys kicked her hard in the ribs, even as she tried to use her arms to shield her head. She wondered if this was it, her time, if she was going to die now. If she did, who would take care of Dad and Mikush and Angela. And then, with a last, vicious kick, they were gone, laughing together, as Sophie lay huddled on the sidewalk, murmuring a prayer.

CLAIRE WAS at the Xerox machine, making copies for herself, when she caught sight of Michael down the hall. He was coming toward her, his briefcase in hand, his topcoat over his arm. She steeled herself for his overly polite greeting as he passed. Since their shopping trip a few days ago, he'd been distant and professional, to the point where his courtesy seemed exaggerated.

Then the telephone rang at his secretary's desk. Michael paused while she picked it up. Eileen listened for a minute, then motioned Michael to come back.

Claire pulled the last of her copies from the bin and straightened. She seemed to have a sixth sense about Michael, or maybe it was just that she was always conscious of his presence, of the way he moved, the way he sat.

Something was wrong.

Michael wasn't taking the call in his office, but was still standing at Eileen's station, his whole body curiously taut as he listened, the receiver to his ear. Concerned, Claire headed toward him.

She knew for certain something was wrong when she got close enough to see the color of his skin; it was gray, and the area under his prominent cheekbones looked sharply dented and shadowed.

"Yes, yes, I can be there in fifteen minutes..."

Claire shot a quick, questioning look at Michael's secretary. "His mother's in the hospital," she whispered. "Emergency."

Claire put her hand on his arm, and Michael stared at her blindly. The knuckles that gripped the telephone were white.

Claire tried to get his attention. "Let's go to the hospital. Come on."

He hung up the telephone, and fumbled in his pants pocket for his keys, telling Eileen, "My mother was mugged. They say she's hurt, but she'll be okay." He found the keys and began to stride down the hall, tossing his next words over his shoulder. "I've got to get to the hospital. Can you cancel my appointments?"

"Sure, Michael. Hey, I hope everything's all right. Let us know." Belatedly, Eileen added, "I'll see that your appointments are canceled too, Claire."

Claire gave her a quick thanks, then said to Michael, "We'll take my car. I'll drive."

For the first time, he seemed to notice that she was beside him. "I can drive. I can handle it."

"Michael, you're upset, and no wonder. Let me drive you."

Claire pushed the elevator button; an interminable time passed before it arrived. Michael punched the button with his palm, once, twice. "Damn it, come *on.*"

As they got on the elevator, Michael closed his eyes for a long second. "Some bastards hurt my mother, pushed her down. The nurse said she's stable, but I don't know..."

"How about your father? Is he there with her?"

"No, he had a stroke seven months ago. He can't take care of himself. But they said he's taken care of. I'll need to check that, too, as soon as I get to the hospital." Michael watched the numbers over the door light up.

Then they were finally in the parking garage. "Did you mean it about driving me?" he asked.

"Of course."

"Then please drive my car. I've got a car phone, and I'll need to make some calls."

They found his black Jaguar and Claire slid in the driver's seat, fumbling until she adjusted it to compensate for her shorter legs.

Michael had to give her directions to the hospital. It was in an old, residential side of town, and she was unfamiliar with the narrow streets. All the time she drove, Michael talked on the phone. His initial shock had given over to an eerie, efficient sort of calm, as he insisted on information and talked to one person after another.

By the time they got to the hospital parking lot, he had discovered that his mother was in Orthopedics and that the social worker from his father's therapy clinic had taken his dad to a nursing home temporarily. "Thank God they're both all right," he said, clicking off the telephone.

Claire stayed with him as he met with the doctor and discovered that his mother's broken ankle was being set. A muscle worked in Michael's jaw, but otherwise he sat still, listening as the doctor explained the extent of her injuries.

"I can show you the X rays," the doctor told him. "It's a nice clean break. She's in shock, and she's got some bruises on her ribs that are going to make her uncomfortable. She's very fortunate not to have broken her hip."

The doctor shoved his hands in the pockets of his white lab coat. "We gave her a little something to settle her down. She was pretty upset, and for a while we couldn't get her to speak English. Finally, we found somebody who spoke Polish. She kept saying she had to get home to your father."

Michael nodded. "He's had a stroke. He's..." There was the slightest hesitation. "He's totally helpless, and she's very protective of him."

The doctor nodded. "You might want to reassure her about him. I don't think she quite believes us that he's taken care of."

The doctor told them it would be a while before he could see his mother, so after Michael had looked over the X rays, he and Claire sat down to wait.

The wait stretched on for hours. Michael stood, paced. Then he sat again. Then stood. Then paced. He was obviously deep in thought. The muscles of his jaw moved rhythmically, as if he were chewing something that was difficult to swallow. His shoulders were tense. Whatever Michael was thinking, it was not good. He seemed more than upset about his mother, he was angry. Claire almost asked why, but at the last minute discovered some inner source of tact. He was worried; he had a right to be. If he wanted to tell her what was on his mind, he would. She forced herself to look at the magazine on her lap, even if she couldn't concentrate on the words.

Finally, Michael went to the window and stared out over the parking lot to the shadowed houses behind. "I told my mom a long time ago that the neighborhood wasn't safe anymore. God, nobody knows better than I do how many criminals are roaming the streets. I told her I'd find them a safe place to live. She just won't listen." He balled his fists. "This is my fault. I should have packed my parents up and moved them out of there bodily."

Claire put the magazine aside. "You can't make a grown woman move, Michael, not if she doesn't want to. Besides, she's your mother. She's always going to think she knows more than you do."

He sighed. "I had this great condominium picked out. Modern, and really nice. I thought my mother would like a new kitchen to cook in. Instead, when I took her to see it, she told me she preferred her old gas stove and that the carpet in the new place was too fuzzy and soft."

Claire came up to stand beside him. "My mother has never understood why anyone would want to live anywhere but Hespin. I'd never get her to move voluntarily." She tried a small smile. "We women tend to put down roots."

"She's stubborn, that's all. Used to doing for herself, she says."

Well, so that was where Michael got his stubbornness. Claire's smile turned bittersweet. Seeing the concern on Michael's face, she was forcefully reminded that under the cool exterior was a man capable of intense love and loyalty. It was very hard to know that this intensity of feeling would never be offered to her.

But for now she would take whatever relationship he offered. Claire thought for a moment. "You know, Michael, I haven't met your mom. But from what you've told me about her, if I were going to look for another place for her to live, I'd help her choose a house instead of a condo, maybe something not too modern, maybe a little closer to the neighborhood she's used to."

He shrugged. "I don't think it'd make any difference." He glanced at his watch, then said, "I'm going to go back down to X ray and see if I can find out what's taking so long."

Claire nodded. He hadn't asked her to stay, but she settled down to wait. Michael needed someone tonight. There had been stark fear in his eyes when he'd gotten the news about his mother, and his features had been set in cold, hard lines for hours. More than anything, Claire wanted to be here, to help him through this ordeal. She wished that when he came back, he would sit by her, allow her to touch him a little, reach out and smooth away the gleaming lock of hair that kept slipping onto his forehead.

Claire was leaning back on the worn vinyl couch, her shoes off, her eyes closed, when Michael returned a half hour later. A tattered copy of *Newsweek* was open across her lap. Strands of her hair had come loose from her ponytail and hung around her face. Her scarf had been pulled from the neck of her plain silk blouse, and Michael could see now that the scarf sported the image of a brilliant green hummingbird, its needlelike beak poked into an equally bright red hibiscus. Quickly, he pushed down the realization of how much he had needed her to get through this night. Claire. Dear God, how did she seem to get under his skin and stay there, despite his best efforts to keep his distance?

He heard his unwanted feelings in his voice. It was uncharacteristically soft, maybe even a touch tender. "Claire, are you asleep?"

She straightened right away. "No, of course not. What did you find out?"

"She has a worse break than they thought at first." He felt his jaw tighten anew. "If I could get my hands on whoever hurt her—"

"Michael." She reached out, put her hand on his arm. "The police will handle it."

Oh, right. They'd handle it as effectively as they'd handled Mary Jo's accident. He turned away from the raw bitterness her innocent words brought. Using the fingers of one hand to rake back that annoying hunk of hair that kept falling onto his forehead, he said, "Look, I hate to ask this—I know I've been a real jerk to you these past few days, and I owe you an apology for that. So I hate to ask—"

"Just ask, Michael. What do you need?" she said gently.

At her words, Michael's heart, so carefully shielded against this woman, was touched. "It's after nine. I've called Angela twice, and she insists she's all right. But if it gets any later, I don't like the idea of her being home alone." He reached into his pocket, absently fiddling with some change. "I know Angela's thirteen, and she's too old for a baby-sitter, but I think she might be worried about her grandmother."

"Would you like me to go sit with her?" Claire asked.

"If you don't mind."

She was already standing, pulling the black velvet band from her ponytail and quickly redoing it into its customary sleekness. "I'll leave right now. You'll have to tell me how to get to your place. I'll take your car, and when you call, we'll come back and pick you up."

He couldn't help smiling at her decisiveness. It was the first time in a long time someone was volunteering to take up some of his burden. "No, don't come back for me. When I'm done, I'll call a cab. I don't know how late I'll be."

"All right."

He held her coat as she slipped it on. When she turned, she was standing close to him. Too close. She was so near he could see the fine grain of the fabric of her red cashmere coat, and he could smell the tangy tropical-flower scent she wore.

Move, he ordered himself. But before he could make his legs take a step back, she brought her fingers up and lightly touched his cheek. Just that, the merest contact between her skin and his, was enough. In slow motion, he moved his own hand up, up, to cup her fingers and prolong the contact. Helplessly, he brought the tips of her fingers to his lips.

"Michael." She breathed his name, rather than spoke it.

The sound snapped him out of his trance and he took an abrupt step back. What on earth was he doing, taking advantage of friendship and sympathy this way, misleading Claire? "Please see about Angela." His voice was gruffer than he'd meant it to be,

She stood there, looking uncertain, but smiling a little.

Just then the nurse called him to see his mother, and Claire turned to go.

Michael had planned a speech during the long hours he'd been waiting—some cheery words about how Dad was doing fine and how his mother would love the attention and hate the hospital food. But the touch of Claire's hand had left him shaken, and when he saw his mother lying in the hospital bed, he couldn't think of a word to say.

Sophie Chalinski was a sturdy woman, short but strong-boned, her body made more for function than grace. But now she looked small and frail, with her propped leg swathed in a thick plaster cast and one side of her face smeared with some kind of white ointment.

Michael leaned forward and kissed her good cheek, and for a moment his throat was so tight he thought he was going to break down. With superhuman effort, he forced a smile. "How are you?"

"Fine." She couldn't quite manage an answering smile. "How's Dad?"

"He's real good, Mom. He's in a very nice nursing home."

Her hand fluttered. "I knew you'd take care of him. Thank you, Mikush."

He settled into a chair next to her bed. "Is there anything you want? Something to drink, or should I turn on the television?"

"No, thanks. But you should be working. You don't have to sit with me."

"It's nighttime," he told her, but he'd have come no matter what time of day it was and she must know that, too. He didn't have to say it, did he?

"Angela shouldn't be alone at night."

"Don't worry, Mom. I've got someone to stay with Angela."

She nodded, and at the news that everyone was taken care of, finally relaxed.

For a while, Michael sat there, talking occasionally. Sophie drifted in and out of a light sleep. After a long time, the noises of the hospital faded and the hall lights dimmed. "It's time you got some real rest," he said finally.

She nodded slowly. "I'm tired. You go on home, too, Mikush."

"Don't worry about me. I want to stay awhile."

"Are you all by yourself?"

"Now I am. But someone drove me down."

"Good, a friend."

"Someone from the office, that's all."

She perked up momentarily. "Boy or girl?"

He sighed. "A woman. Her name's Claire. She's the one who's with Angela."

"A girlfriend. That's good, Mikush."

It was useless to argue with her; she was in pain and feeling the effects of whatever pill she'd been given. But he knew her. "Claire is not Polish, Mom."

He thought that would be the end of it, right there. Instead, she surprised him. "You know what, Mikush? I don't care." She sat up a little to punctuate her words, wincing at the pain. "I want you to be happy, and if a girl was nice enough to bring you down here and then see to my Angel, that's plenty good enough for me."

CHAPTER FOUR

CLAIRE WALKED down the hallway, looking for the number of Michael's condominium. The apartment was in an expensive neighborhood, not too far outside the Loop.

When she knocked, the door was opened almost immediately, by a slight, blond girl.

"Are you Miss Logan?"

"I'm Claire." She smiled. "And you must be Angela."

The girl didn't smile back. "You didn't need to come. I told my dad I had everything together here."

Claire wondered what to say. She agreed with Michael that Angela was too young to stay by herself late at night, but she knew that wasn't something Angela would want to hear. She tried another smile. "Well, I'm here. Couldn't I come in for a while? Your dad wouldn't worry, then."

"Yeah, okay." Angela held the door open wider. "You're right. If you're here, maybe Dad won't be calling every fifteen minutes. You can put your coat over there." She gestured toward a Louis XV chair, and Claire shrugged out of her coat and laid it across the back. Then she walked into the living room, going over to the wide window that overlooked the downtown Chicago skyline.

"Um, would you like to sit down, Miss Logan?"

Claire turned. "Sure. But you don't have to keep calling me Miss Logan. It makes me feel like I'm about seventy-two."

The girl hesitated, then smiled for the first time. "You're not that old."

"Well, thanks. I think."

"Really, you look okay, not old at all. I mean, I really like your earrings, and your scarf." Angela looked away and fiddled with the buttons of her pink cardigan.

"Thanks," Claire said again, seating herself in the recliner that faced a wall of bookshelves and a big-screen television. The moment she sat down, it struck her that she must be sitting in Michael's favorite chair. The rest of the room was fussy, the upholstery covered in hard, shiny damask. But the chair she sat in was wide, soft from use, and the arms were worn. A copy of the *American Bar Association Journal,* and a paperback by an English mystery writer were on the table next to the chair.

Still standing in front of her, looking awkward and very young, was Angela. Michael's daughter. Claire suddenly felt rather awkward, herself.

Angela tossed her braid over one shoulder. "Um, would you like something to drink?"

"Sure. What do you have?"

"Pepsi. Milk. My dad has some wine in the fridge."

Claire asked for a Pepsi.

Angela brought it, then sat on a fringed ottoman and fiddled with the remote control for the television. The screen jumped to life, but she didn't put on the sound, just sat staring for a minute at the images.

"Your grandmother's going to be all right, Angela," Claire said softly, although Angela hadn't asked about either her grandmother or her father.

Angela swiveled swiftly to face her. "Is that true? Really true or something you're just saying?"

"She's okay, Angela. She has a broken ankle and she was upset, but she's going to be fine. I was there when the doctor spoke to your dad."

Angela's lower lip wobbled.

"Didn't your dad tell you all that, when he called?" Claire asked.

"Well, he did, but I thought maybe he wasn't telling me the truth. He's always watching out for me, like I was some kind of kid or something."

Claire smiled. "Fathers are like that."

"He doesn't realize I can stay by myself. He keeps calling and I have to get off the phone with Sabrina to answer his phone."

"He loves you, Angela."

"He loves me too much," she grumbled, but her cheeks turned red.

Claire felt a sudden urge to put her arm around Angela and give her a quick hug. But she suspected the girl would think she was being treated like a kid. Claire kept her voice even. "And because he loves you, you should think about cutting him some slack."

Angela shrugged, looking away. "I guess."

"But he can be a bit much, sometimes, can't he?"

"Yeah."

"And he *is* very stubborn."

Angela brightened and turned toward her again. "Yeah."

"Like somebody else I know?"

"Who?" She looked puzzled.

"You," Claire said, leaning forward. "You want to make darn sure I know you didn't need anybody tonight, but I bet you felt alone and scared about your grandmother."

Two spots of color appeared on the girl's cheeks, but she smiled, a quick, almost shy smile. "My dad said I'd like you."

"Did he?" Claire was pleased.

"Yeah. So, are you hungry, maybe?" She stood. "I don't know if you're on a diet or something. Not that I think you need to be or anything," she added hastily. "I mean, I kind of am, but I only ate yogurt for dinner and I was thinking of a bagel with peanut butter on it, and some diet Pepsi."

"Bring on the peanut butter," Claire said, and she followed Angela into the kitchen. She helped Angela slice and toast bagels, and tried not to raise her eyebrows at the quantity of peanut butter Angela slathered on her own bagel.

"Are you a friend of my dad's?" Angela asked as they took their places at the table in the breakfast nook.

Good question, Claire thought. Well, she was in his condominium, watching over his daughter. Doing so gave her a warm feeling. "Yes," she said.

"I thought so." Angela took a sip of Pepsi. "He *said* you were somebody he worked with, but I figured you were his friend."

Claire hid a smile.

"I mean, he's never had a lady come over before, and I meant it about liking your earrings. They're cool."

Claire took a thoughtful bite. It was a relief that Angela didn't seem to mind the idea of Michael having a female friend. And it was, well, interesting, that Michael had not had a woman over to his condominium. But she shouldn't make too much of her own presence here, Claire cautioned herself. The call about his mother had been an emergency; Michael had had no one else to turn to this evening. It didn't mean anything that he'd asked her to stay with his daughter.

"You've only got one hole pierced in each ear, though," Angela said. "My friend Sabrina has two holes in her right ear, and three in her left. Her left ear has a real sapphire stud her mom bought her. I *love* three holes."

Claire laughed out loud. The kid reminded her of herself at that age. "I don't think they'd go for three holes at Haynes, Haynes, Collingwood and Crofts, so I guess I have to make do with one earring per ear." She glanced down at her bracelet, with its dangling enameled elephants. She was already pushing things at the firm. Showing up with three earrings on one earlobe would probably send George Fanal into orbit. "You don't have your ears pierced."

"Nope. Dad won't let me. I thought maybe when I was thirteen he would, but he bought me a phone, instead." Angela paused. "I guess I like the phone better. Dad would probably pick out some ugly little roses for me to wear, anyway." She took a bite of her bagel. "They'd be pink for sure. Dad always buys me pink."

"You look good in pink, with your coloring," Claire said. But she had wondered about Angela's choice of clothing. She was wearing flannel pants, a simple sweater and a lace-trimmed blouse. Claire's experienced eye could tell the outfit was costly, but it did nothing for the girl.

"I *hate* pink!" Angela's sudden vehemence was startling.

"So, don't wear it," Claire replied in a reasoning tone.

"Nobody buys me anything else. I've been saving up my allowance, though. I'm going to get myself a vest or something. Maybe a purple one."

"I love purple," Claire said.

Angela smiled, a friend-to-friend smile. "Me too."

When the telephone rang, Angela got up to get it. "It's Dad," she told Claire. "Again!" After she had talked a minute, she handed the phone to Claire.

Michael's voice was rich, and deep with concern. "I'm glad you got there okay. Angela's not too upset about her grandmother, is she?"

"We're fine," Claire assured him.

"I'm coming home in a few minutes, but it might take me a while to find a cab this time of night. Are you hungry? Can I bring you something to eat?"

"No, thanks, I've been having peanut butter and Pepsi with Angela."

There was a pause, a beat too long, Claire thought. Before she could wonder what it was she'd said to cause it, he was speaking again. His voice sounded more neutral this time. "Well, I'll see you both soon, then."

Claire hung up and she and Angela took the last of their Pepsis to the living room.

Angela curled up on a cushion on the floor, and Claire took the recliner again.

"Claire? Could you maybe take me shopping for my vest?"

A shopping trip with Angela sounded appealing. Claire knew exactly what kind of clothes would enhance Angela's delicate looks. It would be fun, and a nice change from the endless hours she'd been putting in at the firm. "Would it be all right with your dad?"

"Oh sure, I'll ask him tomorrow. When can we go?"

"Would Sunday be okay? I usually have to work on Saturdays."

"Sure."

Now Angela was really excited. She began talking about the kind of outfit she envisioned, hardly letting Claire get a word in.

"I could ask Sabrina to go with me, but she'll tell me what to buy, and I just want some help, not somebody to pick it out."

Sabrina again. Michael had mentioned that Sabrina was Angela's friend, and had also said something about not liking the girl very much.

"Sabrina shouldn't push you into anything," Claire ventured, "even if she is your friend."

"Sabrina's cool. And if Sabrina wasn't my friend, I wouldn't have any friends at all."

"Oh, Angela, I'm sure that's not true."

"It *is* true," Angela insisted, her face red. "When my parish school closed down, Dad thought I should go to Baldwin Academy, because it's a really good school. But I couldn't make any friends there, till Sabrina. The kids are rich, and they have cool clothes. I don't."

Ah, thought Claire.

"But you must be smart, and you must have worked hard in school, to have been accepted there." Baldwin Academy had a sterling reputation for academics, even stronger than its reputation for being expensive. "That's something to be proud of."

"Who cares?" Angela tossed her head. "I don't want to be smart. I mean, I don't care if I'm smart, but I wish everybody liked me."

Claire suddenly felt as if she were in a time warp. Her sister, Amy, had been a cheerleader, but as a teenager Claire had been tall and chubby and graceless. Somehow being captain of the debate team just hadn't cut it, compared to the girls who knew what to say to boys, how to use a curling iron and eyeliner, and how to sound sophisticated while they talked about nothing. Claire had never been good at chitchat. *You're too smart for a girl, you know...* How she'd hated being different!

"Oh, Angela," she said, impulsively sliding out of her chair to join the girl on the floor.

Angela turned to her, and her tone was fierce. "Don't feel sorry for me, Claire. Everybody knows my mom is dead and my *busia* picks out my clothes, and just because I'm smart and I want a friend, I have to—" She broke off. "What would you know about it, anyway?" Angela, face aflame, drew her knees to her chest and wrapped her arms around them.

"What do I know about it?" Claire asked, surprised that even after all these years she still felt so strongly about what she was going to say. "I know *all* about it. When I was a teenager, I couldn't do anything with my hair and I wanted to look good and I didn't know how. And I wanted a boyfriend, but all the guys thought I was too smart. I would beat them at debate, every time we had a match. And then I'd go home and cry."

Angela turned to look at Claire, her eyes shining with interest. "Really? Did you—" she fiddled with the cuff of her sweater "—well, you know, ever think of maybe not doing so good at the debate, and letting a boy you really liked win?"

"Never." Claire paused, knowing she needed to be honest. Angela wanted the truth. "Well, I thought about doing that, a lot. But I never did, because I decided I needed to be who I was, no matter what."

"I know, you mean having self-respect." Angela rolled her eyes.

"And you know what, Angela? After a few years, it didn't matter so much. I still wanted to look good, so I figured out what looked right on me. My hair is stick-

straight and won't hold a perm, so I just put it in this
ponytail and try to make it smooth. And I'm too tall and
way too curvy to be fashionable, so I sort of dress to scale.
I've learned to wear bright colors when I'm not at work,
and big jewelry all the time." She smiled ruefully at the
elephants dancing around her wrist. "I still don't feel
beautiful, but I feel like me. The real me. And that's a
very good feeling."

Angela cocked her head. "And you do look good,
Claire," she said generously.

"And now I get paid to be smart, to be a good lawyer
and, let me tell you, that feels great." Claire gave in to an
impulse and gave the girl a hug.

It was nearly one in the morning when Michael returned home.

He put his keys, wallet and tie on the dining-room table, and walked into the living room. The first thing he
saw was Angela curled on the floor, asleep, her braid
falling across her neck. The sight startled him; he hadn't
expected her to become so comfortable around a stranger
that she would actually fall asleep. At some point, Claire
must have covered her, because a blanket was tucked
around the girl's shoulders.

Claire was lounging next to her, reading, her back
against a stack of cushions. Her shoes and suit jacket were
off. Seeing Claire with Angela like that, so comfortable
and casual, caused his heart to give a tiny lurch.

Just then, Claire saw him. She got up and came to him,
her index finger holding her place in the book she'd been
reading. He could see now that it was Angela's copy of
Ethan Frome, which her English class was reading.

"You didn't make Angela go to bed, I see," he whispered, and, despite his weariness, he smiled.

"Hey, do I look crazy enough to try to put a thirteen-year-old to bed?" She smiled back, a luscious, no-holds-barred smile of welcome. "How's your mother?"

"Good. Sleeping." He took off his coat and suit coat. "I suppose I'd better wake Angela and get her pointed toward bed." He looked doubtfully toward his daughter.

"Why don't you leave her for a while, Michael, and have something to eat? You must be exhausted."

He *was* exhausted. He really should wake Angela; she had school tomorrow. Then he should thank Claire and call a cab for her. But maybe it was because he was so weary that he suddenly couldn't bear the thought of sending her home right away. "I'm starved. Did you and Angela polish off every bit of peanut butter?"

She laughed softly and he led the way to the kitchen. He made himself a peanut butter and jelly sandwich while she got the coffeemaker going.

When they were seated, he found that for the first time in a long time he felt like talking, and for the first time in a long time he had someone with him he really felt like talking to. He missed his father, the way they'd talk for hours, and he missed his mother's soothing cup of tea with a plate of sweet *pacznki* and the directive to "Talk, Mikush." Because of his father's stroke, Michael no longer felt he could burden either one of his parents with his lingering sadness.

He finished one sandwich and went to the counter to make another one, while Claire sat at the table, sipping coffee. They talked about his mother's mugging.

"Maybe the police can do something," Claire said without much hope in her voice. "We'll have to let them handle it."

Michael put the sandwich down on the counter, then turned to face her. "Oh, yeah, they'll handle it, all right.

Do you know how many muggings take place in a city the size of Chicago? And if the criminals are caught, do you know what the penalty is? *If* some hotshot defense attorney doesn't get them off, and *if* miracle of miracles, they actually have to go to prison, they'll be out in less than a month. The prisons are overcrowded. Believe me, I know. Nobody's going to handle this.''

He saw Claire glance toward the kitchen door, and that's when he realized his voice had risen. He'd closed the door when they'd first come in so their conversation wouldn't disturb Angela. Now, though he couldn't stop the words from pouring out, he made a real effort to modulate his tone.

"You know, when I was doing criminal law, I was damn good. I got more guys off than anyone in the department.''

He was so focused on what he was saying that he didn't hear Claire approach in her stocking feet. But suddenly she was right there, beside him. She covered his hand with her own warm one.

"Michael, you're not responsible for what happened to your mother. No one is responsible except the men who did it.''

He turned to look at her. She meant well, but she didn't understand. "Don't you realize,'' he said slowly and deliberately, "that those sons of bitches who hurt my mother could have been some of the very defendants I got off?''

"Michael, it was your job. You were supposed to do the best you could for those men, even if they were guilty. You took an oath to do that.''

"Yes, you're right. That's what they teach us in law school. But sometimes knowing it's your job just isn't enough.''

She slipped an arm around his waist, and almost instinctively, he turned toward her, toward the succor she so freely offered.

He gathered her into his arms. She was tall, but he was taller, and the top of her head fit just under his chin. When he used a hand to tuck her head against him, the perfection of that fit startled him. She held him, and he held her, for a long moment. Desire shot through him as her warm curves pressed against his chest.

Suddenly, he realized her breathing was uneven, as uneven as his own.

It was unfair and wrong of him to mislead her.

He had to let her go.

He gathered his strength, gathered his thoughts. "Claire," he said, his voice a hoarse whisper. "I think it's time I told you about Mary Jo."

When she tilted her face to his, he saw that her cheeks were flushed. "Okay," she said, and her shoulders straightened. "Tell me about your wife."

"Why don't we sit down," he suggested.

"No, go ahead. Tell me about Mary Jo."

Claire's dark eyes gleamed in the bright light of the kitchen. He didn't want to hurt her. But he needed her to understand that there couldn't be anything between them.

He took a deep breath. "Mary Jo was pregnant when she died."

Claire winced, and he had to look away from the sympathy that sprang into her gaze.

"We'd been trying for years to have another child, and Mary Jo was on her way to the doctor's when she was hit by a drunk driver."

"Oh, God, Michael—"

"I was at work. I was always at work, getting criminals off," he interrupted, determined to get the whole story out while he still had command of his emotions. She stood beside him at the kitchen counter, listening, her gaze direct, her body as taut as his own. "She died that day, at the hospital. I managed to get there before she died. I held her hand. At first, she kept asking about the baby, and I didn't know if I should tell her the truth, that our baby was..." He could not go on.

"Oh, Michael, I'm so sorry. I didn't know any of this. I knew you'd lost your wife, but not the whole story." Her eyes were moist, and she reached out and touched the back of his hand with her fingertips.

He took a deep breath. "I loved Mary Jo so much."

There was a pause, and then she said, in an even lower voice than his, "I know."

"Claire, the man who killed her was never prosecuted. I used to have all these connections, and I thought I was a real hotshot at the public defender's office, but I couldn't make the prosecutors seek an indictment. I've always thought if I could have done that, if I could have made sure that guy paid for what he did to Mary Jo, if somehow I could get her justice... But I couldn't, and I had promised her I would."

"You still love her," Claire said very softly.

"Sometimes it feels like she's been gone forever, that life's just one monotonous ache. But sometimes it feels as if she's still here, when I touch something in this apartment and remember that it was hers too." He swallowed. "That's why I haven't had the heart to change anything, not since she died."

She looked up at him, her eyes dark and wide with sympathy and caring. They stood there, neither of them moving, for a long moment.

Then he cleared his throat. "I'll call you a cab," he said finally, going over to the telephone and picking up the directory.

Her voice was very soft. "Are you really okay? Would you like me to stay a while, keep you company?"

"That's all right." He wanted her to go, he told himself. If she stayed, he'd end up taking the comfort she offered, and maybe more.

He hated to discuss Mary Jo's death. He hated, too, admitting that he'd failed, that he hadn't been able to get Beske prosecuted. But something hard inside had shifted as he'd talked to Claire. He resisted the notion that telling *Claire* had made him feel better; it had just been time to tell somebody.

A few minutes later, Michael walked Claire down to the lobby to wait for her cab. It was very late, and no one knew better than he how mean the streets of Chicago could be after dark.

They were quiet as they waited. The lobby, with its ultramodern steel-and-glass decor, was dim. The only light came from the street outside and the lights around the bank of elevators. There were some canned spotlights in the corner, showcasing some plants in silver tubs. The security station was vacant.

"I'll stop by and see your mom," Claire said.

"You don't have to do that." But he was grateful for the offer.

He intended to do nothing more than take her hand, to tell her he appreciated all she had done. He should not have touched her. Because as soon as his skin touched hers, he was lost.

Desperately, roughly, before his brain could kick on to tell him this was wrong, wrong, *wrong,* he pulled her into his arms. His hand tipped her chin up, and his lips came down on hers. He felt her initial shock, then a relaxation as her whole body melted against him. He held her to him with a hand on the back of her neck, his palm cradling the mane of her hair, her full breasts pressing against his chest.

Her mouth was warm and . . . alive, so very alive under his. She parted her lips, and he parted his. With a will of its own, his tongue surged into her mouth, and she met his tongue boldly with hers. As she kissed him back with a fervor that matched his own, he knew there was nothing to think about but her lush, willing body against his and—

No.

He broke from the kiss. "Claire." He breathed the single syllable as if he'd just run a long way.

Her voice was breathless, too. "Oh, yes, Michael." She placed her hands on his face, one on each cheek. They were trembling.

He lifted his own hands, covering hers in an effort to still them, at the same time trying to fling off the desire that had broadsided him the moment he'd touched her. "I shouldn't have done that."

She stiffened. For a second, they just stood there, locked in a frozen embrace. Then Claire pulled herself out of his arms and turned away from him. She fumbled in her pocket for her gloves. She wouldn't look at him.

He had no idea what to say. "Claire, I'm sorry—"

"Please, Michael. Don't say any more." She bowed her head for a moment, and when she spoke again, her voice quavered before gaining strength. "It's been a long night." She drew a deep breath. "And my cab's here."

Without another word, she pushed through the heavy-plate glass doors into the night.

Michael followed her. He paid the driver far more than the fare required to get Claire home. "The extra is for you to wait until she lets herself into her building," he said to the driver. "I want her to be safe."

Then he watched the cab pull away from the curb. He imagined he could still smell the contradictory scent of Claire—sharp citrus and sweet, tropical flowers. It seemed to linger in the cold night air. Most of all, he was sure he could taste her, feel her lips moving, responding to his need.

When he went back upstairs, would he feel Mary Jo's presence in the rooms she had decorated? Or, would he picture Claire curled on the floor, reading his daughter's schoolbook, the lamplight shining in her dark hair?

CHAPTER FIVE

"HAVE YOU GOT IT?" Sabrina Simmons whispered, standing very close to Angela.

Angela reached up to the top shelf of her locker, pretending to look for something among the litter of pens and papers. "Hi, Sabrina," she said over her shoulder.

"You didn't call me last night." There was a familiar petulance in her best friend's voice.

"My dad came home early and we went out to eat and then to see my grandmother in the hospital. It was too late to call when I got home. Your mom said no calls after ten, remember?" Angela fished for a purple marker and waited for Sabrina to ask how her grandmother was. Angela was eager to tell her, because her *busia* looked good. Angela had been really scared about how she was doing, even though her dad and Claire had told her she was okay, and she wanted to tell her best friend all about it.

"I worried that maybe you didn't have it done, or that it sounded too much like yours. You could have called me. I could have told my mom it was a wrong number or something."

Angela sighed and turned around. She adjusted her notebooks, putting her notes for physics, her next class, on top. Sabrina was waiting, tossing her perfect blond hair over one shoulder, exposing the gold loops in her ears, cracking her gum with impatience.

Angela had what she wanted. But Angela suddenly decided Sabrina could wait. For one thing, she had never even asked how her *busia* was doing. A friend should remember to ask.

"Hey, Sabrina." Randy Warner came up and lightly punched Sabrina on the upper arm. He didn't kiss her or anything, even though Angela had seen them kiss, twice, while they were outside the building, waiting for their rides home. Baldwin had a lot of rules, and one was no kissing in the school building. Baldwin had a lot of stupid rules, even though Randy Warner was almost sixteen. Almost grown-up.

Randy Warner was so cool, more cool even than Sabrina. And he had a best friend named Joel Tate who looked sort of like he was Tom Cruise's younger brother. Angela liked Joel a whole lot.

Sabrina tossed her head and laughed at something Randy said. Angela had tried tossing her head that way, at home in front of the mirror, but it didn't look right. Maybe it was this stupid braid she wore, that just... flopped all over the place.

"Hey, kiddo, you dropped this." Randy handed Angela her marker, which had fallen to the hallway floor.

Angela hated it when Randy called her kiddo, but she smiled anyway and talked with Sabrina and Randy about the soccer match that was scheduled for a week from Friday. Joel Tate played forward for Baldwin Academy.

Out of the corner of her eye, Angela saw that Rachel Kellermann had come to her locker two doors down and was listening to the conversation, too. Angela smiled at her, and Rachel curved her lips in an almost-smile in return. Rachel was shy, and sort of chunky. Her parents had German accents and her father was some kind of scientist—a mad scientist, Sabrina always claimed, wiggling her eyebrows and laughing. Rachel's parents seemed different from the other parents who had kids at Baldwin. At least, Angela thought, her own father drove an awesome car and had a tailor make his suits. Rachel Kellermann didn't ever seem to fit in anywhere.

I could be like Rachel, Angela thought, *lonely, standing by my locker and listening to the cool kids talk.*

Instead, she was one of the cool kids, and she was lucky that Sabrina had started a conversation with her one day outside of fifth-period English, and that they had got to be best friends. Angela looked down at her plaid jumper. For once, it wasn't pink, but it was so out of fashion. She knew, frowning at it, exactly how lucky she was, to have Sabrina for a friend.

"We could take the El after the game, and get a pizza, and play the videos," Randy was saying. "Can you go, too, Angela?"

Angela shot a glance toward Sabrina, to see if Sabrina minded her horning in on her date with Randy. Angela was still unsure how it went with dates; she'd never had one herself.

"Can we get somebody for Angela?" Sabrina asked.

"I asked Joel," Randy said. "I told him maybe Angela would be coming, and he said okay, if we don't mind waiting around until the coach lets the team go."

Angela's heart did a little flip. "You told him I'd be going? And he said okay?" Even though she tried to sound casual, she heard a breathless note in her voice.

"I *told* you Angela has a thing for Joel," Sabrina said to Randy, and Angela blushed to the roots of her hair. She was thinking fast. Her dad probably would say she was too young for a date, but on Friday nights she stayed over at Sabrina's. It could work out.

She glanced toward Rachel Kellermann. Rachel blushed and looked away. So, Angela thought, she wasn't the only one who had a thing for Joel Tate. Suddenly, she felt sorry for Rachel. Sometimes she and Rachel talked about school and things, even though one time Sabrina had seen them and later said, "Why are you talking to *her?*"

The warning bell rang.

"I need my paper, Angela," Sabrina said. "We've got English fifth period."

Angela hesitated again. It wasn't as if it was really cheating, or anything. Angela hadn't written all that much about *Ethan Frome* that Sabrina couldn't have got herself from the Cliff Notes.

Only... only Sabrina hadn't got the information from the Cliff Notes. Angela had written the whole paper, and she'd tried hard to make it sound different enough from her own so that the instructor wouldn't find out what was going on.

She'd thought it would get easier, now that she'd done this four times. The first time Sabrina had insisted she write a paper for her, Angela had felt terrible, scared that her dad would find out. He'd be furious, and disappointed in her. She heard all the time at home about how her *dzia dzia* had fought the Nazis and then the Communists in Poland, and how in America everyone had rights but also responsibilities. Now that she was thirteen, Angela was embarrassed when her dad talked about doing the right thing, about standing up for what you believed in, about things like pride in your work.

But as irritated as she was at him most of the time, Angela didn't think she could stand it if her dad was disappointed in her.

He just didn't understand. He was sad and he missed her mom, and he was trying to do everything the way he thought her mom would do it. Only he didn't really know how her mom would do it. Nobody would ever know, now.

Angela bet her mom would have understood that the most important thing in the world was your friends.

Slowly, feeling like crying, Angela fumbled through her notebook for the English paper. When she pulled the essay out, she held it toward Sabrina.

Sabrina gave a little squeal and snatched the essay out of her hand, reading rapidly. Sabrina was bright, but she was more interested in Randy and her hair than her classes.

"God, Angela, couldn't you have written more than four pages?"

Angela caught Randy's gaze. He rolled his eyes and grinned, sort of a with-women-it's-never-enough look that seemed so sophisticated.

"Four was the minimum."

"But I could have got extra credit," Sabrina said.

"You'll get a good grade."

"Oh, Angela, I'm not upset with you, really. You're so smart, you know."

Her dad said she was smart, too, but he also always said that what he was most proud of was how hard she worked...

"Give it back," she said suddenly, holding out her hand.

"Hey, no way." Sabrina gave her a teasing smile and tossed her hair. "You gave it to me, and I'm using it." Then her eyes narrowed. "Are you going to be a scared little Catholic girl about all of this? Because if you are, just remember that if I get in trouble, so do you."

Angela's stomach hurt.

"Nobody's going to get in trouble." Randy slouched away from the locker. "Unless you both miss the final bell."

They hurried away. Angela and Sabrina turned left at the next hallway, Randy right, toward the high school end of Baldwin. "Angela, I'll tell Joel you can make it next Friday." The words were tossed over his shoulder.

Sabrina squeezed her hand. "See? Everything's cool. You just do a few things to prove you're my friend. That's what friends are for, and we'll have a blast."

Sabrina was right. And now Angela had until a week from Friday to plan what might count as her first date. And it was with Joel Tate! Would he kiss her? No boy had ever kissed her before, but Sabrina would give her pointers, and Angela would practice in front of the mirror, to make sure she didn't look weird or anything.

It was worth it, Angela thought, having to write an English paper or two for her best friend. And really, it wasn't that big a deal.

FIVE DAYS LATER, Michael stood in the kitchen, pouring himself a second cup of coffee. He needed it. He hadn't slept well last night, not after he'd been awakened by another dream, this one downright torrid, featuring dark hair, and a red, red sweater over white skin, and an enameled bracelet, made up of a bunch of elephants. Elephants, for God's sake. Now he hoped the coffee would give him a boost.

Angela appeared, looking scrubbed and neat in a denim skirt and rose-colored turtleneck. That was a surprise. Angela got to stay up late on Saturday nights, and on Sundays she was sometimes hard-pressed to get up by ten.

"What have we got for breakfast?" Angela peered into one of the cupboards, then chose the low-fat cereal she insisted the housekeeper keep in stock. After she poured it into a bowl, she doused it with about a quarter cup of sugar. Michael smiled ruefully. Maybe he should lighten up about her dieting.

He sat down with Angela at the kitchen table, and while she was eating, showed her the advertisement for an exhibition that was beginning its run at the Art Institute.

"So, what'll it be today, Angel? Matisse or ice-skating?"

She chewed for a moment, swallowed, and then in an overly casual voice, said, "Oh, didn't I tell you? I'm going shopping."

No, she certainly hadn't told him. Sundays were *their* days, a day Michael tried hard to save for his daughter. And she'd said *I'm,* not *we're.*

He set down his coffee cup. "Okay," he said carefully. "Shopping's fine with me. Where do you want to go? Marshall Field?"

Angela wouldn't look at him, and there was a spot of color on the cheekbone turned toward him. "Actually, I'm going with Claire Logan."

Michael was stunned. When had she made a date to go shopping with Claire? And hadn't he explained to Claire that his Sundays with his daughter were precious, the high point of his week?

"I see," he said, telling himself he was angry with Angela for making plans without consulting him, not hurt that his daughter wanted to spend her Sunday with Claire rather than him. He thought Angela enjoyed their outings as much as he did, thought it meant something to her that they were spending time together. And these days, it seemed, he could never escape Claire. He saw her at work, now he heard her name at home. No wonder he was having dreams about the woman!

Angela turned to him. "I've got money saved, and Claire's going to help me pick out some clothes."

His mind's eye flashed to the red sweater in the shop window, the ugly one with the plaid Scottish terrier and fringed yarn whiskers that Claire had admired, the sweater he kept imagining cuddled next to her skin. He glanced at his daughter, wondering what on earth she and Claire would pick out.

"If you needed new clothes, I would have taken you to get them," he said, though Angela had a closet full of clothes. "Or your *busia* would have made you—"

"Oh, Dad, you don't understand. I *hate* my clothes!"

She'd said that before—he'd put it down to his daughter turning thirteen, the time when all the books said Angela would be dissatisfied with everything.

Now he wondered. He didn't pay much attention to what kids were wearing, and he'd always thought Angela looked fine. But for Angela to have saved her allowance to buy clothes instead of CDs... And to ask Claire for help...

Angela was staring at him defiantly, no doubt waiting for him to say something—anything—so she could burst into tears, rush to her room and slam the door.

Mary Jo had liked feminine, classic clothing. He opened his mouth to remind Angela of what her mother had preferred, then stopped.

He remembered something Claire had said. *What's her style, Michael? What colors and styles does she like?*

He'd been so sure Angela was too young to have a "style." Maybe he'd been wrong.

Without a word, Michael left Angela in the kitchen and headed to his bedroom. On the dresser, his wallet lay next to a picture of Mary Jo. As he picked up the wallet and extracted his gold card, his gaze went to the picture. *Mary*

Jo, I wish you could give me some advice. It's damn hard for me always to know the right thing to do. Mary Jo smiled, that serene, airbrushed smile that suddenly seemed a bit unreal. He was on his own, here.

In the kitchen, he sat beside his daughter again. Michael noticed she'd been crying a little. Clothes weren't important, not as important as his relationship with his daughter. He reached out and patted her hand awkwardly, wondering if he was doing the right thing, or if he was spoiling her too much. "Here," he said finally, handing her the credit card. "Get what you want." He tried to smile. "Just remember, I'm a father, okay? Try not to shock me too much."

"Oh, Dad." Suddenly, she was out of her chair and hugging him fiercely, and he heard a sob against his neck. *"Thank* you."

WHEN CLAIRE GOT to the door, she told herself she was prepared for awkwardness. Although she had seen Michael a few times at the firm since his mother was hospitalized, both of them were careful to keep their encounters short and confine the conversation to business. She couldn't forget the other night, when she'd managed to make a fool of herself, practically begging him to kiss her. Even now, she was embarrassed to look at him, to remember the all-encompassing need that had coursed through her body the moment she'd felt his lips on hers.

He had been hurting, and he'd just told her about his wife. Surely she could have allowed him to hold her, without becoming embroiled in passion, using her body and mouth to urge him to a desire that proved nothing more than that he was a man. He needed a friend. She needed a friend.

Claire had felt the pain and the longing, the desperate longing that had hardened Michael's mouth, caused it to so thoroughly take her own . . .

A longing for Mary Jo.

Claire would have stayed home, but for her promise to Angela. She smiled in relief as Angela came to the door. "Hi there. Are you ready to go?"

"I'll just get my jacket. Come on in."

As Claire stepped into the foyer, determined not to go any farther and take a chance on encountering Michael, the man himself walked into view.

"Claire." He smiled at her, a reserved, wary smile, and shoved his hands into the pockets of his jeans.

The gesture drew her eye. Nobody did things for an expensive suit like Michael Chalinski. But the sight of him in a trim, thigh-hugging pair of jeans was enough to set her heart humming again. Her reaction made her nervous, even though she had decided there would never be a repeat of that humiliating scene in the lobby of this building.

"I won't have Angela out too long," she said, and then without waiting for a comment from him, hurried on, "We'll take the El, and go to a couple of boutiques off Michigan. I can never find much that I like in the department stores, but I've discovered a couple of little shops that carry interesting pieces." Involuntarily, she glanced down at her vest. It was new, and when she'd put it on that morning, she told herself that wearing it had nothing to do with the possibility of seeing Michael. It was a fitted patchwork of dark red velvet and blue denim, sporting six fake-gold pocket watches, with attendant chains.

Michael, too, was looking at the vest, and it suddenly struck Claire that the lines of the darn thing emphasized her full breasts much more than the clothing she wore to work. Oh, no, he didn't think she was coming on to him, did he?

She could feel her cheeks growing hot as his gaze lingered, so she just blabbed. "And, ah, I'll see that she gets some lunch, and if we have time, maybe we'll go to a music store...I mean, all kids like music, but I'll have her home before dinner, no matter what..." She finally ran out of things to say. Where *was* Angela, anyway? "Angela?" she blared, way too loud.

The sound brought Michael abruptly out of his reverie, and Claire could have sworn a quick flush darkened the area around his prominent cheekbones. "I'll get her." He turned, obviously glad for the chance to make his getaway.

"I'm right here." Angela appeared in her coat, looking from one to the other. "I had to go to the bathroom."

"Oh," both Claire and Michael said at once.

Claire stood aside to let Angela precede her out the door. Then Angela turned. "Dad? Would you like to go with us?"

A split second of surprised pleasure swept Michael's features, before he assumed a carefully neutral expression. "I thought you wanted to go with Claire."

"You can come, too," Angela offered again.

"Sure, we'll show you the meaning of the word *shop.*" Claire aimed for a light tone.

He looked uncertain. Claire figured he would have jumped at the chance to spend time with Angela, which meant that he simply didn't want to be with Claire. A stab of hurt went through her. He was in love with his wife. He liked Claire, as long as she didn't push. Why couldn't she get that through her head, stop letting him get to her? He wasn't the first man she'd wanted who hadn't returned the sentiment.

"Okay, let me get my keys. I'll drive us." With a boyish smile that turned Claire's mental lecture on its head, he retrieved his keys and pulled on a suede jacket.

Claire directed them to a boutique where she bought her favorite things. Angela was delighted with the outing, and her good spirits were catching. Claire found herself talking with Michael more easily.

At the boutique, Angela pawed through the racks. Claire discovered Angela had a good idea of what she wanted, and Sandy, the clerk who always saved the quirkiest things for Claire, was having a ball showing the girl some blouses. Claire settled into a chair next to Michael while Angela and Sandy took what they jokingly referred to as load one into the fitting room.

Michael stretched his legs out, looking outsize and male in the fragile chair. "I was surprised Angela wanted me along," he admitted. "She doesn't think I have good taste in clothes."

"Well, your clothes are fine, but Angela's are a little out of style," Claire said as gently as she could.

"So I've been hearing. I thought I was doing the right thing, letting her *busia* pick things out. But my mother is seventy, and she's always concerned with how practical something is. I figured, what the hell do I know about a little girl's clothes?" He shot her a look. "The part I don't get is why on earth it's so important to her. Mary Jo and I didn't bring her up to be this materialistic."

"It's important to her because, for one thing, she's not a little girl anymore. She's thirteen, Michael." Was the man that dense? Did he really not understand what it was like to be a thirteen-year-old girl, on the edge of womanhood and so confused... Claire brought herself up short.

Of course he didn't know; how could he? At that moment, the full magnitude of the task Michael had set himself, his desire to be both father and mother to Angela, hit her.

Michael worked seventy hours a week, eighty if he had a big case pending. His star was rising at the firm; he was making excellent money. Many men in his situation, she thought, would have hired someone to care for their daughters while they got on with their own lives, professionally and personally.

Many of the seniors at the firm were divorced. A position in a big law firm, with the grinding hours and winner-take-all hustle, wasn't conducive to marriage. Thinking about it, Claire realized that most of the single men she knew enjoyed dating and socializing. Michael was so good-looking, surely he could live that life if he chose. It might even help his career. Instead he chose to spend his time trying to be both mother and father to his daughter.

"In some ways, she's still a little girl," Michael said after a moment's reflection. "But, you're right, she is growing up." He drummed the fingers of one hand on his jean-clad knee. "In a way, I don't think I've wanted to face that. I knew I hadn't been enough of a father to her before we lost Mary Jo, and I guess I wanted to pretend I had plenty of time to fix things, to build a relationship with her." He sighed. "Instead, I may have blown it."

"Oh, Michael, you didn't blow it, not by a long shot." Impulsively, Claire squeezed his hand, and then left hers covering his; she was thrilled when he didn't pull away. Instead, he turned to face her more fully. It struck her then that Michael badly needed reassurance on this point.

"Do you know what I would have given for a father like you when I was a girl?" she said. "My father belittled me, thought I should hide how I really was inside. You can't imagine how that felt, knowing that to have the approval of the one male who mattered to me, I had to deny everything about myself I liked.'' Suddenly, she felt the hot prick of tears behind her eyelids. ''So you make mistakes with Angela, but you're there, not off with some little doll you prefer to her mother. Angela told me how you encourage her, praise her for how hard she works in school. She's got to know how much you love her, so there's no way you can go wrong.''

''Do you think so? Really?''

''I do,'' she said. Then her treacherous heart betrayed her again, because now she was imagining she saw him take a deep breath, his lips softening, his eyes half closing, and she was imagining he was bending toward her, here in a little crowded boutique...

His eyes flew open. ''No,'' he said, his body stiffening, and for a split second, Claire thought she had suffered another embarrassing rejection.

Then she followed his gaze. Angela was standing a few feet in front of them, in a shiny, skintight pair of leggings and a royal purple crop top. The top had long sleeves, but her entire midriff was bare, and the fabric and cut magnified the points of her small breasts.

Angela had been smiling, a half shy, half defiant smile, but at her father's reaction, defiance pushed to the forefront.

Michael was clearly furious. ''No way. No way are you walking around wearing that. You look like a—''

''Michael.'' Just in time, Claire held up a cautioning finger, and he fell abruptly silent.

Beside Angela, Sandy tried to pull the top lower on one side. She shot Claire a helpless look.

"I *like* this outfit." Angela had planted herself in place. "It makes me look older."

Claire felt the tension in Michael.

"It's a great color, Angela," Claire said, deliberately not commenting on how tight and revealing the girl's choice was. "And I know you like purple. But it's too bright for you. You're more delicate than I am, and the thing is, you need to find your own look."

Angela fastened an uncertain gaze on Claire.

"That's why you brought me here, isn't it?" Claire asked, using the calm tone she reserved for unreasonable clients. She stood. "Let me go through some of these racks with you. Sandy, have you got something in yellow?"

Relieved, Sandy started looking through racks. "Maybe we'll have better luck with load two."

Claire finally found what she was looking for, a sweater she had spotted the week before. She held it out toward Michael. "How about something like this?"

His mouth set in a grim line, his expression doubtful, Michael eyed the sweater, with its swirling purple triangles on a butter-yellow background. "Isn't it a little bright?" he asked finally.

"Yellow will look good on her. Try it on, Angela," Claire urged. Sandy found a matching pair of leggings and disappeared into the fitting room behind the girl.

Claire stood by Michael, her hand on the back of his chair, while they waited. When Angela appeared, her shining eyes and the blush on her cheeks were enough for Claire.

"Oh, Angela, you look terrific."

"Dad?" Angela stood in front of her father in the loose, soft sweater and the leggings, which didn't seem so tight with the sweater covering her hips.

Michael cleared his throat. "You look very pretty, Angel." His voice was gruff.

Angela beamed at him and sauntered a few steps toward a full-length mirror. "I've got just the place to wear it to, next Friday night, when I go to the soccer game and then after—" She cut herself off, then tilted her head, examining the effect.

Claire hid a smile, remembering all the times as a teenager she had practiced everything from debate to dance in front of a mirror, and how often she was disappointed with the images she saw. A warmth crept into her as she watched Angela. Angela was clearly pleased at her reflection.

"Claire? Could you maybe tell me what to do with my hair?" Angela was holding the end of her braid in one hand and looking at Claire as if she were a miracle worker. "I was thinking, maybe I'll get it all cut off, spike my bangs or something."

Michael shifted uncomfortably in his seat.

"Let's try something less drastic, first," Claire suggested. "Sandy, have you got a scrunchie that would match this outfit?"

"What's a scrunchie?" Michael asked.

Angela said, "Oh, Dad," at exactly the same time as Claire said, "Don't worry, a scrunchie doesn't bite." He slumped back in his chair, looking defeated.

When the clerk held out the little band of gathered fabric, Michael realized a scrunchie was what Claire used so often to hold her ponytail. He liked Claire's hair, that sleek black satin that never seemed out of place. At least a hundred times, he'd imagined teasing that little band out of the way, and feeling the full, smooth cascade of hair flowing down her back.

After Claire unbraided Angela's hair, she didn't put the scrunchie around the hair at his daughter's nape, as he had expected. Instead, she caught up Angela's curls, securing the band over one ear, so that her hair fell over her shoulders on one side in a tumbled mass that made her look downright beautiful.

"Oh, wow," Angela said.

Michael relaxed then, realizing that Claire knew what she was doing. He watched from his place by the window, as the three of them, Claire, Sandy and his giggling daughter, picked out one item after another—tights, jeans, T-shirts. Sometimes Angela came to him for approval, but most often she turned to Claire.

And Claire didn't seem much older than his daughter as she held one item after another against Angela's slender frame. "Oh, God, that's ugly," she exclaimed once over something Sandy had produced, and all three women burst into laughter.

Michael had never thought shopping could be so much fun. He watched from the sidelines, feeling indulgent toward his daughter and warm toward the whole world.

Angela had taken a sweatshirty something into the fitting room when he turned to Claire.

"Claire, do you remember that red sweater?"

She looked blank.

He had no idea why it felt so important that she remember. "That red sweater. The night a few weeks ago when we went window shopping, and you liked a sweater with a Scottish terrier appliquéd—"

"Oh, yes." Her expression, which had been frowning in concentration, cleared. "The one with the brass button for an eye and the—"

"Whiskers," he finished before she could. "Did you ever go back and buy it?"

He sounded too intense, he knew, but she answered anyway.

"No, I didn't. I looked at it a few times, but that boutique's too expensive. I need to save the biggest part of my clothes budget for suits to wear to work."

He felt a stab of inexplicable disappointment.

But the day was still almost . . . magical. He had never felt so loose and mellow, to the point that when Angela asked if she could have her ears pierced, he said yes without hesitation and headed over to Marshall Field. There, after her ears were pierced, Michael bought her a tiny pair of real gold studs, and Angela kissed him on the cheek.

As the three of them shared a pizza late that afternoon, Michael watched his daughter. He felt almost overwhelmed with love. He'd have to protect her, watch over her. But he had to realize that she was growing up too, and give her more freedom. He felt a surge of gratitude toward Claire, for helping him begin to find his way back to his daughter.

Finally, he took Claire home. When he walked her to the outer door of her apartment complex, he knew he didn't dare follow her inside. With Angela waiting in the car, he was safe. He couldn't pull Claire into his arms, not where his daughter could see them. Well, he could kiss Claire on the cheek, couldn't he? Today proved they could be good friends, and a friend could give her a light peck of thanks.

But he didn't trust himself to stop there. So he took her hand and gave it a brief squeeze, and knew that when he thanked her for the day his voice sounded unnaturally husky.

It was only later, out of Claire's presence, that some of his good cheer left him. Angela took her packages down the hallway to her room. A few minutes later, passing her closed door on his way to the shower, he heard the beeps of her phone, signaling she was calling Sabrina.

He had hoped that Angela's newfound attachment to Claire might mean his daughter would cling less to Sabrina. Obviously, that had not happened.

In the bathroom, feeling vaguely unsettled, he pulled a towel from the linen closet and turned on the hot water. Standing under the shower, a realization hit him. He saw what had seemed so different about today.

He had not missed Mary Jo.

Suddenly, Michael felt cold, despite the hot water pouring over him.

Instead of keeping Mary Jo's image alive, he'd enjoyed his time with Claire. Maybe he'd even pretended that the three of them—he and Angela and Claire—were a family. He'd struggled to get closer to his daughter today, and he'd gained some insight into what made Claire the woman she was, why she needed to shine at the firm.

On the way to all this understanding, was he losing his precious memories of his wife?

He turned off the shower, then realized he hadn't rinsed his hair. Damn. Claire could make him forget things.

Mary Jo had been gone less than two years. Okay, so he was a normal, healthy male whose body wanted a woman. But that was as far as it went, he assured himself. His attraction to Claire was physical, a reaction he should have expected to come sooner or later.

And besides, this was only one day, a day suspended out of time, a day that was not part of his real life. He should simply remember it that way.

Sighing, Michael turned on the shower again and rinsed his hair. When he was through, he toweled off enough to yank on a pair of sweats.

On his way back down the hall, he noticed Angela had already completed what must be the shortest Angela-to-Sabrina communication on record. The light over her bed was on, and she was reading. He paused in the doorway.

"What's the matter? Wasn't Sabrina home?"

"Oh, I talked to her." Angela set her book aside. "I was telling her how great Claire was, and, you know..."

He waited.

"Sabrina said Claire was taking me shopping so she could impress you." Her new ponytail still hung jauntily over one ear, but her eyes looked large and somber in the light. "I got sort of upset, but I didn't want her to know, so I said I had things to do and had to hang up." She paused. "Dad, do you think that's why Claire took me shopping, just to impress you?"

"No, I don't." He was sure of that much. Claire was too honest to be manipulating the situation the way Sabrina suggested. "Claire would never do something just to impress somebody. She likes you." He paused. "But in a way, I'm glad Sabrina said something, so you never get the wrong impression about Claire and me. We're just friends. Okay?"

She smiled. "Okay, Dad."

His daughter had what almost seemed like a crush on Claire, Michael realized as he moved away from the doorway. Not a crush, exactly. More like hero worship. What would Mary Jo have thought of that? he wondered. Would she have wanted Claire to spend time with her daughter? Not for the first time, he decided Mary Jo might not have even liked Claire. Where Mary Jo was quiet and shy and traditional, Claire was talkative and outgoing and modern. It was baffling to him that he could find two such very different women attractive.

It was baffling... and unsettling.

THE RINGING TELEPHONE jolted Michael out of a deep sleep, and automatically he reached for the receiver. His bedside clock said 1:00 a.m.

"Is this where I can collect the reward?" It was a feminine voice, sounding crisp and confident over the telephone line. "Are you the one offering the reward in the *Tribune?*"

Instantly, Michael was wide-awake. He gripped the receiver hard. "I'm offering a reward. For information. Did you see the accident on Cavendish and Petrove on April third, almost two years ago?"

"Oh, sure," the voice said. "The guy who hit that car was drunk."

Oh, God. Drunk. Over the past twenty months, as his classified advertisement had continued to run, there had been a number of callers, all seeking the reward. None of the others had volunteered the information that the person at fault was drunk.

Was he finally going to be able to nail Beske?

Over the rush of adrenaline, his lawyer instincts kicked in. It was the middle of the night. The comment might be nothing more than a clever guess. After all, many fatal accidents were caused by people who had had too much to drink.

"Please. Tell me exactly what you saw that day," he said.

"Well, the driver was drunk. Weaving around. How much is the reward?"

"It could be substantial, if you're willing to testify to what you saw. Tell me more, please. How exactly did the accident occur?" His heart was pounding. In the dark, he fumbled amid the items on his nightstand for a pad of paper and a pencil.

"Well, you know, he just hit it," the caller said. "Damaged the car real bad." Michael picked up the slightest hint of slyness creeping into the voice.

"What kind of cars were the parties driving? Who did he hit, a man or a woman?" Please, God, he thought, don't let this be another person just calling for the money.

"He hit a woman."

Yesss.

"And the cars they were driving?" He held his breath.

"Maybe we could meet somewhere, talk this over."

"What kind of cars?"

"Um, hers was kind of... blue?" The last word was drawn out into a question. Anger and disappointment, both bitter as gall, flowed into Michael's veins.

"Her car was red," he said. "Red, damn it! You didn't see anything, did you?"

"Oh, yeah, red. And his car was black."

Beske's car had been red, too.

Ever so gently, with exquisite care, Michael hung up on the caller. Then he lay back on the bed, and flung his arm over his eyes.

CHAPTER SIX

"So, WHAT DO YOU think, Claire?" Stuart Tyler III put down his pen and looked across the teak conference table toward Claire. Stuart hadn't bothered to ask anyone else for an opinion, Michael noted, although all seventeen associates were gathered for the case conference.

"I don't think you should offer more money to settle," Claire said thoughtfully.

"For now there's just one plaintiff." Stuart loosened his tie in a nervous gesture. "But they're threatening a class action if we don't cooperate."

Michael sat at the head of the table, presiding over, but not participating much, in the case conference. Once every two weeks, the associates in his half of Litigation got together and hashed out some of their cases. Unlike many other law firms, Haynes, Haynes, Collingwood and Crofts didn't go in for case conferences. The partners thought associates should talk over their cases with their senior, period. But Michael liked the conferences, thought it gave the associates a chance to defend their ideas in an atmosphere of support.

Stuart continued to outline the possibility of a class action suit in his products liability case. A new brand of cleansing powder with an unusual herbal ingredient had caused severe skin rashes in a number of users; the plaintiff in question had nearly died from an allergic reaction.

"The class could number two thousand, at least," Stuart was continuing, his voice going slightly lower at the wonder of having two thousand plaintiffs for his company client to negotiate with. "I'm going to recommend we settle at the first opportunity. Who could take this big a risk?"

Michael sat up straighter. A class action suit was a trial lawyer's worst nightmare. But it was early, yet; negotiations had just begun on the case. If there was a time to take a risk, Michael felt it was now.

He was careful not to allow his opinion to show. The purpose of the case conferences was to let the associates find their own way. "Okay," he said finally. "Stuart's shared with us the risks if we hold out on a bigger settlement offer. Anybody want to comment?"

Claire said, "I do." She leaned forward. "Stuart, they're demanding at least a third more than our client ought to pay." Glancing at her legal pad, she continued, "I checked the Illinois court records for the last ten years, and the plaintiff's demand is way off. After all, the company knows it screwed up, and they're willing to pay fair compensation." She smiled wryly. "Lord knows, that's a plus, compared to some of our clients."

Michael wasn't really surprised that Claire had looked up the information about what similar cases had cost companies over the years, even though the case wasn't her own. She always prepared diligently for these conferences. A quick glance around the table revealed that none of the associates, except perhaps Stuart, had gone to the trouble of researching precedents. They had all learned something. Now he waited for Stuart to defend his position. After all, giving away a lot of money now might prevent a several-million-dollar verdict in a few years.

Instead, Stuart gave Claire one of his puppy-dog looks of admiration that always managed to set Michael's blood pressure soaring. Lately, the gossip mill around the firm had been full of the news that Stuart and Claire had been seen together a couple of times at the coffee bar in the lobby, and that Stuart was working up the courage to ask her out.

Stuart pushed his glasses higher on the bridge of his nose. "Do you really think we shouldn't settle, Claire?"

"I think it's too early. The other side might get tired of paying out costs and fees, and eventually they might be willing to listen to reason. They've been watching too much television. My bet is, they'll end up accepting something reasonable if we don't give in too easily." She paused. "But don't take my word for it. What does everyone else think?"

A few others gave opinions, but none were based on facts and figures as Claire's had been. Stuart listened carefully.

Stuart was a smart and pleasant-enough guy, if a little too cautious. In working with him, Michael had become convinced that the man would never have the go-for-the-jugular instinct that was essential in a good trial attorney.

But Stuart was a good lawyer, in his way. Michael was already considering the best way to ease him into Probate or Real Estate, where his talents might shine.

"Maybe you're right, Claire," Stuart said, and when Claire smiled at him, he flushed.

A surge of emotion went through Michael, and it was so foreign that for a moment he wondered what it was that squeezed his gut so tight. Then it hit him.

He was jealous of Stuart Tyler III because Claire Logan had smiled at the man.

His gaze slid to Claire. She was joining in the discussion with animation, holding up a finger occasionally to signal that she was—again—wading in with an opinion. Stuart was so besotted with her that it must have been obvious to everyone in the room. However, looking at Claire, Michael was sure that she didn't have a clue that the guy was half in love with her.

Michael was so engrossed in his thoughts that he didn't notice that someone had come to the open door of the conference room. A slight movement drew his eye.

Slowly, the discussion died down, and all eyes were on the man in the doorway.

George Fanal, the partner in charge of Litigation, Michael's boss, stood waiting. There was no way of knowing how long he'd been there.

Michael stood. "George, come on in. We're just going over the Woffing products liability case."

"Michael." Fanal came into the room, clasping Michael's hand in a show of shared power clearly designed to impress the associates. They *were* impressed, staring openly at Fanal. Slaving away in their tiny offices or the law library, Michael knew that they rarely saw the partners who ran the firm.

Fanal settled himself into a vacant chair. "Thought I might come down and see one of these case conferences everybody's been talking about," he said easily. "Some of the other firms have been using them to advantage, I hear." Absently, he fingered his tie. Michael's eye was drawn to the diamond stud he wore through it, in the shape of a horseshoe, just ostentatious enough to be at odds with the corporate image the partners worked hard to convey. "Now, don't worry about me, just continue with your discussion. I'm only here to observe."

Nobody said anything. The easy atmosphere of a few minutes ago had vanished. Finally, Michael spoke. "We're glad to have you, George."

Michael knew why Fanal had stopped down. Lately, Russ Mallory, the other senior in Litigation, had been passing the rumor that the conferences were eroding Michael's authority. Michael told himself that his associates could handle a visit from a partner. Some were stars, some not, but all were competent and used to the give-and-take of the conferences. In fact, working with them gave him the only real satisfaction he got out of his job these days. "Stuart, why don't you summarize your case for George."

Stuart did a good job, but by the time he'd gone over the case, his upper lip was sweaty.

"And you want to settle." Fanal thought it over. "A class action suit is a damned pain in the ass. It might be a good idea to settle."

There were murmurs of agreement from a number of associates—including those who'd just argued the opposite position.

"Well, I don't think so." Claire's voice was calm and to the point.

Like at a tennis match, all eighteen heads in the room swiveled to Claire.

"I've got the figures for other settlements in allergy cases, Mr. Fanal. The plaintiff's lawyers are loose cannons and the plaintiff wants too much."

Fanal's eyebrows drew together in a frown. "Well, if the plaintiff's lawyers are loose cannons, all the more reason to settle. We can't have our lawyers devoting a lot of time to a case where the other side is pulling a lot of shenanigans."

Claire seemed to settle herself more firmly into her seat. "It's Stuart's call, but he asked to bring the case to our conference to get other opinions. Frankly, I don't think we want a reputation for settling cases on their nuisance value alone. Long term, that could spell trouble for the firm.''

Over at his end of the table, Fanal stiffened.

Michael shot a glance at Claire, silently urging her to be quiet. The other associates sat in a frozen tableau.

''The partners give us overall strategy, Claire,'' Michael reminded her mildly, feeling he should rebuke her before Fanal had a chance to. ''Our job is to win cases.''

''Which we can't do if we settle everything because we're afraid to take a few risks,'' Claire retorted.

Fanal sat up very straight. ''I take it you think this firm is afraid to take risks.''

Claire's cheeks turned pink, but her gaze was steady. ''Yes, I do. In Real Estate, Larry Oliver made me settle at least three cases I thought we had a chance of winning at trial.''

Fanal angled his head, whether in curiosity or annoyance or both, Michael wasn't sure. ''Unlike the associates, the partners have to worry about things like win percentages. Do you know what would happen if our firm took a big case to trial and lost? Our clients are conservative. They'd rather pay out a lot of money now than lose a trial and provide headlines for the *New York Times*.'' He smiled at her indulgently, as though he found her eagerness charming but her reasoning faulty. ''Now, Michael has filled me in on this Woffing case. I know we have evidence problems. The hearsay rule will give us trouble. You know these technicalities. The Hathaway case could be applied by the court in a way that is not good for our client.''

''The Hathaway case was good law when you won the case, Mr. Fanal,'' Claire said. ''It was good law for twenty years. But four months ago it was overruled.''

Oh, damn, Michael thought. Claire had done it now. The Hathaway case was Fanal's breakthrough case, the one which had propelled him to partner, the one he liked to talk about even more than he liked to talk about his stable full of racehorses. At every Christmas party, Fanal cornered one associate or another and replayed his big win in Hathaway.

Under his Jamaica sun–induced tan, Fanal turned pale. "Overruled? It's not good law?"

Fanal, like most of the partners, didn't really practice law anymore. Their job was corporate in nature. Of course Fanal didn't know that Hathaway had been overruled, Michael realized. Nobody would be stupid enough to make a point of telling him, unless it had a direct impact on a case.

Now it did have a direct impact on a case. And Michael was dismayed that the one person in the firm who would tell Fanal his precious case had been overruled was Claire. The woman didn't have the good sense to keep her mouth shut when firm politics demanded. At the same time, he had to admire her for sticking to her guns.

"It was in the *Northwest Reporter* a few months ago." Claire's voice softened. "Your reasoning was sound, Mr. Fanal, for its time and place. But there are new technicalities in the law and—"

Fanal held up a hand. He was silent for a moment, and the associates also held a respectful silence.

"Well, that does change things. If we have a better-than-average chance at trial, it might make sense to wait and see how things develop."

Still no one said anything.

"You have strong opinions, Ms. Logan," Fanal finally continued, but his tone was only half-rebuking. A grudging respect had edged into it.

"Yes, I'm afraid I do," she said, smiling a little. "Michael's always trying to rein me in, too."

"And obviously not doing a very good job of it."

Inwardly, Michael groaned. Claire had just managed to make it abundantly clear that Michael did not run his half of Litigation with the iron fist that most of the seniors used in their departments.

He felt a surge of anger. Was Claire Logan going to be his downfall? The woman who coaxed him into playing hooky, who dragged him off shopping, who dressed his daughter in brilliant yellow leggings . . . who kissed with a fervor that sent heat shooting through his whole body . . . who invaded his dreams. . . . On top of everything, was she going to screw up his chances for a partnership?

A HALF HOUR after the conference broke up, Claire found herself in Michael's office. He remained seated behind his desk. So far, his tone had been mild, but Claire knew he was not pleased that she had challenged George Fanal at a public meeting. Stubbornly, she ignored his invitation to sit down.

"I thought the purpose of the conference was to discuss the case," she said. "That's what I was doing."

"What you did could have been political suicide."

Claire's chin came up. "What are the partners paying me for, if not to express my professional opinion?"

He was upset, and she was sorry for that. She was also sorry she had blurted out that bit about Hathaway at just the moment she did, but Fanal would have had to hear about his case being overruled someday. In the law, nothing stayed the same forever.

Michael raked his hand through his hair in a gesture of utter frustration. "It's not *what* you said, but *how* you said it, and especially *when* you said it. Look. If you won't take care of your career, I'll do my damnedest to protect you. But you have to help me by knowing when to keep quiet sometimes.''

Claire felt anger shoot through her. She would have expected this from her father, from Larry Oliver, from Fanal himself, but not from Michael. She'd thought he was different. "I make my choices, Michael, and I live with them.''

He paused for a moment. "All right," he said finally. "But your choices may affect other people as well. I'm supposed to be a friend of yours. If nothing else, how can you justify making me look like I don't have control over the associates?''

"That's ridiculous." But for the first time, his argument had an impact. She did make her choices, and she'd lived with some wrong ones. But she didn't want Michael to suffer for her decisions.

She must have hesitated too long before replying, because Michael obviously saw his advantage. "I can't let you screw this up for me, Claire. I want a partnership. I *need* a partnership.''

"Why?" she challenged.

"Why?" he repeated, his voice rising in disbelief. "For the same reason every other person in this firm wants one. For power. For money. For security.''

"Come on, Michael. You don't have enough money?''

He leaned forward in his chair, and his fingers gripped the edge of the desk, so hard his knuckles were white. "I have a daughter. She goes to an expensive private school and soon she'll be going to an even more expensive college. My mother and father have exactly nothing, although my dad worked his butt off in a stamping plant for twenty-seven years. They spent everything they had getting me through Yale." He took a deep breath. "My father's medical care could be a staggering expense in years to come. I'm all they have. I have no choice."

"Oh, Michael." In a rush, all the anger went out of her, to be replaced with tenderness. "You don't like your job."

"I do like my job." But for the first time, his gaze wavered.

Ah, thought Claire. She knew he found satisfaction in supervising his associates; he never lost patience with them. He'd never pulled rank, until today, with her. But for the rest of what went on at Haynes, Haynes, Collingwood and Crofts—the pressure to bill, the under-the-table wheeling and dealing, the relentless gossip—Claire had always been secretly convinced Michael was too honest and idealistic to really enjoy the game.

She took a step toward him. "Your reasons for sticking with your job are admirable. But I wonder if all this sticking with things to the bitter end is part of how you try to control everything."

"Claire." He shifted restlessly. The one word was a clear warning.

Claire could not stop. "No one can control everything, Michael. Not even you."

He was out of his seat in a flash. A few quick strides took him to her.

"Listen to me."

He was too close. Claire had to look up. His eyes glittered, harsh and gold, as he gazed down at her. Claire felt a sudden shiver, and then had the strangest sensation that she had poked at a sleeping tiger.

"Damn it, Claire! Let me protect you."

His nearness made her nervous. "Why?" she whispered.

"Because," he muttered, his gaze still locked with hers.

For a long, charged moment, neither of them spoke.

Michael's intercom buzzed, and he jerked from her as though he'd been burned.

"Michael? Are you there?" It was his secretary's voice. "Henry Campbell of Allen and Associates on line one."

He leaned over and pressed the button. "Take a message, please, Eileen."

Michael clicked off the intercom, sat down abruptly on the edge of his desk and looked away.

Claire finally said, "I guess I should have waited with that news about Hathaway, picked a time more private to tell Mr. Fanal his case had been overruled."

He nodded, still not quite meeting her eyes. "You value your reputation as a lawyer. You work harder than any associate in this department. I don't want you to blow your chances to rise in the firm because of scenes like that case conference."

"Okay." He spoke the truth, and now she had acknowledged that fact. But she still felt very awkward.

"Okay." He sounded relieved, and turned immediately to his desk and picked up a file.

A few moments later, Claire headed for the coffee area. As she poured her decaf, she tried to sort out her feelings. Michael was trying to pretend there was nothing between them but business, but no matter how hard he tried, a tension that was purely personal stretched between them. But he didn't want a relationship with her; that was plain. And that hurt.

But suddenly, she had another thought. It seemed Michael was going to extraordinary lengths to protect her from trouble with the partners. Why?

Michael tried so hard, maybe too hard, to protect those people he . . . cared about. He was overprotective of his daughter, and he worried about his parents.

And now, at some level, anyway, Michael seemed to have added Claire Logan's name to his list.

CHAPTER SEVEN

SOPHIE CHALINSKI was finally going home. It didn't seem right, going home without Mike, but she had no choice. She knew once she was well enough her husband would come home, too.

Her ankle hurt, the cast got in her way, and the crutches made her underarms sore.

Normally Sophie would have hidden her discomfort. But she had an ulterior motive. So instead of pushing herself as she would have usually done, she hobbled and moved her crutches forward a few inches at a time and complained about the pain in her ribs, so that Michael and Claire, on either side of her, reacted by being very solicitous. Michael carried Sophie's suitcase. Claire had Sophie's flower arrangement from Michael's office in one hand, and the smaller, prettier one from the Saint Stephen's Ladies Altar Rosary Society in the other.

The two were behaving strangely, Sophie thought. Claire had given her the impression she and Michael were good friends. But from the moment they'd arrived at the hospital to take her home, Sophie had noticed that they didn't look at each other. And both spoke mostly to Sophie.

Well, whatever was going on today didn't matter a bit in the long run. She was used to thinking ahead. She'd had plenty of time to think, being stuck in that hospital, and she had made quite a few plans.

The walk to the car took forever, with Sophie having to stop and rest frequently. That scared Michael, she could see. He was used to her being peppy.

She let Claire put down the flowers and get into the back seat, and then with a groan that was only partially feigned, let her son make a great production of getting her settled into the low-slung passenger seat and sliding the crutches back to Claire.

"We got your groceries already, Mrs. Chalinski," Claire told her as soon as they were moving. "We didn't want to tire you out with shopping, so we picked out some frozen dinners. I made you some vegetable soup, too."

"Thank you, Claire," Sophie said, biting her lip for real this time, because every bump in the road sent pain up her leg. "Did you remember the chocolate chip cookies? From Domeniak's?"

"I got them, Mrs. Chalinski. The ones from Mrs. Field's."

Sophie chuckled. She'd known Claire less than a week, and already they had a joke between them, she thought with satisfaction. The day after she'd been admitted to the hospital, Claire had stopped by to introduce herself and visit. Sophie had been impressed by the gesture. She'd happened to mention she missed her chocolate chip cookies. Every morning at home, she ate chocolate chip cookies for breakfast, with milk.

"Oh, that's a terrible way to eat. They're so fattening." Involuntarily, Claire's eyes had gone to Sophie's well-padded figure, and the girl had blushed deeply.

"That's all right," Sophie had said. Mike used to say he liked his woman with a little meat on her, and she was seventy years old, for heaven's sake.

"It's not okay," Claire had retorted. "I'm sorry. I sort of blurt things out sometimes."

A few days later, Claire had been back. Sophie had asked about Michael, and work. Then Claire had talked and *talked* about him, saying she admired his legal abilities. But all the time she talked about his expertise, her cheeks had been bright red, and her eyes had sparkled, and there was a rich warmth in her voice. And when she got up to leave, she'd handed a paper sack to Sophie, and in it had been six of Mrs. Field's cookies. Those cookies were better than anything Pete Domeniak had ever stocked.

"Mrs. Field must have some Polish blood in her somewhere," Sophie said now. She turned her head, but she couldn't see Claire. Reluctantly, she faced forward. It didn't seem polite to talk to somebody while facing straight ahead, but she couldn't help it. "I'd like to hear more about your family in Nebraska, Claire. They wouldn't happen to be Catholic, would they?"

Michael shot his mother a quick, sharp glance, then turned his gaze back to the road.

"No, we're Congregationalists," Claire replied, "going back a few generations. My mom cooks with the ladies for funerals. My sister, Amy, does, too."

Churchgoing folk, then, Sophie thought. A Congregationalist. Not Catholic, but Sophie decided that was all right. It wouldn't interfere with her plan.

She was going to ask if Claire was seeing some nice young man back in Nebraska or here in Chicago, but thought better of it. Michael would be on to her immediately. She'd just have to wait and pick her time; she didn't want to scare Claire off, either.

"My mother has a business, baking wedding cakes at home," Claire was saying. "She used to be a housewife, but—" She stopped, then continued, "She had to learn to make a living, so she got great at decorating cakes, and she knew everybody in town, so she got business. It was hard, though, and one of the reasons I decided to be a lawyer was so I could support myself."

Sophie liked her reasoning. The world could be a hard place, and it was good that nowadays a woman could earn a living if she needed to, to take care of her family.

Claire's voice became wistful. "I miss her and Amy, and Amy's kids. I can't wait to go home for Christmas. I only managed to get home once this summer. Of course, summer's not a good time to go to Nebraska. It's even hotter than Chicago."

"Really?" Sophie asked encouragingly. "But I'll bet winter's not so bad. Winter in Chicago is terrible."

"Oh, no, it's much worse in Nebraska. We have blizzards, and the wind blows the snow so hard that if you're driving, you can't even see the road." And Claire was launched, then, as Sophie had intended, into a description of her town, and the weather, and her mother's house.

All Sophie had to do was listen as she held her foot off the floor of the car to lessen the pain in her ankle. When Michael made a turn, she lost her balance momentarily, but quickly recovered. This Claire was a nice girl. Anybody could tell she'd been raised right. As soon as Sophie had asked, Claire had agreed to help Michael bring her home from the hospital.

Claire was kind of pretty, too. Sophie liked that big red satin rose she had pinned at her throat, but she couldn't say much for that navy blue blazer that looked like something a man would wear.

Surreptitiously, Sophie watched Michael drive. He was quiet, pretending not to be listening, but there was a very tiny smile in the corner of his mouth.

Ah-ha. So, she hadn't been wrong. Her boy liked this girl. The way he and Claire were behaving—the tension between them—didn't change that. If anything it reminded Sophie that Michael needed her help. Since Mary Jo's death, Michael's world had been Angela and work, work, work. Sophie had loved Mary Jo, but God had taken her, and a family was a father *and* a mother and children.

They were turning into the network of streets with names that ended with *ski,* signaling they were near home. Home. The very word brought a tightness of anticipation to Sophie's chest. "I can't wait to show you my house, Claire. We don't get too many visitors, Dad and me. When he comes home, you can meet him, too."

"That sounds nice, Mrs. Chalinski." Claire knew she was only being polite; there would be no reason to return to this house after today. If Sophie herself hadn't asked for assistance, Claire would be at the office right now, working on a brief for a breach of contract suit.

Michael was pulling up to a small, neatly kept house, which looked to be about sixty years old. The white clapboard bungalow with its wide front porch was laid lengthwise on the narrow lot. There wasn't six feet between the Chalinski house and the nearly identical yellow bungalow next door.

Michael held his mother's arm as she went slowly up the steps on her crutches.

Claire couldn't help a little, private smile. It wasn't hard to see where Michael got his stubbornness. Mrs. Chalinski was feisty, with a kind of inner strength that Claire admired.

Claire followed behind Michael, carrying the crutches and Sophie's old cardboard suitcase. Michael got his mother settled on the couch and went back to the car for her flowers and the groceries.

Claire sat in the armchair across from the sofa. The two women talked a bit while Michael made a couple of trips back and forth. Once, when he was out of the room, Mrs. Chalinski leaned forward slightly and lowered her voice. "Claire, will you come visit me sometimes? Not with Michael, just by yourself. Have you got time to come out here once in a while?"

Claire didn't, not really, but she decided immediately that if Mrs. Chalinski wanted her to come, she'd make time. After all, if this were her own mother, Claire would want someone to come by and cheer her up. "Why, of course I will," she promised.

Mrs. Chalinski leaned back again, a smile of satisfaction on her lips.

Claire figured she would come at times when Michael was at the office. There was no reason for their paths to cross.

Michael had taken the last bag into the kitchen, and Claire could hear him banging cupboard doors as he put things away.

"Look around, Claire," Mrs. Chalinski urged. "Michael wants me to move, you know, but this house is solid. They don't build houses like this anymore, with real plaster and plenty of wood trim."

Claire remained seated, but she did take advantage of the opportunity to look around. Other than a fine dust that had settled on everything over the last few days, the tiny room was almost painfully clean. The lace curtains were pulled tight, presumably against the weak winter sun. In the half moon of the bay window was a round table, and on it, standing regally atop a doily, was a beautiful doll. Its porcelain features were angelic, and a tiny golden crown was nestled into its curly hair.

"How exquisite," Claire exclaimed, getting up to examine the doll more closely. It was dressed in a rust-colored velvet gown, and the tiny china hands grasped a single stalk of wheat. Now that she was close, she could see that the doll was very old.

"Do you like him?" There was no mistaking the eagerness in Sophie's voice. "It's an Infant of Prague, Baby Jesus. He was my grandmother's, and I brought him all the way from Poland, fifty years ago. We Polish women like to dress them for the seasons. Of course, Thanksgiving is an American holiday, so I had to make his gown myself. But I thought he should have something for Thanksgiving because looking at him reminds me to count my blessings."

"He's beautiful."

Michael came into the room. "And he will look just as good in a new house, Mom."

Sophie winced.

"You brought up the subject of moving yourself, in the hospital."

"I was upset, then. And scared."

"You have reason to be scared. And it's time to make plans." His voice was soft, his eyes were dark with emotion as he looked at his mother. "You have courage, Mom. But you have to face reality. You can't stay here anymore. The Bushinskis' house was broken into two weeks ago, and a week before that, Manya Delenek was robbed. I've talked to a few of my old buddies on the police force. They're willing to make an extra drive by the house for a few days, as a favor, but they agree with me that for your own sake, you have to move."

Claire looked from Mrs. Chalinski to Michael. His mother looked stricken, Michael sad but determined.

"There's no rush," Mrs. Chalinski said.

"There's a big rush." His mouth tightened as his gaze slid to Claire. "As long as you invited yourself along today, Claire, how about helping me convince another stubborn woman that she needs to do something for her own good."

The man was impossibly arrogant, Claire decided. He meant well, but his approach left a lot to be desired. "I didn't invite myself along. Your mother invited me. And, you might recall, you offered me a ride from the office."

"Because you insisted on coming."

"Because your mother asked me."

"I needed her," Sophie confirmed, looking from one to the other. "And you two sound like kids."

Michael flushed. "Look," he started again. "You can't stay here, Mom, and you know it. Claire, I could use some help, here."

Claire hesitated. Michael was going about this discussion the wrong way, but he was right. Mrs. Chalinski loved her place, but Michael loved *her,* and he was trying to insure her safety.

"Maybe you could look at a few houses, Mrs. Chalinski," Claire suggested. "You know, another nice old place, not too far from here."

"Michael always wants me to find something new."

Michael shot Claire a look and sighed. Finally, he went over to his mother and took the seat beside her, careful to avoid jostling her injured leg. As he picked up her hand in his, Claire was struck by the tenderness in the gesture. She swallowed a lump that rose in her throat.

"I want it to be new," he said softly, "because I love you. I want you to have the best, after all these years."

"I like old things, Mikush."

"That's what Claire thought." A reluctant, wry smile flashed across his features. "Okay, so we'll find something old." Michael laid her hand back in her lap. "If you want a stove you have to monkey with and a hot-water heater that runs out in five minutes, who am I to deny you?"

There was a long pause.

"Oh, Mikush, all right," Mrs. Chalinski finally said. She looked suddenly older and very weary.

Michael reached out again, and squeezed her hand. "Thank you, Mom," he said simply.

Michael let go of his mother's hand and stood up. "Now," he said, pulling a small leather notebook from his back pocket, "since you're laid up, I'll call a real estate agent and make arrangements to take a preliminary look at some places. *Old* places," he added. A new briskness had entered his voice. "Then, as soon as you're on your feet, you can take a look."

Mrs. Chalinski shifted. "Don't, Mikush. Not yet."

"Mom—"

"I said not yet, Michael." As she spoke, Sophie adjusted the position of her leg, and pain flickered across her face. "I know I have to do it. But not right now."

Michael sighed in frustration. "Damn it, Mom—"

"Don't swear, Michael Francis Chalinski. Not in my house. And, by the way, you didn't need to have my neighbor, Theresa, move in here. I could have managed on my own."

Claire cut in quickly before Michael could reply. "That's a nice idea, your neighbor helping out."

Mrs. Chalinski was undeterred. "*And,* Michael, you shouldn't have told Theresa you were going to pay her. You hurt her feelings."

Michael shoved the notebook back in his pocket. "I thought she was going to be doing a lot of work, and that she should be paid, that's all."

"Theresa is my friend. She doesn't want money to help me." Mrs. Chalinski gave her son a reproving look. "You've been away from Polaski Street too long, Michael, if you can't understand things like that."

Michael didn't reply. Finally, when the silence became awkward, Claire made a few attempts at conversation. But Mrs. Chalinski was obviously tired. Finally, his mother allowed Michael to settle her on the sofa for a nap. Claire stood up to leave as Theresa Panski arrived.

"Now, make sure you go see Dad," were Mrs. Chalinski's last words to Michael.

"Don't worry about a thing, Michael. I'll take care of your mother," Theresa reassured him as she walked them to Michael's car. "But don't get me wrong. I expect you to be over here a lot more than you've been lately."

"Damn it, those two women make me feel like I'm ten years old," Michael grumbled as he got the car started.

"Don't swear," Claire reminded him.

"Cut it out, Claire," he warned, forcing a smile. He knew she was trying to get him to lighten up. He *had* been pretty heavy-handed in there, but it drove him crazy that he couldn't get his mother off square one on this issue. All through their argument, he'd had an eye on Claire. She clearly sympathized with his mother. But Sophie wasn't *her* mother.

Claire adjusted her seat belt. "Mrs. Panski seemed to feel she had a right to scold you. She must have known you for a long time."

"Forever," he said. Threading the car through the narrow streets, he noticed again how many of the storefronts were closed, their shop windows boarded over with graffiti-marred plywood. The bakery was long gone, and even the American Legion Hall and the station where he'd once picked up newspapers for his *Tribune* route had closed. Trash had been blown into small heaps against the curbs. He passed Saint Stephen's on his left, and the brick that surrounded the stained-glass windows looked sooty. His childhood, his heritage, seemed swallowed up in grime and ugliness. No wonder his mother was clinging to the part of the past that was still clean and good.

All of a sudden, he felt, well, alone. It was hard, impossibly hard sometimes, to be head of a family, the one everyone relied on. Since Mary Jo had died, he'd felt this way more and more. He was glad, he thought with a mental groan at the realization, that Claire had come along. She had helped sway his mother, and he'd always be grateful for that.

Michael had planned to take Claire right back to the office. But all of a sudden, he found himself taking her on a tour of his old neighborhood and telling her about the people.

"Theresa Panski was something of a second mother to me. She's lived next door to Mom and Dad for as long as I can remember." He downshifted for a stop sign. "I never learned to speak much Polish—my dad thought it would be better for me if he and Mom spoke English at home. But Theresa Panski would scold me in Polish if I'd get out of line, and in case I didn't understand, she didn't hesitate to give me a little swat."

"No wonder she was upset when you wanted to pay her for staying with your mother."

"She doesn't have much, so I thought the idea would work out all around."

Claire turned to look at him fully, and her gaze was so direct and perceptive, it made him want to squirm. "She's part of your family in a way, isn't she? And you offered to pay her because you always take care of your family, don't you?''

She read him too easily. And once again, Michael was reminded that, despite his best efforts, he couldn't take care of them all. His wife was dead, and her killer was free; his mother was in a situation that scared the hell out of him every time he thought about it, and his father was trapped in a stroke-induced silence.

One of the neighborhood taverns was open on Romanek Street, and it seemed to be the one business that was thriving. Suddenly, he had a craving for a Rathdenburg beer.

"We're stopping?'' Claire asked as he swung into the parking lot.

"How about a beer before we go back?''

"Well, okay,'' she agreed, sounding surprised.

Inside, the tavern looked as if it hadn't been redecorated in thirty years. Worn red-vinyl stools lined a long bar, and the air smelled of peppery tobacco, slightly burned popcorn, beer and strong coffee. It was just after quitting time at the nearby stamping factory, and the room was about half filled with guys who had just come off the assembly line. They were talking in a relaxed, weary cadence that rose and fell as the steins of beer clinked on the bar, were emptied and topped up again. Against the wall, a popcorn machine put-putted away, and from the jukebox came the haunting melody of a Polish folk song.

At the bar, Michael paid for two Rathdenburgs and led Clair to a quiet table near a window. The ill-fitting panes let in a cold draft. The beer and the air seeping in added a pleasant coolness to the dry, overheated air. Belatedly, Michael realized that Claire was the only woman in the room. She didn't seem to notice, as she speculated about Michael's childhood and compared it to her own.

Michael sipped his beer. He was enjoying being with Claire. He always enjoyed her company. And that was precisely the problem. He had been in love with his wife for thirty-odd years, and what he'd loved most about her was her quiet support, her shy gentleness. It made no sense that he would care for a woman who was so different from Mary Jo. So what he felt for Claire had to be nothing more than overdeveloped lust.

For a moment, he let fantasy draw him in. To make love with Claire, to pull off that hideous satin rose she wore at her throat, to open her silk blouse, button by button, and kiss his way down to her luscious breasts. Yes, sex with the right woman—one who accepted his attentions for what they were—that would be all right. But with Claire—

"I love this Rathdenburg beer, Michael," she was saying. She had also said she loved his mother's doll, and thought the old neighborhood was interesting, loved the stained-glass windows at Saint Stephen's, and she really thought highly of his mother.

Wordlessly, he drained his beer and signaled the bartender for another.

Sex with this woman was out of the question. Under her competent exterior, there was vulnerability; he'd seen a blush on her cheeks once too often. She held herself open, willing to be hurt . . . And Michael Chalinski was damned if he would be the man to hurt Claire Logan.

Friends, he thought. Claire kept talking about their being friends. And friends would be very nice, if he could keep his physical desire at bay.

"Thank you," he said suddenly, "for helping with my mother."

She beamed; it was the only word for the wide, wide smile she gave him. "There. Was that so hard?"

"Was what so hard?"

"Saying thank you."

He picked up his second beer. "I guess not. God, I was a jerk today, wasn't I?"

"Yes, you certainly were."

He was startled; she wasn't supposed to agree with him when he said things like that. For a moment, he just stared at her.

And then he laughed.

It felt good to laugh. And when he laughed, her eyes lit with amusement, too. They were so dark and liquid they caused a stirring in his blood, all over again.

They sat for a few minutes. Michael switched to coffee, Claire to diet Coke. Guys came into the tavern; some left. The door opened and shut, each time with a blast of cold air. At the end of the bar, a group of men whooped with laughter.

Then Michael felt a hand on his shoulder and turning, stared into a face he'd once known well.

"Mikush. Hell, man, it *is* you!"

Michael stood up immediately, and pumped the other man's hand. "John, hello."

John Persecki hesitated a second, then folded Michael to him in a quick, self-conscious bear hug.

Michael had only seen his old friend once in ten years—at Mary Jo's funeral. Just about everyone in their high school graduating class had come. Now, looking into that genial, round face that had grown even more round with the passage of time, he knew it had been far too long since they'd talked. "John, can you sit with us?"

"For a minute or two. I just came in for a quick beer and then I've got to get home. Cindy knows I'll be a little late, but she'll have supper waiting."

Michael introduced Claire as a friend and colleague at the firm. John squirmed a little, the way he'd done through all the years Michael had known him, whenever he thought a girl was pretty. "Do you really want company?" he asked as he shook Claire's hand.

"Oh, sure, have a seat," she said pleasantly.

"Let me earn my keep. I'll get us a basket of popcorn."

Soon he was back, easing his huge, muscled frame into the big old wooden chair. "So, Michael, how's life in the city? Last I knew, you were still with the public defender's office. And now you're with this law firm. What was the name again?"

"Haynes, Haynes, Collingwood and Crofts. I'm in litigation, but we also do real estate, probate, the whole nine yards."

"So, how impressed am I supposed to be? Is this the big time?"

He chuckled. "It keeps me busy."

John paused, thinking. "Well, then, tell me this. What kind of car do you drive nowadays?"

Michael hesitated.

"A Jaguar," Claire supplied.

"Wow." John was awed. "It *is* the big time."

Claire smiled at him. "Not for all of us. I bought my car well used, and it sure isn't a Jag."

John smiled, and took a swig of beer. There was a pause, then his expression grew sober. "So, Michael, how are you doing, really? We should have stayed in touch after Mary Jo..." He paused, clearly searching for the right words. "After Mary Jo..."

"Passed away," Michael said quietly. He hated this part of meeting some of the people who'd known her, hated listening to those words that everyone found so difficult to say.

John cleared his throat. "And Angela is adjusting? And you're doing okay?"

"Right," Michael said shortly, trying to keep the bitterness out of his voice. All of a sudden, he felt uncomfortable, very conscious of Claire, seated across the slick, dark wood of the table.

John used his napkin to swipe at the ring his glass had made on the table. "I'm glad you're doing well," he said. "I think about you sometimes. I'm sure you still miss Mary Jo a lot, but she's been gone nearly two years. So it's good to see that—" he looked at Claire, then continued "—that you've gotten on with your life and found—oh, hell," he interrupted himself. "I'm really sticking my nose into it now."

He looked so pained and awkward that Michael felt he should say something. His first thought was bitter. John acted as if Michael was supposed to just "get on with life," but what was less than two years when you'd loved someone for more than thirty? But at least John was willing to talk about Mary Jo as a real person. Some of the people he knew never mentioned her at all; it was as if she'd never existed.

"It's okay," he said quietly, and realized as he said the words that it really was *okay*. "You knew her and liked her. And it's okay to talk about her."

John brightened. "Mary Jo was a nice woman, very pretty," he said, shifting his focus to Claire in evident relief. "Tiny and blond. Really quiet. Even when she was with good friends, even when we were all partying, laughing and telling crazy stories, she wouldn't say a word. She'd just smile and squeeze Michael's hand. She had a nice smile, though.''

"She sounds lovely." Claire spoke the truth. She could imagine the petite, pretty woman Mary Jo must have been. And quiet. Claire was never quiet. Heck, at a party she was always the one with the crazy stories. No wonder Michael kept his distance. To Michael, Claire must seem like a clumping elephant, tall and graceless and mouthy. Why on earth would he want Claire, when he'd had a woman like Mary Jo for a wife? It was inconceivable.

Claire shot a glance at Michael. He was sipping his coffee, his gaze seeming to see something very far away. Was he imagining—longing for—those old times, where in a crowded room his shy wife reached for his hand?

John shifted, pushing his chair back. "You know, though, Michael—I hope you don't mind me saying this— Cindy and I often talked about how different you and Mary Jo were."

Michael glanced up, abruptly brought to the present. "You did?"

"Well, we liked her. Everyone liked her." John turned to Claire once again. "But Michael was so smart, so driven. Everybody knew he wouldn't be living on Polaski Street forever. We figured he'd be on Wall Street or something, and we were surprised when he and Mary Jo got married. Somehow we thought—" his gaze shifted again to Michael "—you'd end up with somebody more modern or something. You know, somebody who liked to talk politics, maybe somebody you met in college." He took a big swig of beer. "Hell, this is the beer talking. Forget I said anything."

Claire glanced over toward Michael, and realized with a start that he was looking straight at her, staring, really. His gaze was intent, deep, dark...and she had no idea what that gaze meant. "Mary Jo was perfect," Michael said with finality, addressing John, but looking at Claire. And the odd thing was, Claire got the impression that he was talking more to himself than to her. A shiver went up her spine.

"Yeah, she was perfect." Oblivious to whatever was passing from Michael to Claire, John gave his old friend a little punch on the arm. "Too perfect for the likes of you, buddy."

Claire sat there, feeling confused. Michael had loved Mary Jo; she was perfect. But now he was looking at Claire so strangely...kind of surprised, maybe...but that made no sense.

"As a kid, this guy was too weird," John was saying to Claire.

"Really?" she managed to say.

"Oh, yeah, he was my best friend, but I never understood him."

Michael abruptly broke her gaze, then took a swig of what had to be cold coffee. "I wasn't so hard to understand."

"Oh, yes, you were, Mikush, you and your dad. Lord, that guy was the greatest, though."

Michael smiled at his old friend, a genuine, warm smile, and Claire wondered if she had imagined that intense exchange. After all, she never had really understood men.

"Let me get you another beer," Claire offered. When John protested that he had to get home, Claire urged him to stay a few more minutes. She was thoroughly unsettled; no way was she ready to be alone again with Michael right now. "Your next Rathdenburg's on me, as a bribe. I want to hear stories about when Michael was a little boy." She gave a nervous little laugh, feeling distinctly chatty, the way she always did when she was tense.

She made sure her tone was light. "I mean, was he stuck-up or what? Now, don't leave out the funny or dirty parts."

With a grin, John settled back, and Claire signaled for the bartender.

John scratched his chin, thinking. "Well, let's see. Michael was the smartest kid at Saint Stephen's, by far. He pitched for the softball team. After supper, if you'd go by his house, though, he'd be inside with his nose in some book or, more likely, out on the stoop arguing about something with his old man."

"They didn't get along?" Claire asked.

"Oh, no, Claire, not that kind of arguing," John said. "They'd be all red-faced and excited about something, and when you'd ask what they were arguing about, it would be like—" he frowned, thought hard, looked at Michael as though that would help him focus "—the Hungarian Revolution or something. Real deep. And Michael's dad was always talking to us boys about how this was America, and we were free, and we could never let the Communists take us over like they had in Poland. We had to take responsibility for our country, be willing to fight for it, die for it. To a kid, it was heady stuff." His voice was soft, reflective. "Michael's old man, well, he was something else, smart like Michael. And idealistic, I guess you'd say."

"Michael's father sounds wonderful," Claire said softly.

"You make me sound weird as hell, though," Michael complained, but he was now relaxed, and obviously wasn't offended in any way. "I didn't just read books, you know. I had a bike and a skateboard and water skis, too."

John nodded. "And at the proper time in your, ah, development, you kissed my sister."

"How in the world did you know that? I never told you."

"No, Beth did. She said your mouth was all wet and you kept pressing it on hers and you tasted like Red Hot candy and that you were one lousy kisser. I remember it exactly, because I was going to make damn sure I did a better job than you when I kissed a girl."

Michael's grin was sheepish, and he looked everywhere but at Claire.

And that was fine with Claire; she couldn't look at Michael either, not while she was imagining a boy's innocent, cinnamon-candy kisses, and a man's passionate, hard lips, molding, shaping her own, coaxing fire. Oh my, yes, Michael had learned a lot over the years.

And suddenly, reminiscing wasn't funny.

Claire felt a fierce stab of jealousy. For the first time, she fully understood why they called jealousy a green-eyed monster, it was so irrational—and so intense. With a twist in her heart, Claire focused on Mary Jo's perfection, imagining the kisses—and more—she and Michael had shared.

"Michael, I have to get back to the office," she said suddenly.

"Ah, John, how is your mother?" Michael asked at exactly the same moment, his attention fixed on his friend.

"My mom's okay, but worried all the time," John said.

"Is someone sick?"

"Naw, it's my baby brother. Nick has just turned eighteen, and I guess Mom should have moved out of the neighborhood a long time ago. There are some pretty tough kids around, and Nick's taken up with a few." John finished the last of his beer. "I feel kind of responsible for him, since Dad's passed away and I'm the only one who's stayed in the old neighborhood.''

Michael exchanged a glance with Claire. As much as Claire wanted to leave, she could tell this was important to Michael. She nodded slightly.

Michael explained to Claire that he had never known Nick, who had been born to John's parents long after their other children were grown. ''Has your brother been in any real trouble?'' he asked John.

''Sort of. Two shopliftings at the mall. Tapes and CDs and stuff.'' He looked embarrassed. ''Not anything big, but it's getting worse, because he's mouthing off to Mom all the time, staying out until four in the morning, and she calls me crying in the middle of the night—'' He broke himself off, stood, and reached for his jacket. ''I'm taking him bowling along with the kids tonight, so, really, I've got to get a move on. Sorry about ending this on a down note. It was great to see you again.''

''If you have a legal problem, if Nick gets in any more trouble, you know where to find me.'' Michael handed him a business card.

John studied it a moment. ''I don't know much about law, but even I know we can't afford you nowadays, Michael.''

''We'll work something out,'' Michael said easily.

John shifted. ''I'll get him straightened out. I've promised myself I will.'' He zipped his jacket and turned to Claire. ''Sorry about all the reminiscing, but this guy and I go back a ways. And that stuff about Nick, I hope you won't think he's a bad person. He's just going through a rough period.''

Claire nodded, touched his arm. ''I enjoyed your stories. It was nice to meet you, John.''

Claire and Michael followed John out into the now-dark parking lot, both of them quiet. Claire was lost in thought, thinking for a moment about John Persecki. Michael's friend seemed to feel an extraordinary sense of family responsibility. She had seen the same thing in Michael. She admired the quality in both men. After all, maybe if her own father had put his family first, she would not have had to endure those terrible teenage years.

Claire felt a kind of bittersweet melancholy settle on her as Michael quietly drove them back into the heart of the city, where the skyscrapers were glittering columns against the night sky. There was a world of difference between the Loop and Michael's old neighborhood, but both were Chicago, and both had made him the man he was. And Michael was a man she admired, respected, responded to like no other man she'd ever met. But the very thing that drew her was what kept Michael at a distance—an abiding love and loyalty to a woman. Another woman.

Michael pulled into the parking garage of the firm, then to his assigned space. There were still several cars in the garage, belonging to the die-hard associates who'd be working for some hours yet. Claire and Michael got out of the car, and she came around to his side.

She looked at him. "Why do you suppose it is that John—"

She never got the rest of the words out. Without warning, Michael kissed her. The car heater had been running full blast, and Michael's lips were warm. Claire was startled, but in less than a second she could feel herself yield. His mouth pressed, moved. It nibbled and coaxed, and then finally, inevitably, demanded.

Claire threw her arms around his neck. He smelled of fine, rich after-shave and buttered popcorn.

She didn't want to think, she only wanted to feel—feel the rough stubble of a man's beard, the crisp line of his hair, the hard wall of his chest, the hot demand of his arousal pressing into her.

Her coat was open, and his hand came up between the lapels of her suit jacket to cup her breast.

Then Michael groaned, and with the sound came the knowledge that his hand on her breast pleased him, excited him. Claire felt answering heat flash across every nerve ending. He stroked her nipple through the thin silk of her blouse, and it was her turn to moan as her nipple beaded under his palm.

Michael bent his head to rake his lips down the side of her neck, his mouth so hot in contrast to the cold night air. He moved on, to bury his face for a second in the satin rose she wore at her throat.

When he pulled away from her, Claire almost cried out at the loss. She wanted him to warm her, to fit against her, to let her feel the tangible evidence of his desire. She started to sway toward him.

He grasped her shoulders, steadying her. "Ah, God, Claire, that wasn't supposed to happen."

Claire was trembling all over. "For something that isn't supposed to happen, it seems to happen a lot," she whispered.

"It's just that I can't seem to... help it." Michael dropped his hands, looked away and swallowed hard. "I like you. You can make me laugh, the way I haven't laughed in so long. And I can't help... touching you."

Claire's heart lurched at his words, but something about his tone made her uncertain. "But that's good, isn't it, Michael?"

He was still looking away, and now it seemed as if there was so much space between them, much more than the mere step that would take her into his arms again. "I'd convinced myself it was just sex, this attraction I feel toward you, and that I could handle it." He gave a short, bitter laugh. "You see how well I handle it. In my dreams, I'll see that red rose you're wearing." He shoved his hands in his pockets, and his voice lowered. "But that's not all. Sometimes, late at night when I lie awake... I can't help wondering if there could be more between us."

Oh, yes, Claire thought. *There could be more—much more—but you have to let it happen.*

He finally turned to look at her, and when he spoke, his tone was one of utter finality. "But I can't...."

"Why not?" she whispered. "You know I care for you, Michael—"

"Don't," he interrupted. "Don't ever say you care for me, because I have nothing left. Nothing to offer a woman like you."

"You have plenty to offer. You're a wonderful father, and a caring son, and you work hard—"

He shook his head, and his eyes were dark and winter-bleak. "I'm empty inside." There was a long pause, and when he spoke again, his voice was quieter, more reflective. "Sometimes I think, maybe if I could get the guy who killed Mary Jo, if I could just do that, even if I wasn't able to protect her... Well, then, maybe I could go on. But I've never had a chance to find out."

Claire ached for him. "You did the best you could, Michael. Do you really believe you don't deserve to be happy because no matter how hard you tried, you couldn't put her killer in prison?"

Michael straightened his shoulders. "Don't you understand how it tears me up inside to know I couldn't keep my promise to the woman who was carrying my baby when she died?"

Claire reached out and took his hand. His palm was hard, big and square, and his fingers were so very cold. She could warm them. She could warm *him*, if he'd only give her a chance. "Michael, listen to me. All we can do in this world is our best."

Michael didn't reply, but looked away, across the gray concrete and rows of parked cars, toward where the winter wind was gusting, pushing tiny, hard grains of snow into the garage.

Claire shivered, from the chilled air and from the bleakness she had seen in Michael's eyes. And from fear. She was afraid for him, afraid, too, for her own heart. Maybe she couldn't do enough for Michael. Maybe she wasn't woman enough, or maybe she wasn't the right woman.

CHAPTER EIGHT

AFTER LUNCH, Angela took her tray to the conveyor belt that ran along one wall of the cafeteria. Sabrina was on one side of her, and Jenny Franklin, one of the girls Sabrina hung around with, on the other.

"It's not cheating," Sabrina said, putting her milk carton into the trash. "It's just helping out a few friends. All you have to do is flash your answers to Jenny. She sits right next to you. No one will ever know."

Angela separated the disposables from the rest of the items on the tray, and plunked them into the trash can. She knew that if she put her paper on the desk in a certain way, and Jenny saw it, and used her answers, that wouldn't be Angela's fault. If anybody was cheating, it would be Jenny. In a way, it didn't seem as bad as writing an English paper for Sabrina. But she had only written those papers because Sabrina was her best friend.

"Please," Jenny said softly. Jenny was usually so confident. Yet, today, she seemed nervous. "I have such a hard time with physics."

"I could help you study," Angela offered. "It works for me."

The touch of sarcasm was lost on Jenny, though Sabrina shot her a sharp look.

Jenny shifted her books. "I've tried studying. I just don't get it."

The three girls left the cafeteria together. Angela had trigonometry sixth period, Sabrina and Jenny geography, so they prepared to part as they entered the hallway. The hall was filled with kids heading to class.

Angela turned toward Sabrina to say something, and unexpectedly caught the eye of Joel Tate. Joel was standing with his back to a column of the turn-of-the-century building, and he looked tall and impossibly grown-up. He gave her a half cocky, half sheepish grin, exactly the kind of grin Tom Cruise did in the movies.

Angela looked away immediately. She couldn't possibly talk to him. No way. Joel had kissed her, after the soccer game. Right up until the night of their date, Angela hadn't quite believed she was going out with Joel, was sure she had somehow misunderstood the situation. And really, when they were at the pizza place it hadn't seemed like a date, even though they had sat next to each other across from Randy and Sabrina. Joel and Randy had eaten an awful lot of pizza and talked mostly to each other. Sometimes it was like Joel wouldn't quite look at her, and that had made her so nervous.

But afterward, they had all walked back to Sabrina's apartment house, and they had lingered on the path leading to the entrance. Then Joel had taken her by the arm and drawn her away from the others to the shadowy side of the building. He'd kind of dipped his head, like he was shy all of a sudden, and he'd kissed her. He didn't push her hard against the wall or press his body up against hers, like they did in the movies. He just sort of held her by the shoulders, closed his eyes, and pressed his warm mouth to hers. Angela was thrilled and eager and scared, all those feelings pushed and mushed together. When she went into the apartment lobby with Sabrina a few minutes later, her heart was beating way too fast and she wondered if she was in love.

And he hadn't called, not even once. He'd left her in an agony of waiting, wondering if he liked her or if she hadn't done the kiss right or something.

Sabrina had seen Angela's reaction to Joel. She looked at him, then at her. "I'll tell Randy to ask around, see if Joel really likes you, Angela, or if he's just leading you on," she promised, squeezing her hand. "Randy can find out."

"Okay, just don't let Joel find out it's me who wants to know," Angela whispered, watching as Joel got slapped on the shoulder by another guy and went walking down the hall without a backward glance.

"He'll never find out," Sabrina promised. "And if he doesn't have a thing for you, I'll pass the word around school that you were the one who wasn't interested."

"Thanks, Sabrina." Angela felt overwhelming relief. You needed a friend for this stuff. You *had* to have friends.

Angela had started to turn away, when Jenny stopped her. "Are you going to help me with the test?"

Jenny was pretty nice. And, since she was Sabrina's friend, she was Angela's friend now, too. "I'm not going to hide my answers," Angela said. "You can do whatever you want."

"Thanks." Jenny's relief was evident.

All of a sudden, Angela's mind conjured an image of Claire Logan. Claire had said all those things about being proud of being smart, of being sort of honest with yourself. But Claire was a grown-up, and things were different for kids nowadays. Claire would be disappointed in her if she knew what Angela had done, and what she was planning to do, and that made Angela feel bad.

But Claire would never know.

"TERRIFIC JOB, Michael." Standing at the back of the legislative hearing room in Springfield, Gordon Lyle slapped Michael on the back. The young state representative was pushing for greater penalties for the crime of driving under the influence, with a special focus on kids who drank. "Did you see Representative Stark sitting in the corner during your testimony? He was listening, man. He was listening. And he controls the committee with the bucks to see this bill gets enforced."

"Great." Now that his testimony was completed, Michael began to relax. When Lyle had first contacted him, asking him to testify at a legislative hearing on behalf of the bill, Michael had said no. Lyle wanted testimony from people who had lost loved ones to drunk drivers, and he wanted the testimony to be emotional. "Touchy-feely" stuff, he'd called it, asking Michael to talk a bit about how it felt to suddenly be a single parent.

At first, Michael had loathed what Gordon Lyle was suggesting. To call what he'd gone through a "touchy-feely story" had made him want to throttle the guy.

But Lyle had persisted, calling him over and over again at the office, then at home. And Michael had eventually seen past Gordon Lyle's flippancy to the other man's heart. Lyle genuinely wanted to make sure kids learned the consequences, at an early age, of drinking and getting behind the wheel of an automobile.

Lyle was still talking. "I'll give you a ring Friday night, let you know how the votes stack up. But I feel good about this one. I can smell a win."

"Okay, give me a call." Michael's calm words didn't betray how much relief he was feeling. As hard as it had been to talk about what had happened, he was glad he'd been able to bring himself to do so. Mary Jo would have wanted her death to count for something. Even though he hadn't said much about how Mary Jo's death had affected him—he'd focused on Angela and the things she would miss, by not having a mother—it had been enough. As Gordon Lyle had said, they were listening.

Later, as Michael headed back to Chicago, he spent a half hour on his car phone, handling a couple of matters concerning his own caseload. Then his secretary put Amanda Richmond on the line. She was a young associate he supervised, and she had just lost her first case.

"I was so humiliated," she told him. "Judge Chadwyck made me look like an idiot every time I opened my mouth to object. By the time the trial was winding down, I was so self-conscious I was sure I was going to fall on my face, whenever I approached the witness stand. I *know* the jury picked up on the judge's attitude."

Michael knew how she felt. He shared a story of one of his own early courtroom experiences. Why the hell, he thought, did some judges enjoy "initiating" a young lawyer this way? And women lawyers seemed to get that initiation in spades.

Amanda sighed. "So, what's next, Michael? Am I fired, do you think?"

It took guts to even ask the question, Michael thought. Amanda had all the right instincts to make a fine trial lawyer someday. Michael had been careful, for her first trial as the lone attorney, to give her a case where the stakes weren't too high. The client wasn't a make-or-break one for the firm.

"I'll talk to George Fanal, let him know how much you prepared, and your trouble with the judge," he promised. "It might help if we sit down with George together, so you can let him know losing isn't going to be a routine occurrence for you."

"A meeting with Mr. Fanal? Where I tell him where I think the case went wrong and how I'm not going to let a judge walk all over me next time?" Even over the slight static of the cellular phone, Michael heard her anxiety. "God, I don't know if I can."

"You can, Amanda." He tried to convey his own confidence in her. "Times are changing, but it's still brutal out there for women trial attorneys. Fanal knows that. What he'll need to know is whether you can handle it." Michael slowed for a road-repair truck creeping along ahead of him. "You're one of my best associates, and there's no way we'll let Judge Chadwyck have the last word on what kind of lawyer you're going to make."

There was a long pause as Amanda presumably thought it over. "Okay, I'll do it. Go ahead and schedule a meeting with the old man. How about if I talk to Claire about this, ask her how she'd handle explaining to a partner how the case went awry? She doesn't let Mr. Fanal intimidate her."

Michael felt a grin forming, even as he saw a sign at the edge of the road promising a twelve-mile, one-lane road-repair zone. The traffic ahead of him had slowed to a crawl. "Talk to whoever you want, but don't take all your advice from Claire. I think George is still feeling suckerpunched, after finding out Hathaway was overruled."

Amanda chuckled, and Michael knew by the sound that she was feeling better. Sooner or later, every attorney lost a case; it was what you learned from that loss, and how quickly you rose above it, that set the talented trial lawyer apart.

"Hey, Michael, thanks."

"No problem."

"No, really," Amanda said. "Before I called you, I was tempted to clean out my desk and leave. Your support means a lot."

Michael clicked off the button on the telephone a moment later, conscious of a strange sense of peace. It had been a good morning in Springfield; maybe something would actually be accomplished by his testimony. And he could make sure Fanal got the proper perspective on Amanda Richmond's case.

The traffic ahead was at a standstill, but Michael's thoughts raced. He knew what he should be concentrating on. Mary Jo, and continuing to do whatever he could to make sure she hadn't died for nothing. Amanda Richmond, and the sixteen other associates who were counting on him to teach them trial skills and keep their careers on track.

What he should not be concentrating on was Claire Logan. Never mind that he had wondered once or twice today, whether Claire's influence had helped him open up a bit.

Distance. He would simply put distance between them, spend no more time with Claire than he did with the other associates. It didn't matter that she made him laugh, it didn't matter that he looked forward to case conferences with her, where he could challenge and be challenged by her agile mind. And it certainly didn't matter that she smelled like sultry flowers and citrus, and her glistening hair and outlandish jewelry set him to dreaming...

Distance.

It had started to snow, wet flakes that would make the roadway sloppy. But at least traffic was moving again. Michael pressed his foot to the accelerator.

"IT'S BAD, MICHAEL." John Persecki sat in Michael's office, nervously turning the soft-brimmed wool hat he held in his hands. "This time it's really bad. I got a call from the jail where they have Nick and the deputy said I could go to a judge and ask for a public defender. But then I thought of you. It's going to kill my mother if Nick goes to jail. He's her baby."

Maybe he should be in jail, Michael thought. The way John told it, the police had picked Nick up last night. Nick had been drinking, as had his passenger, Bobby McNair. The passengers in the car they hit, a boy and girl coming back from a date, had both been injured.

Nick and Bobby had escaped without a scratch.

Wasn't that always the way?

Abruptly, Michael got up and went to the window behind his desk.

From behind him, John spoke. "Look, I know this gets you where you live, Michael. I mean, with what happened to Mary Jo. I wouldn't have come to you, but after I saw you the other day, and you gave me your card..." His voice trailed away, then he sighed. "If you could recommend a lawyer, maybe somebody we could afford, I'll leave. I'm scared to take my chances without a recommendation." There was a pause. "He's my baby brother, Michael, and it's not been easy for him since Dad died."

Michael stared out the window, his mind not registering the images of the cloudless winter day, or the sun gleaming against the glass and steel of the nearby skyscrapers. John waited. The man had been his best friend all during his childhood, and Michael had told him in no uncertain terms to come to him if Nick got in trouble again.

But hadn't Michael been through enough? Did he really have to defend this kid now?

"How badly hurt were the occupants of the other car?" he asked, half-turning toward John.

"Scrapes, bruises. The girl broke her wrist and the boy twisted some muscles in his neck."

Relatively minor, then, Michael thought. But no one knew better than he how much worse it could have been...

"Ah, Michael? Also, in the trunk of Nick's car, the police found some sterling silverware." John's voice became even more hesitant. "I'm, well, I'm pretty sure I know where that silverware came from." His voice lowered. "Manya Delenek described it to Mom and me a couple of weeks ago, after she was robbed."

Michael turned, aghast. "Your brother is one of those thugs who've been beating up old ladies in the neighborhood?"

"God, no. Nick wouldn't do that. He's not really bad. He just—"

"Steals," Michael said flatly, his fists clenched by his sides.

John's face was pale. "He's been charged with receiving stolen property."

Michael turned again and pretended to look for a law book on the shelf under his window. John wasn't kidding when he'd said this case would get to him.

Mary Jo and his mother.

He was sure, from his mother's descriptions of her attackers, that they were quite a bit older than Nick Persecki. But the robberies in the neighborhood? The break-ins had always occurred when no one was home. Nick would probably know, thanks to Mrs. Persecki, which ladies would be away from home at the most opportune times.

Michael would recommend a good lawyer for John. It was the least he could do.

No, he thought. He owed John more than that. People from the neighborhood took care of their own.

"What did he blow on the breath test?" Michael's voice was carefully neutral as he settled himself into his desk chair and pulled a long yellow legal tablet toward him. He was a lawyer, and when he accepted a client, it was his duty to represent him to the best of his ability.

"A point-one-nine."

"God."

"I know." The hat in John's hands went round and round.

Michael's voice softened. "You need to realize, that's a lot more than a beer or two, John."

"I know," John said again.

Michael asked several questions about Nick's previous criminal record and last night's accident, about the flatware in the trunk, about Bobby McNair. He made notes on the pad.

"Are you going to be his lawyer?" John asked.

"Yes. But for you and your mom, not for Nick."

John smiled for the first time. "Thank you, buddy."

"Now, John, listen to me. Nick is just eighteen, but with this juvenile record of his, a judge could send him to adult jail. Jails are full of career criminals. Believe me, I know. There was a time when I knew half the people in them, and I'd see kids like Nick go in for something relatively minor, and come out knowing the best way to hotwire a car or hold up a bank. No matter what, we've got to keep him out of jail." There was no point in telling his old friend, Michael thought, how physically brutal life in prison was for young men.

The hat stopped turning. "You see it like I do, Michael," John said in relief. "He's just a baby."

Very deliberately, Michael put down his pen and leaned forward. "No, John. Nick is not a baby. He's an adult who chose to take an illegal drink—several drinks—and get behind the wheel of a car. He's an adult who allegedly chose to participate in at least one burglary against people we know and respect. Frankly, if he's guilty, and at this point I suspect he is, he deserves to go to jail."

John sat very still. His face had gone from pale to white.

"I'm sorry, John. Your treating him like he isn't responsible for what he does isn't going to help Nick."

"But you said Nick shouldn't go to jail."

"No. Not this time."

"How are you going to keep him out?"

Good question, Michael thought. The police might have screwed up the testing procedures on the breath test. It was always a possibility, but they didn't make too many mistakes like that nowadays. And it was going to be damned hard to argue about the silver in the trunk, as long as the police had followed standard evidence-gathering procedures. "I don't know yet," he said finally. "It's why you've got a lawyer, though, John."

"Thanks, Michael. I mean it."

Michael swiveled to his intercom. No way did John have the three hundred and fifty dollars an hour that was Michael's going rate at the firm. For the sake of his friend's pride, Michael would probably charge something, but John wouldn't have to know it would be a fraction of the firm's usual rate.

The associates on his staff did their share of *pro bono* work. Russ Mallory didn't require it for the attorneys in his half of Litigation. It was insane, he'd said to Michael more than once, to have the lawyers working on anything but billable cases. But Michael figured charity work was a good way for some of them to begin to understand that their law degrees brought some community responsibility, not just a job in a high-rise building and enough money to make the payments on their first Corvettes. And the extra experience wouldn't hurt, either.

He pushed the intercom button. "Eileen, who's up for the next *pro bono* case?" Michael always did the *pro bono* work as a team with his associates on a rotation basis.

"Hang on, Michael. I'll check."

In a few seconds, she was back. "Claire Logan is up next."

Inwardly, Michael groaned. Less than three days ago, he'd resolved to keep Claire at a distance. But if he bumped over Claire in the rotation, it would be noticed by Eileen, as well as by the other associates. And the way things went at the firm, that fact would be gossiped over. He didn't want speculation that her supervisor thought Claire couldn't handle a case, when in reality it was her supervisor who couldn't handle his emotions. "Eileen, can you check and see if Claire's available right now? If she is, please send her in. I've got a case for the two of us, and it needs some work, right away."

NICK PERSECKI had been arrested in one of the small cities that ringed Chicago proper, and it was a long ride from downtown to the jail where he was being held. Claire was excited about the case, her first criminal case. It was challenging. The evidence seemed so clear against Nick Persecki.

"I've done some preliminary research, Michael," she said as he headed the Jaguar down a crowded stretch of the Dan Ryan. "Looking at the police report, I don't think the police made any mistakes in administering the breath test."

"The police didn't make any mistakes in the procedure of administering the test. But was the breath-test machine calibrated right?"

"I don't know yet. But I plan to check as soon as I can."

"Good."

That was typical of the way the conversation had been going. Strictly business, with short to-the-point responses from Michael. Something was bothering him. He hadn't looked at her once since they'd got in the car, and he seemed to grow more distant with every mile.

"Michael, do you want to talk about it?" She asked quietly. "After all, this must be very troubling, to help a young man beat a DUI charge, when the man who killed your wife got off without—"

"Never mind, Claire," he interrupted, his jaw set.

"Really, Michael, I understand." She was hurt by the fact that he didn't want to confide in her. "You can tell me how you feel."

"How I feel is irrelevant. I'm a lawyer. Nick Persecki is my client."

"I know that. But surely you can't help having some feelings about—"

"I have no feelings about it," he said flatly. "And Claire, I really think that if you're going to be so persistent, you could concentrate on how you'd like to handle your approach with Nick Persecki."

Well, to heck with you, Claire thought, stung. He was deliberately shutting her out, and she had no idea why. She replayed those moments when they'd stood together in an echoing parking garage and shared that intimate kiss. Michael had actually confessed to caring about her. She was at a loss to know how to rekindle that moment of sharing.

Now Michael was a stranger again. A distant, polite stranger. Her supervisor, her boss. Nothing more.

They were nearing the jail where Nick awaited them, before Michael spoke again. "I don't know how Nick will be when we meet him, but I'd be prepared for some show of bravado, Claire. He's only eighteen, but his record indicates that the severity of the situations he gets involved in is increasing. That's a bad sign. Many of these kids feel they have to be cocky and in control. The sooner you show them you're calling the shots, the smoother things will go as you work the case."

"Okay, Michael," she said. "I'll handle it."

He nodded, as if he was sure she could, and it mollified Claire somewhat. If nothing else, she appreciated his quiet confidence in her ability.

They stopped on the first floor of the jail and made arrangements for Nick to be released on his own recognizance, when John came to pick him up. The deputy in charge remembered Michael, but asked to see Claire's identification card from the Illinois Bar. When they passed through the first security gate, and the door slid shut behind her, Claire paused for a moment. This jail might be in a wealthy suburb, it might be modern and clean, but it was still jail. The place was claustrophobic, especially when she and Michael got on an elevator that had no buttons, only an intercom with a disembodied voice asking them to identify themselves and their destination. How would it feel to be eighteen and locked in such a place? How could having a few beers and getting your hands on some silverware be worth being put in here?

As if reading her thoughts, Michael said, "This is when these guys are usually most vulnerable. If you can get through to them while they're in here, you may have a chance."

Claire could do little more than nod because they had reached their floor and were being led to a room by a deputy who had met them at the elevator.

They waited for Nick to be brought to them. At the table in the center of the room, Michael sat down on one of the four chairs, and went over his notes again, clearly oblivious to his surroundings. But the gray walls and the barred door gave Claire the creeps. She sat down too, and got out her own notepad, determined to be as casual as Michael.

"Hey, my lawyers. Cool. Now I'll finally get out of this hole." Michael and Claire looked up as Nick, clad in an ill-fitting orange prison jumpsuit, was led into the room. Grinning, he gave Michael and Claire a thumbs-up sign. The deputy angled a disgusted look at Michael.

"Has he given you trouble?" Michael asked the guard quietly.

The guard shrugged, said, "He's more of a punk than some," before explaining that he'd wait outside.

As the door closed, Michael looked Nick over carefully. There was a family resemblance to John—the same large, square frame, the straight, sandy hair, the blue eyes. But Nick's hair was longer, and though clean, the badly cut locks hung limply down his back. And where John's eyes were guileless, Nick's had narrowed as he assessed them. Michael met his gaze, but Nick wouldn't hold it; instead, he stared at Claire in a way that was downright insolent.

She didn't seem to notice, standing to put out her hand and introduce herself and Michael. Then she and Michael sat down again at the large table. The top was covered in new-looking gunmetal-gray laminate that was already scarred in places by obscenities and initials.

"Two lawyers. That's cool. My big bro did okay for once, didn't he?" Nick plopped into a seat by the wall, stretching out his legs. "So, when am I out of here? I need a shower."

"John's coming for you soon," Claire explained.

Nick nodded, his head at a cocky angle, but Michael, watching him closely, thought he saw a flash of relief cross Nick's face. Even as he watched, the kid's expression hardened again.

Michael spoke. "We have plenty of time before John picks you up. Now, we need to hear your side of what happened, Nick."

Nick leaned back in his chair. "Everything I say's confidential, right?"

"Right," Claire assured him, picking up her pen. "I assume they told you you tested at point-one-nine on the alcohol breath test. That's quite a bit over the legal limit, even if you were twenty-one, which you aren't. At your age, it's zero tolerance."

"That's a dumb law," Nick said, and the way he kept looking at Claire, the way his gaze would rest a shade too long on her neck or breasts, was beginning to set Michael's teeth on edge.

Really, he hadn't expected anything else from Nick, not at this first meeting. Michael had been here before, seen it before. What surprised him was how much the kid was annoying him. After all, the staring wasn't that big a deal. "Unfortunately, it's not up to you to decide which law you want to break," Michael said. "So, Nick, just tell us. Did you or did you not have anything to drink last night?"

"Did." Nick positively smirked at Claire. She ignored him.

"How much and what?" Michael asked.

"A few beers. I forget exactly how many. Also, two whiskeys with some crummy, warm soda water. I've drunk more. Hell, last night Bobby drank more than I did."

"Well, the fact that you acknowledge you drank," Claire said, "could be a problem. We can't put you on the stand, if this case goes to trial."

"We couldn't anyway," Michael reminded her. "His record would come into evidence that way. If the jury ever heard all the things Nick has been up to these last two years, he'd be D.O.A."

Again, for the briefest of moments, Michael thought he saw anxiety, maybe even fear, cross Nick's features. Seeing an advantage, he pressed his point. "You're in real trouble this time, Nick. You won't be spending time in juvenile hall on this offense. It's adult prison now. I'll bet you've watched enough television to know what happens to kids like you in prison." He paused to let his words sink in. "And if we can get you off on the driving-while-under-the-influence charge, there's still the little matter of the silverware the cops found in your trunk."

Nick licked his lips. "It's just a few pieces, some knives and forks and stuff. It's not worth nothing much."

"It's enough that the cops can call it grand theft, Nick. I think we'd better hear what's been going on in the old neighborhood, don't you?"

"Nothing's going on," Nick said quickly. Too quickly.

Claire also had apparently noticed. "You've got to be up-front with us, Nick. We can't be surprised by evidence. Now, if the police go poking around your mom's house, or looking in your garage, or talking to your friends, are they going to find silverware or other items taken from houses in the neighborhood?"

She had him. Nick was trembling a little. "Naw."

Claire fixed him with a hard stare. "Are you sure?"

Suddenly, Nick seemed to find Claire's demeanor a challenge. He straightened, and perused her body, from the tip of her dark head, skimming along her black wool suit jacket, giving unseemly attention to the modest V of her hot-pink silk blouse, near where a thumbnail-size fake ruby hung from a chain. "Hey, you're my lawyer. It's your job to believe me, babe."

"Ms. Logan," Claire said so fast Michael didn't have a chance to defend her. "My name is Ms. Logan."

"Sure, babe."

Before Michael had time to think about it, he was out of his chair. In one stride, he was towering over Nick. The kid started to stand, but Michael grabbed his shoulders, and pushed him, heavy wooden chair and all, against the wall. The back of the chair thunked against the concrete. "Didn't you hear the lady? Her name is Ms. Logan."

Nick licked his lips, his eyes flickering. "Yeah, I heard her."

Michael put his face very close to Nick's. "Now. Let's try this again." He enunciated each word. "What—is—the—name—of—your—attorney?"

The kid swallowed. "Ms. Logan."

Michael kept his hands firmly planted on Nick's shoulders. "Now, pal, listen up, because I'm only going to say this once. My services are worth a good chunk of change, not to mention the cost of the legal services of your other lawyer, Ms. Logan. We might just be good enough, both of us working together, to keep your sorry ass out of jail, if you cooperate. You with me so far?"

Still pinned, along with the back of his chair, to the concrete wall, Nick nodded vigorously. Freckles that had only been faintly visible before, now stood out on his pale cheeks. Out of the corner of his eye, Michael saw Claire staring at them in shocked fascination.

"So, you're going to tell us everything, Nick. And when John picks you up, you're going home, and you're going to be a model citizen, and you're going to treat your mother with respect. If you don't, you're going to answer to me. Me, not your big brother John, whose only crime is he loves you too much. If you so much as make a move that might be construed as illegal, Ms. Logan and I are off the case, and you can take your chances on the next public defender." He paused, letting his voice drop to a husky whisper. "And you want me for your lawyer, don't you, Nick?"

"Yeah, I want you." Nick sounded awed. Michael resisted the urge to smile to himself at how young Nick suddenly seemed. When it was all said and done, the kid was a pussycat, easily cowed. Michael felt intense relief. When he'd seen Nick's record, he'd been genuinely concerned that the kid was a hard-core criminal at eighteen. Now he seemed more like a scared kid. Good. A scared kid was malleable. Maybe there was a chance for Nick Persecki. And with that thought, Michael knew exactly how he was going to handle the case.

"Now, when I let you loose, you're going to sit in that chair and cooperate. Got that?" When Michael finally let go, Nick sagged into the chair.

Michael sat and turned to Claire. "Ms. Logan, would you please ask our client the questions you prepared?"

Immediately, Claire snapped to attention. "Ah, sure. Now, Nick, how did the silver come to be in your trunk?"

Nick used a finger to worry the collar of his jumpsuit. "I didn't steal it," he said, casting a nervous glance Michael's way. "I swear to God."

"So, who did?" Claire held her pen at the ready. "Bobby McNair?"

Sweat broke out on Nick's upper lip. "I can't say," he said.

"It was Bobby McNair? How do you know that? Were you with him when the silver was taken?"

"I can't say... Ms. Logan."

Claire cast a frustrated glance Michael's way.

"You'd better say," Michael said quietly. "The way this could go down, Bobby McNair could tell the judge you were the one solely responsible for that theft. And the police already have you on the drunk-driving charge. And the police might decide that Nick Persecki is responsible for every unsolved burglary in the old neighborhood.

"Then, of course—" he paused for emphasis "—there are those muggings. Not many, but they all involved old ladies. A jury isn't going to like the old-lady part, Nick. I figure, with Bobby testifying against you, you could get maybe—" he stopped and pretended to peruse the law book he had open on the table in front of him "—oh, ten years, or so."

"Ten years. No way, man." Nick looked about half the size he'd looked when he had first come into the room, as if his body had shrunk in the worn orange jumpsuit.

"Of course, if you behave yourself in prison, you could be out in six or seven years," Michael added helpfully.

"I can't rat on Bobby! He wouldn't rat on me, man."

"He'd rat on you in a nanosecond. Have you ever heard the expression about there being no honor among thieves? As a former defense lawyer, I can tell you it's the truest saying there is."

Nick's forehead creased. "I don't understand. No honor among..."

"You puzzle it out, Nick." Michael stood. "You should have plenty of time to puzzle it out, waiting in this hole for your brother to pick you up. But you puzzle it out carefully, because I'm your lawyer and I'm right about how this will go down." He gathered his papers and the law book and shoved them into his briefcase. "Are you ready to go, Ms. Logan?"

Claire put down her legal pad, clearly surprised. Several lines on the paper were filled with questions, questions she had not yet asked. "Ah, yes, sure, Mich—" she cast a hasty glance Nick's way "—Mr. Chalinski."

They were at the door, leaving a scared Nick Persecki still seated at the table. "Wait," he called just as the guard was letting them out. "When am I going to see you again?"

"I'll let you know," Michael replied, and then, pausing to let Claire go ahead of him, went through the door without a backward glance.

CHAPTER NINE

"I'M SORRY, I jumped in before you finished your questioning," Michael said as they headed back into the city. "But I wanted to leave Nick with some serious thinking to do."

"It's okay," Claire answered. "I certainly trust your instincts. But I have to say, I had no idea you could talk like that."

His eyes were on the road. "Talk like what?" he asked. He sounded serious, but an incipient grin was twitching the corners of his mouth.

"Like you were some television cop or TV lawyer or something. Starring in a new, hard-edged, top-of-the-ratings show called 'Chalinski—For the Defense.'"

Michael laughed, and Claire joined him, although for her the sound came out a sort of nervous chuckle. She'd made light of Michael's handling of Nick Persecki, but in truth, he had awed her. In that dark, gray place, where Claire had felt a bit intimidated, he had seemed overwhelmingly masculine. And she hadn't missed that his tactic was just what Nick needed. She already knew Michael was well-thought-of at the firm. Now she realized what a stellar public defender he must have been. She'd seen his eyes as he'd seated himself again at the table, after taking some of the cockiness out of Nick—his eyes were a snapping golden brown, alive and warm.

"How did you know Nick needed you to act so tough?" she asked.

He turned to her for a split second before again facing the road. "Didn't you notice how he was looking at you? His eyes running down your figure like that? Stopping at your—chest." His hands flexed on the wheel.

"Well, yes, but I figured I'd just ignore it."

"I couldn't ignore it."

Claire felt a little thrill run through her. "Oh."

"Yes. Oh."

"Well, it worked," she said lamely.

"Yeah. For now." Michael slowed for a curve. "I didn't really plan my approach, but as soon as I had Nick against the wall, I could feel his fear. Smell it, kind of. And I knew then I had to keep up the pressure, see how quickly he'd crack." He smiled, a genuine smile of satisfaction. "He cracked quick, thank God. Some of the guys I've represented, even the kids, were so hard, Claire. Nothing and nobody could reach them." He accelerated. "Those were the ones who usually ended up in prison for a very long time. Or dead."

"But you can do something for Nick."

"I think so. It's really too soon to tell, but I think so," he said frowning. "The thing is, Claire, the neighborhood he lives in is rough now. A kid has to act hard to get along there. And when kids like Nick have been doing that for a long time, they think that's the way to get on in every situation. Look at how reluctant he was to say anything negative about Bobby McNair, even though I'd just scared the hell out of him." He downshifted as he joined the predictable backup of cars on the Dan Ryan. His hand stayed lightly resting on the gearshift.

"We couldn't really get off the case," Claire noted after a moment. "Even if Nick doesn't follow your instructions, once we've decided to represent him, we're stuck as long as he wants us as his attorneys.''

"Nick doesn't have to know that."

"True." Claire stopped and thought. "So, Bobby McNair would sell out Nick in a—" she couldn't help grinning "—a nanosecond. Which is a legal term of art, I guess."

He grinned, too. "Of course. They didn't teach you that word in law school?"

Claire felt tingly warm. Michael was riding high, clearly relieved at making a connection with Nick, and it made him seem so much more approachable than he had been on the way to the jail. He was joking with her, and there was warmth and camaraderie in the small car.

Could she keep these warm feelings alive, hold them close to her heart, and prevent Michael from closing her off again?

"You were thinking?" Michael prompted after a moment.

"Yes. How are we going to get Nick to jump the gun and testify against Bobby? And if he does, will it keep him out of prison?"

"I don't know. I'm pretty sure that Nick didn't take the stuff. So that would leave just the drunk-driving charge. But Bobby McNair's juvenile record isn't one-tenth as long as Nick's. I know, I checked."

"Oh. So he isn't as bad as Nick."

"Or Bobby's just a lot smarter."

Claire pulled her legal pad from her briefcase and made a note on it. "Well, we have to see if the prosecutor will recommend some kind of deal that the judge will accept. We also have to see if Nick would be willing to turn in his friend. We have a lot of work to do."

Traffic was moving slowly, but it was moving. Claire glanced at Michael's strong hand on the gearshift, and thought how much she liked his hands, spare and competent and masculine. She realized she didn't care if traffic was backed up for miles.

Michael spoke. "Assuming we can pull this off, Claire, and keep Nick out of prison, which is a big if, it still won't be enough. Somehow, we have to figure out this kid. If we don't, it'll just be a matter of time before he gets into trouble again, and that time he probably will go to prison. Somehow, we have to reach him."

"How, Michael?" Claire asked.

He shook his head. "I don't know. But we need to try. I'm a father, and I know kids get mixed up sometimes. Not that Angela would ever pull something like Nick has, but in trying to take care of her, I've realized that it's very hard for some kids to grow up."

Claire nodded.

Michael was slowing for one of the numerous tollbooths. He tossed some change into the bin, and accelerated after the gate opened. "I'm sure, if anyone can convince the judge to give Nick a chance, it's you, Claire. You'll just keep arguing with the prosecutor, pointing out evidence and statistics until the poor slob gives in."

Claire smiled. "I think there might have been a compliment buried in there somewhere."

"Sure I'm complimenting you," he said, completely serious. "You do excellent work."

He rarely complimented her. Most of the time he disagreed with her strategy, argued with her. Sometimes he suggested ways she could prosper in the firm, ways that would never suit her. The compliments were few and far between. He dished out both praise and advice in almost equal measure with the other associates. Claire had often wondered why he was so careful with her. But no way was she going to second-guess him now. For once in her life, she wasn't going to push.

So, "Thanks," was all she said now.

A few minutes later, he slowed for another tollbooth, then another and another. Most Chicagoans hated this gauntlet of tollbooths and the traffic slowdowns they produced. Now Claire found herself wishing there were a hundred more, a thousand more, before she faced the inevitable moment when Michael dropped her off at her car.

Somehow, she must have communicated her thoughts, or maybe he was just as loath as she to part company, because as they reached the rim of downtown, he suddenly asked, "Are you in a hurry? Have you got time for me to show you something?"

His voice sounded casual. Almost too casual, as though he invited her along for little jaunts all the time. "Sure," she said, careful to match his tone.

In a few minutes, he was headed into a part of town Claire wasn't familiar with. However, it wasn't far from where Mrs. Chalinski lived. "Are we going to see your mother?" she asked.

"Close," he said. "I'm going to show you a house I think she might like." He hesitated. "You seem in tune with her somehow, and I thought maybe you'd give me your opinion before I take her to see it. I know I'll never get her to help me really hunt for something, but I thought if this pleases her, I'd buy it."

As he spoke, he pulled up to the curb.

It was dark, but Claire could make out a two-story house with the broad eaves and deep porch that suggested it had been built in the 1920s. Claire could also see that the house was in poor repair. The bushes were overgrown; the paint was peeling off in large slabs.

"This is only a few miles from the old Polish neighborhood, but it's still safe. They have this block patrol thing where the neighbors patrol the streets, the real estate agent told me."

Claire popped the button on her seat belt. "Your mom would love to be part of that."

He gave a frustrated sigh, and Claire almost smiled as she sensed the touch of resignation in it. "I'll go crazy, worrying about a seventy-year-old woman, out patrolling with her neighbors."

"Don't you see, Michael? You want to protect her, but your mother doesn't want to feel helpless, either. No woman does." Impulsively, Claire put out her hand and covered his where it lay on the gearshift.

Warmth, then a charge that was almost electric, seemed to surge through her at the feel of his skin against her palm. Claire was stunned at the power of the sensation. But she didn't let go, and for a timeless minute, the two of them sat in the dim light of the fading day, his hand under hers.

Finally, Michael shook his head as if to clear it. "Well, this isn't showing you the house, is it?" Resolutely turning from her, he opened his door.

Claire got out and came around to the curb. "How will we get in?"

He pulled a set of keys from his pocket. "The agent dropped these off this morning. I looked at the house over the weekend. The agent was coming with me for a second look this morning, until I got sidetracked with the Persecki emergency."

There weren't too many steps, Michael explained, putting a light hand on the small of Claire's back as they walked up to the porch. He said he was sure someone could build a ramp for his father's wheelchair.

"Isn't this place in pretty poor repair?" Claire asked after he'd opened the door and flicked on the light switch.

They were standing in the living room. A dusty fifties-style dish chandelier was tilted at a crazy angle, throwing garish shadows off the walls. The walls had been painted pea green, and the draperies that still hung at the windows were an even more unpleasant shade. For a moment, Claire just stood looking around in dismay.

It seemed very warm in the house after the chill of the winter air. Michael shrugged out of his topcoat and took Claire's, draping them on a low railing that separated the living room from a formal dining room.

"Lord, how long has it been since anyone lived here?" she asked. "Look at those cobwebs." Dust had collected on the wide baseboards. The staircase that rose along one wall of the living room was remarkably similar to the one in the Chalinski home, except there the newel posts had been rubbed and polished till they gleamed.

Ah...

They don't make houses like this anymore, with real plaster and wood trim.

Claire spun around. Oh my, yes—it was there, in the west wall—a big half moon of a bay window.

"It looks like your old house," she whispered.

"You see it, too," he said, his voice as hushed as her own. "You see what it could be."

His eyes were dark pools in the greenish light. That same light highlighted the planes and angles of his face, that stark, masculine, Slavic face. He took a step toward her.

"Claire, I..." He reached out his hand to her; she raised her own.

It was her fault, Claire thought later. Because she was the one to go into his arms a split second after he said hoarsely, "I should show you the rest of the house."

With hands on his cheeks, she tugged his face down to hers. Uncertainty, maybe even resistance, flickered in his eyes before his face hardened in the lines of powerful passion. Then his eyes closed as Claire kissed him. Boldly, she threaded her fingers in his hair, then brought her hands to the back of his neck. As he bent to her, she lifted herself to reach him better.

This is right, she thought. There might be problems between them. Michael might not think she was the kind of woman for him, and in truth, she had doubts herself sometimes ... But not now. This was right. Any doubts evaporated with the first touch of his skin to hers.

And his skin under her hands felt right too, rough and male. She wanted more. With Michael, she always wanted more.

With a groan, Michael deepened their kiss, at the same time bringing her hips flush against his.

That groan, and the sound of their mingled breaths, were the only sounds they made as they clung to each other. Then Michael lifted her slightly, took a few steps. Dimly, Claire realized the wall was against her back. But she hardly noticed because Michael was pressing against her. Around her, there was a faint smell of dust and time, but mostly there was only Michael; he dominated her senses.

There was a certain fierceness in the way he lifted her again, fitting her more tightly against his body, bracing her against the wall. Claire used her knees around his thighs to keep herself in place as he held her with one hand on either side of her head and kissed her hard. She opened her eyes, and her vision was filled with Michael, and his own eyes were wide and dark and a little wild.

Her skirt had hiked up, and Claire welcomed the feel of him, his erection pressed so intimately against her. Pleasure pooled and centered between her legs. Under his suit jacket, her arms went around his back, and she felt fine cotton broadcloth, heated by the muscles of his back. Almost involuntarily, it seemed, his hips pulled back slightly, then with a groan, he thrust against her.

Almost frantic with desire, Claire fought to get a hand between them, reaching for his belt buckle. Then she had it, and she tugged, trying to get it open.

"Claire, please," he finally whispered harshly, but whether he pleaded for restraint or for the joining she longed for, Claire didn't know.

A knock sounded at the door.

Against her, Michael froze. Claire stiffened.

The knock came again, an insistent, staccato sound.

Wordlessly, Michael took a step back, and Claire slid to her feet. For a moment, her legs felt too shaky to hold her. Her gaze went to the door, and then to the window next to it. Thank heavens the curtains were drawn.

"I'm sorry, Michael," she whispered, and looking grim, he shushed her.

Claire smoothed her skirt and straightened her ponytail. She was still trembling. Good Lord, she thought, she had wanted Michael. That wanting had been building between them all day, but still she was shocked at how quickly things had got out of control in a house that didn't belong to them.

Michael shot her a quick, are-you-okay? kind of glance; Claire nodded, though she felt anything but okay. Michael opened the door.

Standing on the dark porch were two women and a man, all elderly. Each carried a large flashlight, trained on the porch floor.

"We're the block patrol," one of the ladies said. "We saw the light and decided to check things out."

"What are you doing here?" asked the man.

Michael, with remarkable composure, Claire thought, explained they were looking at the house. Her own legs felt like jelly.

"At seven o'clock in the evening? And where's Mrs. Caraballo, that real estate lady? How come she's not with you?" The second's woman's voice rang with suspicion.

Michael fished in his pocket for the key. The real estate company logo was on the key chain. Still, it took a couple of minutes of explaining, including an offer for them to call Mrs. Caraballo, to reassure the three on the porch.

"I told you they could be looking to buy the house," the man finally told his two companions.

"Well, like I said, I still don't see how a man who could afford one of those fancy sports cars would be wanting to buy this kind of house," one of the women argued.

"He's thinking of buying it for his mother," Claire explained.

"Oh, well, if that's it . . ."

The others were still skeptical, clearly in no hurry to leave the porch.

"Ah, I think we're done here, anyway," Claire said, "Aren't we, Michael?"

"We sure are." His tone was grim as he helped Claire into her coat under the collective eye of the block patrol. They crowded the open doorway, peering at Michael and Claire.

But they stood aside as Michael locked the door. He didn't say another word, instead helping Claire down the concrete walkway to the curb.

"We got your license number, just in case you're up to something fishy," the man warned as Michael opened the passenger door for Claire.

Michael came around to his side, opened the door, then sank into the deep leather seat. For a second, he just sat there, then with a weary-sounding sigh, started the engine and pulled away from the curb.

Claire tried to think of the right thing to say as they turned the corner. Words seldom failed her; she ought to be able to explain—excuse—what had almost happened. Michael probably would not want her to make a big deal of it, she knew, but there was no way to make light of what might have happened, or what she had been feeling.

Finally she settled for repeating what she had said in that dreadful moment after they had been interrupted. "I'm sorry."

"No. I'm sorry," Michael corrected. His tone held no tenderness, only self-contempt. "There was no excuse for my behavior."

"Oh, for heaven's sake, Michael." Claire was suddenly impatient. The timing had been poor, the setting inappropriate, but what was building between them couldn't be denied. "You sound like a Victorian gentleman, taking full responsibility for everything. You might recall that I was the one who kissed you. There were two of us there." She paused, thinking, then tried to keep the wistfulness out of her voice. "But was what we were doing so wrong, Michael? I know we're different, and I know you're still sad, but every time you touch me—"

"Think, Claire." Michael interrupted, abruptly pulling over to the curb. He shut off the engine, and turned to her. "We might have made love. Hell, if those people hadn't shown up, we would have made love. Tell me, would you have stopped me?"

Claire felt her face flame. "No," she whispered.

Michael's hand flexed on the wheel. "And I would not have stopped." His voice was rough. "But I had no protection with me. Are you on—I mean, have you taken precautions of some kind?"

"No, of course not, Michael. I'm—well, surely you know I'm not involved with anyone, or I wouldn't be kissing you..." Embarrassed beyond measure, she let her voice trail away. She was *involved,* there was no other word for it, with Michael. And he had made it explicitly clear that he wasn't ready for a relationship, though his aroused body had been pressing against the most intimate part of hers not fifteen minutes ago. "But, Michael, you say one thing then do another. Every time I add up the evidence, it doesn't mesh."

"We could have conceived a child." Michael looked very sober, and his voice held something that sounded like surprise, even amazement, that he could have done such a thing.

He was right, Claire thought. She hadn't considered protection when she'd been with Michael, she had just been caught up in the wanting and the thrill of knowing that he desired her so fiercely, too. They had been very irresponsible.

She wanted children someday, but a baby now, with all the complications of her relationship with Michael... And Michael would undoubtedly insist on marrying her, if she was carrying his child. Emotions warred within Claire— a flashing vision of a bright-eyed baby, the sick feeling of imagining Michael proposing marriage out of a sense of duty and obligation...

"You see my point." Again, his tone was grim.

"Yes." But she ached for some kind of tenderness, or at least some acknowledgment of the powerful emotion that had gripped them both.

She tried to swallow some of that ache. Always before, when she had something to say, she said it. She spoke now, but her voice was low. "Michael, this is very hard for me, the way you tell me one thing then do another. I know I sound confident about most things, but all my life I've wondered if a man would ever... care for me as I am..." Oh, God, she thought, don't start crying now.

"Claire." Now the tenderness was there, in the thickness of his voice, whispering her name, in the way his hand came over to clasp hers. "It's not you, Claire. It's me." He shut his eyes for a second, and in the dim light she could see his Adam's apple move as he swallowed. "It's just not like me to do what we almost did on the spur of the moment. When I'm with you, everything feels out of control."

She studied him in the dim light. He was clearly not happy about that loss of control. And he was right—it wasn't like him to lose control so quickly. But before she could explore the thought or what that meant, he spoke again.

"I think I'd better get you home." He straightened and started the car. "We need to keep moving. After all, the block patrol posse will catch up soon if we're not careful."

His attempt at humor fell flat. There was too much tension between them, too much unfinished business.

Reluctantly, Claire decided not to push, not tonight. She was still unsettled herself. But, she thought with a little shiver, they still had a lot of work to do on the Persecki case, and they'd be spending quite a lot of time together.

"JENNY FRANKLIN got an A on her physics test," Sabrina confided as they waited on the sidewalk in the sunny cold for the buses that would take them home from school. They stood a little apart from the crush of kids, talking quietly. "What did you get?"

"An A," Angela replied shortly. "But I think you knew that, Sabrina." All she'd done, Angela told herself for the hundredth time, was put her paper in the upper corner of her desk. If Jenny could see it there, and Jenny had got an A, too, well, that could just be coincidence.

Of course, that was the very corner where a column obscured Angela's desk from the watchful eye of Dr. Beth Samuelson, who was the toughest and fairest teacher Angela had ever had. But all that was over now. Dr. Samuelson didn't believe in giving a lot of tests; there wouldn't be one for a while.

Sabrina glanced down the street. "Hey, I think that's my bus." The bus was barely moving, caught in a late-afternoon traffic jam. "You know, Jenny was real happy about her grade. Can I tell you a secret?"

"Sure."

The other girl looked around, careful to make sure no one was listening. "I mean it. It's a real secret. You can't tell anyone, ever." For once in her life, Sabrina looked absolutely serious.

"I won't."

"Jenny's father hits her, if she gets a B, instead of an A."

For a moment, Angela was shocked into speechlessness. Then, "He *hits* her?"

"Shh," Sabrina cautioned. "Don't tell anybody."

Angela's mind raced. Jenny Franklin's father was a lawyer like her dad; he had a job in a bank, and a private practice, too. Her dad knew him, said he was a good lawyer. And Jenny had awesome clothes and she was allowed to put streaks in her hair. She was on the gymnastics team, very popular, comfortable with the guys where Angela always felt tongue-tied. "That can't be true. She doesn't act like her father hits her."

"She *told* me, Angela. She was crying and everything. And how's she supposed to act? *Of course* she has to act cool. Can you imagine what the other kids would say if they knew? They'd all pity her, or something."

Sabrina was right. But still... "We should do something." Angela couldn't think. "We should tell somebody. A teacher, or maybe my dad. My dad would know what to do, I bet."

"Your dad? Give me a break, Angela. He used to work down in the courthouse, and he knows all those cops. He could have Jenny's dad maybe arrested." Sabrina's bus came, but she dropped back a bit to let some other kids board while she and Angela talked. "You promised not to say anything, and a promise is a promise." She pulled her book bag over one shoulder. "Besides, you already helped Jenny. You know how she got her A. All she needed was a little help, Angela. Now you have to let her handle stuff at home. If you told, you'd just make everything worse."

It was true—Angela might have helped Jenny with the test, just a little. For the first time, Angela felt good, in a weird way. "Well, okay," she said uncertainly.

Sabrina got on the bus, leaving Angela on the sidewalk, waiting for her own bus. She stood there, trying to imagine what things must be like for Jenny, but she simply could not. She had nothing to compare it to. Angela's mother had always been soft-spoken. Her dad was louder, and more than once, he'd stood outside her closed bedroom door and demanded she come out, saying she was being a brat. But then later he'd ruffle her hair, and tell her to hang in there, or say something serious about them loving each other.

In a way, she wished she could tell somebody; if not her dad, then maybe Claire. But Angela understood Jenny's wish to keep everything secret. If Angela told, who knew what the grown-ups would do? Everyone at Baldwin might find out, and if they did, how would Jenny stand it? Yes, Angela had done the right thing, just putting her paper where Jenny could see it, and now she'd do the right thing and keep Jenny's secret.

"Where's your bus?" Rachel Kellermann had come to stand beside her. Angela had been too distracted to notice the other girl.

"I don't know. It's late, I guess." Angela made an effort to concentrate, and peered down the street, but there were no buses in sight. She turned back to Rachel.

Rachel stood there a moment. "I wanted to tell you something, Angela. I'm leaving Baldwin at the end of first semester."

"You are? In the middle of the school year?" Angela was surprised. "What's up?"

"Oh, you know." Rachel played with the ends of her plaid scarf, not looking at Angela. "I never did fit in here, and my mom and dad helped me find another school." She worked the ends of the scarf more intently, passing the fringe through her fingers. "They have a chess team and everything at Spencer, and the kids aren't so rich. And they didn't seem so snotty. I spent the day there, and they were...friendly."

"Oh." Angela didn't know what to say. There was no use denying it. Rachel Kellermann was right; she didn't fit in at Baldwin.

"You should think about going to Spencer, too, Angela. They have a modern lit club, where they talk about D. H. Lawrence, and read *Lady Chatterly's Lover*, and everything. You'd like it there."

A tiny part of Angela was tempted, although it would be hard to explain to her father why she'd want to go to a school Sabrina didn't attend. *Well, Dad, Sabrina keeps convincing me to do stuff that really is okay, but I know you wouldn't understand, and I'm really sure you wouldn't like it... And all this stuff keeps happening, and I never know what's the right thing to do...*

"I don't think so, Rachel," she said finally. "But it sounds like a really nice school and everything."

"I was pretty sure what you'd say." Rachel's shoulders straightened slightly. "I figured I'd tell you about it, but I didn't think you'd be interested. You're so popular, here."

"Not that popular."

"Popular," Rachel repeated wistfully. "I always thought we could be kind of friends, but..." Her voice trailed off.

"We are friends," Angela said. It was almost the truth. They could have been friends.

"Right." Rachel turned to go.

"Rachel." Impulsively, Angela reached out to her. Her fingers closed on a bit of scarf. But as soon as they did, Angela felt ridiculous, grabbing on to the other girl that way. She pulled her hand away. "Um, good luck at Spencer."

THE FOLLOWING SUNDAY, Claire, Angela and Sophie were in Sophie's kitchen, making pierogies, which Claire had discovered were little stuffed dumplings. Michael wasn't there, although it was Sunday and his afternoon to be with his daughter. Claire had wondered if he would come. Since the night he'd taken her to see the house, there had been a new tension between them, a kind of... waiting. It colored everything they did together on the Persecki case. Michael never discussed anything personal on those occasions, yet always there were words unspoken.

It was just as well, Claire decided, that Michael hadn't come along. She was coming to care deeply for him, and today, pretending for the benefit of Michael's mother and daughter that she and Michael were nothing more than colleagues would be a tremendous strain. And as it was, the small kitchen was crowded, with just the three women.

"Thanks for coming, Claire," Sophie said for the third time, picking up one of the circles of dough, stuffing it with sauerkraut and pinching the dough closed around the filling so that it was in a half-moon shape. "I hated to let Sister Kasia down. I've made twenty dozen pierogies for the church Christmas festival for thirty-six years, and I would have hated to cancel this year. But this darn ankle..."

"No problem," Claire said lightly, also for the third time. "Really, Mrs. Chalinski, this is fun."

"Call me Sophie, like I told you before. You're my friend, and I feel about a hundred years old when you call me Mrs."

"Okay, I'll try to remember," Claire said. "Anyway, this is a treat for me. You have no idea how good it feels to be in a kitchen with other women." Her gaze included Angela. But Angela didn't look up from where she was breaking egg yolks into a well scooped out of the center of a little mound of flour. "At work, sometimes you get the impression that your whole existence is just within that one building, that winning cases and climbing the corporate ladder are all that matter in the world."

"Family is all that matters in the world," Sophie said flatly.

"Family is important," Claire agreed.

"And you miss yours, don't you?" Sophie asked.

Claire sighed. "Yes. Now that I have all the Christmas presents wrapped, it feels kind of like a letdown, this waiting. But I can't get out of the office before the twenty-third of December." She gave a little laugh. "Actually, I think the partners figure they're being very gracious about it all, giving me a day of travel. After all, the whole firm is closed on Christmas Day, and nobody's billing any hours. That must just about kill their Christmas spirit."

Sophie spooned up a big mound of sauerkraut. "Those partners need to realize what's really important."

It was a simple statement, yet it caught Claire by surprise. Yes, Michael's mother was right. Family was important, and at work, what was most important to her was learning to be a very good lawyer and doing a great job for her clients. She realized her number-one goal wasn't her billing percentage, although the partners tried to foster competition by sending out a weekly computer printout comparing hours billed by all the associates. Michael paid a great deal of attention to that printout. He wanted so much for all of them to succeed, but there was no way they all could....

Michael. She had to stop thinking about him.

"Anyway, I'll be in Nebraska for four days," she said. "I'm dying to open presents with my nephews. I got them this fantastic Lego castle, with little knights and colored pennants and everything. Actually, I can hardly wait to put it together myself."

"Dad was like that," Sophie said. "We'd get Mikush a bicycle or an erector set, and Mike would put it together and take it down three times before we finally set it up under the tree on Christmas Eve." She had put down her spoon, and now her large hand, with its swollen knuckles, gripped the edge of the bowl. "I miss him." Her voice had gone lower with a sudden passion. "I want him here with me, and I'm going to have him back."

"You will, Mrs. Chalinski. I mean, Sophie."

"This darn ankle—"

"Will heal," Claire cut in firmly. "It's just going to take time, that's all."

"How much time do you have when you're seventy?" Sophie sighed and picked up her spoon again. "Well, that's for the good Lord to decide. And I'm in a walking cast now, not on those crutches that gave me blisters under the arms. Pretty soon I'll be able to push Dad's wheelchair, and the day I can, he's coming home." A new briskness had entered her voice. "Now, Angela, I need that dough soon. What's the matter with you today?"

"Nothing." Angela had been kneading dough on the floured board, and Claire, too, now registered that Angela had seemed quiet and distracted, her hands listless as they manipulated the dough.

"Is something bothering you, Angela?" Claire asked.

"I said nothing's bothering me." Angela's cheeks colored, and she didn't look up from her work. But her hands kneaded more vigorously.

Sophie shot Claire a glance, then shrugged a little and switched to the pot of mashed potatoes for the stuffing. Claire continued to roll out the little circles of dough. From the hallway, there came the strains of a Christmas carol, and the unfamiliar sound of the lyrics in Polish made the well-known melody seem exotic.

"I'm glad you're getting to go home for Christmas, Claire," Sophie said. "But if you were in Chicago, you could spend Christmas with us. You could meet Dad. Did I tell you I could almost understand a few words he was saying when I visited him the other day?"

She had—at some length. Claire smiled to herself as she took a huge cookie sheet full of completed pierogies to the freezer. Sophie loved her husband. Claire would like to spend Christmas in the Chalinski home, where all the traditions felt the same and yet different. And Michael would be here...

Claire felt her smile vanish. She liked Angela and Sophie; they were friends. But Michael would never invite her to spend Christmas with him.

Claire put plastic wrap over the cookie sheet, and found room for it on a shelf in the crowded freezer. Michael had insisted the problem was not her, but him. Yet it was hard not to take his rejection personally. When she thought of how eager she had been for his body on hers, how she shivered every time he touched her...

And he'd admitted that he wanted her. They'd come so close to making love.

She shivered now. From the cold of the freezer, she told herself.

"I'd like to spend Christmas here," she told Sophie. "But I need to go home."

"Of course you do," Sophie agreed immediately. "Actually, I'd been thinking of a little party after Christmas. Not a wild New Year's Eve party, but a gathering of friends. Would you come to something like that?"

Claire hesitated.

"I want you to meet Dad," Sophie said. "And I'd do a real traditional Polish meal for everyone. It would be fun."

"Won't it be too much for you, with your ankle?"

"Angela will help me, won't you?"

"Sure," Angela agreed desultorily.

The sparkle in Sophie's eyes was unmistakable.

"I'd love to come," Claire said.

A rather sly smile of triumph lit Sophie's features, and for a moment Claire puzzled over that smile. "Good, then," was all Sophie said.

The three in the kitchen were quiet for a few moments. Sophie scraped the kettle of mashed potatoes, then invited Claire to try her hand at making the little pockets. "Now, pinch the ends good, Claire. You don't want the pierogi to burst when you put it in the boiling water."

Claire pinched. One ragged-looking pierogi went onto the tray. She scooped up the last of the mashed potatoes and put them into another circle. This time her little half-moon was greatly improved.

Suddenly, Angela spoke. "If somebody tells you a secret, and you promise not to tell, is it ever okay to break your promise?"

At the other end of the table, Claire exchanged glances with Sophie. Angela was rolling walnut-size bits of dough between her palms with elaborate casualness. She didn't look up.

"That depends," Sophie said, "on what the secret is."

"Well," Angela said, "what if your best friend told you the secret, and you maybe thought it might be better if you didn't tell? But what if you could also see that maybe you should tell?" The girl's whole body was taut as she spoke.

Sophie looked askance at Claire, clearly unsure what Angela was talking about. But Claire caught the gist of it.

"I guess," Claire began carefully, "it would depend on your reasons for telling the secret. You know, who would be hurt or who would be helped if you told."

Angela frowned. "But how do you know what's right?"

"You ask God," Sophie said.

"It's not that simple, *Busia.*" Angela's voice started to rise. "You always say things like that, but this is something really big."

"All the more reason to talk it over with God."

"Oh, *Busia—*"

"And," Claire cut in quickly, "you think back on what you've learned is right and wrong, and you try your best to do the right thing. Sometimes it helps if you talk things over with someone you trust."

"I can't talk about this. Not to anyone. So, that's that." Angela began stacking the completed pierogies on another cookie sheet, her head bowed.

"Here," Sophie interjected, pulling the tray from Angela. "I wanted to send these last few potato pierogies to Theresa Panski, next door. She loves that kind."

A few minutes later, she asked Angela to run the gaily wrapped plate over to Theresa's. As soon as Angela had gone, Sophie sighed. "I don't know what gets into that girl sometimes. Did you understand what she was talking about?"

"Not really, but obviously something's troubling her," Claire said thoughtfully.

"But what could be so important?" Sophie looked mystified. "She's only a girl, and her father takes care of everything for her."

Claire shook her head, smiling a little. "I remember some grim times, growing up. Maybe something isn't that big a deal to an adult, but when you're thirteen, well, everything can be important."

Sophie sighed again. "I guess you're right. She's growing up all of a sudden. I've been noticing her body is going through changes. I remember, when I was that age, sometimes wanting to cry when there was no reason to at all."

She and Claire exchanged a smile that was bittersweet, each thinking of that time. "Thank you, Claire, for helping me to remember that part of my life. Maybe I should talk to Angela."

Claire began to clear the table, stacking the dishes. "It didn't sound as though she was ready to talk, though, did it?"

"No, at least not today." Sophie came over to the table and picked up an empty kettle. "Here, let me do those dishes."

"You'll do no such thing," Claire said, pulling out a chair and insisting Sophie sit down. When Sophie protested, Claire said, "Now, how are you going to be well enough to have Mr. Chalinski home for Christmas if you don't stay off that ankle?"

At that, Sophie sank heavily into one of the kitchen chairs. "My ankle does hurt a little," she admitted.

"I'll bet it hurts a lot," Claire retorted, stacking dishes.

"All right, a lot." Sophie took a sip of coffee. "You're good for this family, Claire, do you know that?"

Her words warmed Claire. "I like you and Angela."

"Maybe you can get Angela to talk to you."

"If she wants to talk, I'll listen," Claire promised.

She was at the sink, filling it with hot water when Sophie added, "When I said you were good for this family,

I didn't just mean Angela. I also meant you're good for Michael.''

Claire went momentarily still. Michael didn't think she was good for him. Just the opposite, in fact.

"Are you in love with my son?" Sophie asked, point-blank.

Lord, Claire thought, automatically rinsing a plate. What a conversation to be having with Michael's mother!

"He wouldn't welcome any feelings like that from me," she finally said.

Over at the table, Sophie made a sound of disbelief. "He may not know it, but he needs you, Claire."

Claire put down her plate. "He's still in love with Mary Jo," she said, and she could not keep the pain out of her voice.

"We all loved Mary Jo, but she's gone," Sophie said. "The thing is, Michael is stubborn. My Mike is like that. He gives his loyalty and his protection, and that's that. It makes the Chalinski men hard to love sometimes. But it's worth it, Claire, because when they love someone in return—" suddenly, Sophie's voice, usually so brisk, cracked with emotion "—they love totally."

Claire stood at the sink, dishes forgotten, hot tears stinging her eyelids. Oh, to inspire that kind of love from a man.

"I wish he hadn't made that promise to Mary Jo," Sophie said. "Do you know he's still running that advertisement in the *Tribune?* But sending that man to jail won't bring Mary Jo back. Mikush can't let himself be happy. He's fighting a war with himself over it." She paused. "But he needs you, Claire. And I think if you keep on pushing him, he'll admit it."

"If Michael ever marries again, he'll probably choose someone like Mary Jo," Claire said. "One thing I've figured out is that I'm nothing like she was."

Sophie started to rise. "Michael loved Mary Jo, and she was a fine woman. But she wasn't...strong inside. Not like I'm strong. Not like you're strong. In a lot of ways, she let life pass her by."

Sophie had come to stand beside Claire at the sink. "I don't know if I'm saying this right—I don't know a lot of fancy words. But I do know my son. With Mary Jo, happiness was easy. They grew up together, and his dreams sort of became hers, too. This time, he's fighting for his happiness. He needs a woman to fight alongside him. To fight with him. To fight him, if that's what needs to be done."

Struck by the intensity of her words, Claire turned to Sophie. The other woman was much shorter than she was, and when she looked down, Sophie was looking up at her, searching her face. "Claire, he needs you." Her hand clasped Claire's wet fingers, gripping hard.

CHAPTER TEN

"THIS IS YOUR CHANCE. Maybe your last one." Michael sat next to Claire, across from Nick Persecki in the Persecki living room. Mrs. Persecki had hovered, offering a plate of decorated Christmas cookies, refreshments that seemed incongruous with the business Michael and Claire had with her son. At intervals, she would ruffle her son's hair or tell him that everything would be all right. Finally, Michael had been blunt, asking Nick's mother to leave them alone to converse with their client.

"I've spoken with Judge Galen, and Ms. Logan has been negotiating with the prosecutor. Look. We've checked every detail of the police procedures used. We can take the case to trial, but they have you, Nick. You might as well admit that."

"You could get me off. I see on television all the time how guilty guys get off."

"You aren't a celebrity client, Nick," Claire said matter-of-factly. "The world isn't interested in your problems." She glanced at Michael, and he nodded almost imperceptibly.

She leaned forward. "The prosecutor and I have reached an understanding. They'll drop the theft charge and let you plead to the alcohol count. The prosecutor will recommend community service instead of jail. Before you say anything, you need to know something else. Yesterday afternoon, the prosecutor told me Bobby McNair's attorney has been in contact, wanting to make a deal."

Nick looked incredulous for a second, then he cursed. "It was Bobby all along, doing those ladies' houses. Now he's going to say it was me?"

"Looks that way," Michael said calmly.

"That bastard. That lousy, fu—"

"Enough," Michael cut in. "Do you want the deal or not?"

Nick's shoulders slumped. "Yeah, okay, I want it. What do I have to do?"

"Tell us everything, for starters," Claire said.

Nick angled a look toward the kitchen. Michael realized he didn't want his mother to hear what he'd been up to. Good. At least Nick still had some feelings for her. Maybe Michael could work with that. He had no intention of merely getting Nick off on the charge—that wouldn't do Nick, or his family, any good in the long run. But, despite his and Claire's work on the case, and their three previous meetings with Nick, Michael still wasn't sure how to reach him.

"Okay," Nick said again. "Me and Bobby have been friends for a while. Around here, if you're not with a group or something, you need someone. Bobby's big, and the guys pretty much leave him alone. He's kept things cool for me. He's a good friend that way. But Bobby lost his job a few months ago, and he needed money. So, he started to take stuff from the houses. It was just Bobby. Never me."

Again he glanced toward the kitchen. "I was always just home, hanging around Mom all the time."

"Not in school," Claire observed. It was a fact they already knew, having checked Nick's background. He'd been belligerent to teachers, had got in fights. He'd smoked marijuana in the bathroom, and had been truant for days at a stretch. At one time, the authorities had wanted to put him in a boot-camp-style school for juvenile delinquents in an attempt to straighten him out. Mrs. Persecki had refused. Shortly thereafter, Nick had dropped out of school for good.

"Not at work, either," Michael said now.

"I couldn't find anything," Nick said defensively.

"How hard did you look?" Michael retorted.

"I did look, real hard. Everywhere around here. Nobody wanted me." For the barest moment, the tough mask Nick wore slipped. He looked defeated.

Defeated at eighteen.

There was silence. Nick had no skills, and with that hair and attitude, Michael could believe that Nick's search for employment had been a failure. "We can work on things like that," he offered.

"Yeah, right. You're going to get me a job representing a bunch of your big-time clients? We could go out for one of them power lunches." Nick looked away for a moment. "So, what do I have to say, to get out of this fu—" He stopped of his own accord, then continued, "This mess I'm in?"

"Let's start with honesty," Michael said. "If Bobby was behind all these burglaries, how was it that the silverware was in the trunk of *your* car that night?"

Nick got up and paced the small room. In the corner, on a table, was an Infant of Prague, just like at Michael's mother's house. He stopped. "I got my piece," he said finally.

Claire looked puzzled. Michael clarified it for her. "You were involved after the items were stolen. You got a percentage of the price the goods fetched when they were fenced."

"Yeah."

"What did you do to earn your piece?"

"Nothing."

"Come on, Nick. Nobody gets something for nothing, not in your world."

Nick came back and sat down in the chair opposite Michael. "Okay," he said defiantly. "I told Bobby, okay? I told him when the ladies wouldn't be home. My mom knew when they were going places." Involuntarily, he glanced toward the kitchen door once more, then at his fist, which he had balled on his knee. "When I found out what was going on, Bobby had already done three jobs. And my mom always knew when these ladies were going to church, or when they made their shopping trips. You know, they'd talk on the phone with my mom, tell her stuff like that."

"You made your mom tell you when they wouldn't be home?" Claire acted as if, despite Nick's confession, she couldn't quite believe it.

"My mom didn't know nothing about it. Nothing. I'd just kind of ask her things, real casual. She always seemed like she was glad—" unexpectedly, his voice cracked slightly "—that I was interested or something."

A little silence descended over the room.

"But why, Nick?" Claire asked, looking up from her legal pad, where she had been writing down his story. "These people were your neighbors, and they didn't have all that much—you couldn't have got any real money out of all this, just taking a percentage. If you needed a few dollars, couldn't you have asked your brother John for a loan?"

Again there was silence. Finally, Nick looked down, and when he spoke, his voice was hard, challenging. "Look. When I found out what Bobby was doing, he was going to hit Mrs. Ostrinski's place. Mrs. Ostrinski is okay, and she's just a little old lady, for crying out loud. She was real nice to my mom when my dad died, bringing us food for the freezer and doing a novena with my mom, for my dad." His voice lowered, but he still sounded reluctant, maybe even angry to be confessing this part. Michael leaned forward as Nick continued.

"But she's kind of tough in a way, Mrs. Ostrinski. And so I thought, maybe if she was at home when Bobby did her place, well—" He stopped.

"Maybe she'd fight him, and she'd get hurt." Claire's dark eyes had gone soft.

Nick looked relieved at not having to say it. "So, anyway, I figured, Bobby was going to do their places, anyway, you know? So if I knew they weren't home, and I told Bobby, he could take the stuff and he'd never get caught and Mrs. Ostrinski and the other ladies would be okay."

"Oh, Nick—" Impulsively, Claire reached out her hand. Michael quickly put his own over hers, staying her. She looked at him questioningly.

"Nick took money for handing over that information to Bobby McNair," he reminded her quietly.

"But—" She gave him an uncertain look. He's just a kid, Michael could almost hear her saying.

He tried to communicate without words his sure knowledge that they had to hang tough with Nick Persecki. Kids like him respected toughness, and for what lay ahead, Michael needed respect.

Claire looked reluctant, but took her cue from Michael. "All right, Nick. When we tell the police your story, where can they find the items stolen from these houses? Whatever Bobby still has lying around."

Nick talked; Claire listened and wrote. Michael was relieved that, for once, she had taken his advice without argument. He knew how easily Claire empathized with others, how quick she was to reach out.

He also knew that something was building between them. He'd felt it even as he made sure to keep his distance as they worked the Persecki case. A kind of awareness was always present. No matter who was in the room, he was always conscious of Claire, attuned to her somehow. He knew his coolness hurt her. He hated that part, having to hurt her, but it was the only way. Since that night when he'd almost made love to her, Michael no longer trusted himself. And the kind of hurt he was causing her now was nothing compared to the hurt he could cause her if he let their relationship get out of control again.

A few minutes later, as they were driving away, Michael said, "Claire, I know you were trying to offer Nick sympathy, but he already has too many people making excuses for him."

"I know that," she said right away. "I wasn't thinking about that at the time, but I realize Nick's mother excuses his behavior too easily."

Michael nodded. As usual, Claire had caught on quickly. "What's next?" she asked.

"I figure there'll be about a hundred hours of community service ordered in this case. The thing is, most of it's just make-work stuff, like picking up litter by the roadways."

Claire nodded. "I've seen those guys. They go so slowly, it's like they pick up about one piece of trash an hour."

"I'd like Nick to learn something from the experience other than it's better to do community service than go to jail."

"Any ideas, Michael?"

"I'm stumped," he admitted. "Apart from the stealing, I'm also worried about his drinking. I don't know if Nick has a real problem, or not. And somehow, I've got to figure out a way to get him out of that house, where his mother babies him and he's got plenty of time to make trouble."

"He needs a job," Claire said.

"But who would hire him, with his record?" Michael shook his head.

"We'll think of something," Claire promised. "You know, Michael, I think you're doing a terrific job with Nick. I know a lot of attorneys wouldn't bother to do anything more for a client after they'd made the deal with the prosecutor."

She was doing it again, Michael thought. She kept trying to make him into someone he was not. Someone noble...maybe someone closer to the man he used to be.

When would he be able to make her understand that that man was gone forever?

SABRINA SIMMONS, Jenny Franklin and Angela stood by Jenny's locker, speculating about Dr. Samuelson's announcement that there was going to be another test.

"So soon? And right before Christmas? That doesn't make any sense. Dr. Samuelson doesn't usually give too many tests," Sabrina said.

"It's all essay," Jenny said. She made no secret of being nervous. In fact, her cheeks, under her apricot blusher, were downright pale. "Essay, not multiple choice like the last one was. It's going to be hard to explain to my father how I could ace one test, then not do so hot on the next, just a few days later."

"I'll help you cram," Angela offered.

"It wouldn't do any good. Physics is so hard. Even if I spent every minute studying, I still couldn't get a perfect score..." Her voice trailed away miserably.

Angela couldn't think of anything more to say, and Sabrina, too, was silent for a moment. Then Sabrina said, "Well, there's only one thing to do. Angela, you'll have to get that test from Dr. Samuelson's office."

Angela's stomach hit the floor. "I can't do that."

"Sure you can. You're always hanging around Dr. Samuelson. She won't think anything of it if you go to her office with a question or something, and sort of find out where she's keeping the test. Then you just have to borrow it for a few hours so we can make copies. It shouldn't be hard. You know how kind of out of it Dr. Samuelson can be. She'd never notice if a few papers were missing."

Angela felt sick. Dr. Sam...her favorite teacher, the one who was always so excited about teaching. Some of the kids made fun of her enthusiasm for things like motion and gravity and the forces of the universe, but they all knew Dr. Sam cared so much.

Angela tried to push down her panic. All she had done so far was write a couple of English papers for her best friend. Then she had put her test in a place where Jenny Franklin and maybe a few other kids could see it. And now this. Sabrina wanted her to steal the test.

"I can't," she finally said.

"Please," Jenny said softly. Her blue eyes, heavily outlined with brown pencil, were intensely pleading. "Please."

Once, Angela had wanted to fit in so much, and she had assumed girls like Jenny Franklin didn't have anything to worry about, that their lives were perfect. Now she'd learned that Jenny's dad hit her, if she got a B instead of an A. Was it true? Searching Jenny's peaked face, Angela was sure it was.

If she told her dad or somebody what was going on at Jenny's house, Angela didn't know what would happen. Would they maybe take Jenny's father away? She couldn't imagine how ashamed Jenny would be.

"If I do this, it'll be the last time," she warned Sabrina. "Don't even ask me to write a paper for you, or anything, because this is it."

"Sure, Angela. I mean, I agree, no more." Sabrina looked scared, but her eyes were sort of sparkly, too, like it was some kind of adventure or something.

This was no adventure. "Okay," Angela said, feeling as if she couldn't breathe.

"Thank you, Angela," Jenny murmured. "Thanks for being my friend."

Later that day, during study hall, Angela asked for a pass to go see Dr. Sam. If she was going to do this, she had to do it now, this day, before she lost her nerve. Please, she thought, don't be in your office, Dr. Sam. Or, if you're in, don't let me see that test.

But Dr. Samuelson was in. "Hello, Angela," she greeted her. "Have a seat. What's on your mind?"

Angela sat, and asked the questions she had prepared. It was a good thing she had thought over what she was going to say, because otherwise she couldn't have made her mind work right.

It was when Dr. Samuelson was explaining something technical about the Doppler effect that Angela saw it. It was there—the test, right on the corner of Dr. Samuelson's credenza. If she turned her head just so, she could see the questions, with little check marks and what must be sample answers in red ink.

Dr. Sam was going on and on, the way she did when something interested her, and usually everything interested her. "Does that make sense? I know it's complicated but if you think about the sound coming toward you as though..."

Angela lost the thread of the conversation. This wouldn't work. It was impossible. How could she get this test out of the office, with Dr. Sam sitting there right across from her? Maybe she could sneak in between periods or something, and take it and have it back before Dr. Samuelson noticed.

Dr. Samuelson finally quit speaking. Angela started when she realized that her teacher was handing her a book across the desk.

"Here, Angela. This book explains better what I'm talking about. Why don't you look at chapter fourteen."

Angela mumbled a thank-you and took the book. Then Dr. Samuelson said, "Take it with you. I've got to step out to talk over a little matter with the head. And then I have to teach two more classes. But after you've read the section, we can talk about it, okay?"

"Sure, thanks," Angela mumbled.

Right away, Dr. Samuelson rose and left the room. Angela couldn't believe it, couldn't believe that Dr. Sam had just left her alone here, with that test right on the credenza. Angela had been puzzling out how to return and get that test, and she'd been handed a perfect opportunity to take it.

But for a moment, Angela just sat there. She didn't want to do it. Somehow, her own popularity, her place of honor as one of the coolest kids, even the on-again, off-again attention of Joel Tate seemed unimportant. But

Jenny Franklin's dad hit her, if she even got a B, and Jenny Franklin had been about to cry over that test, Angela was sure of it. The weight of knowing that felt so heavy.

Quickly, before she could change her mind, Angela got up, went to the credenza and grabbed the sheaf of papers. She stuffed them in her folder. Then she pulled a couple of books off the almost-toppling stacks Dr. Samuelson kept on the credenza, and placed two big textbooks over the empty space where the test had been. Dr. Samuelson's office was a cheerful scramble of this and that—books, pictures of former students, little models of the solar system and a tiny demonstration volcano, a bulletin board crammed with yellowing notes and a years-out-of-date calendar. If Angela was lucky and Sabrina got the copies made very quickly, Dr. Samuelson would never know the test was missing.

Angela finally left her office immediately. Now there was only her elective literature class to be gotten through, then Sabrina was going to meet her, get the test and make the copies. Angela carefully placed the folder holding the test on the top shelf of her locker, found her novel for lit class and spun the combination lock.

MICHAEL SURVEYED the gaily wrapped Christmas gifts on top of his credenza. The shopping assistant from Marshall Field had just delivered them—wooden boxes filled with mixed nuts for his male associates, little gold-wire baskets of chocolate truffles for the women. Appropriate and impersonal, and he hadn't had to lift a finger, even to wrap them. The Christmas season was almost upon him, and he found himself unaccountably dissatisfied as he surveyed the little array. Claire would probably like the chocolates. Why wouldn't she?

He balked at giving them to her, though. Somehow, it didn't seem right to give Claire the same gift he gave everyone else, the kind of gift you gave when you didn't have a clue about what the other person's personal life was like.

Only—only he had no excuse for giving Claire something different. No excuse and no reason, he told himself firmly as he took one other present, a Cartier gold pen, and approached the bank of elevators. George Fanal had called him up to his office for what had become a gift-giving ritual.

Fanal's office was on the highest floor of the firm, over the partners' conference room and weight room. Michael settled into a butter-soft leather club chair and accepted the brandy Fanal poured from a crystal decanter.

"So, Michael, here's to a Merry Christmas," Fanal said jovially as he raised his snifter in a toast.

"And to a profitable New Year," Michael said, raising his own glass and playing the game to the hilt.

A few minutes later, after Fanal had opened his package and exclaimed over the pen, Michael opened the gift Fanal had given him—a small sculpture of a running horse.

Michael had no particular interest in horses. But Fanal was obsessed with the Thoroughbreds he raised on his farm an hour north of the city, on Lake Michigan.

"Nice little filly," Fanal was explaining, indicating the sculpture. "You can see the form, the breeding in the line of her back..."

Michael sipped his brandy, only half listening as Fanal went on and on, conscious of a peculiar restlessness. Usually when he was in Fanal's office, he was reminded of why he had originally come to the firm. The money, prestige and power were nowhere more evident than in this office, perched as it was over some of the country's most expensive real estate, and decorated with antiques, Oriental rugs and fine paneling.

The money was handy. Michael was honest enough to admit that. But the power, the prestige—the things he'd once thought might help him to nail Beske—hadn't helped at all.

"I hate to intrude on the Christmas spirit with business," Fanal said, finally changing the subject, "but there's a little matter I think it's time we addressed. Stuart Tyler isn't getting the hang of trial work, is he? I've been thinking about that day I sat in on your case conference. Stuart was a flaming wreck over that products liability case."

No, Stuart wasn't making much progress, Michael thought. "I've been working with him. It can take a little longer for some than others."

Fanal grunted and poured himself another brandy. "He's not going to catch on."

"He'd be fine over in Real Estate or Contracts. He has excellent technical skills."

"Lawyers with good technical skills are a dime a dozen." Fanal tipped his chair back, absently turning his snifter to admire the gold liquid within. "Fire him, Michael."

But it's almost Christmas, Michael thought. Where on earth had that thought come from? he wondered an instant later. What bloody difference did it make whether it was Christmas, or not, when you were about to shoot down a man's dreams?

"No," he heard himself say.

Fanal's chair came abruptly upright, and he stared at Michael in astonishment.

"We should try him over in Real Estate first."

Fanal arched a skeptical eyebrow.

Michael pressed on. "The man's talented. I say we give him a chance. If in six months he can't cut it, then we can let him go. But I think you'll find he's an asset to the firm in the right spot."

Fanal paused for long moments, considering. Finally, he said in a mild tone, "The brandy's especially fine this year, don't you think? My wife picked up a case in France. The really good stuff isn't sold over here, you know."

Michael nodded, careful to keep any feelings of triumph from showing on his face. But he knew he had bought Stuart another six months.

Fanal rose and walked around his desk, his snifter in hand. He paused, studying a couple of antique horse brasses hanging on the wall. "I just told you to fire Tyler, and you just refused. Don't you wonder why I'm tolerating what amounts to your insubordination?"

"Perhaps," Michael said evenly, "because you pay me to teach the associates the finer points of practicing law and to give you an honest assessment of their ability. That's what a senior does." Something really strange was happening to him today. In a perverse way, he realized, he was beginning to enjoy this conversation.

"What you just did, making the decision not to fire Tyler, is what a partner does. Not what a senior does."

"Maybe so," Michael agreed.

"I guess that means you're ready to be made partner."

Partner. Was this an offer of a partnership? Michael's mouth went suddenly dry. George was smiling, nodding at what must be dawning comprehension on Michael's face. Michael had wanted this, dreamed of it, planned for it for two solid years. In his best-case scenario, he'd assumed it would take at least two more years of grueling work for the offer to come. Partner!

Fanal came to stand by Michael, and put a hand on his shoulder. "The offer's not official. It can't be until we have our yearly meeting in February. So I'm relying on your discretion not to say a word about this around the firm. But I've got the votes, and you can safely assume the offer will come. Welcome aboard, Michael."

Michael stood in a kind of daze and shook hands with Fanal. A partnership. Finally, everything he'd dreamed of... Of course, partnership meant he'd no longer supervise the associates; he was going to miss working with them... he shook off the thought. He was making partner, and that was all that mattered. Another thought intruded. He wouldn't be spending time with Claire anymore. Well, that was what he wanted, wasn't it? Distance, no temptations, his life on track. And he was going to have both that and his precious partnership.

"Let's have another brandy." This time, after Fanal poured, he sat down next to Michael, as if signaling their equal status.

"Now," he continued, "we've talked over Tyler. But I've been thinking too about Claire Logan."

Michael's body went utterly still. A savage kind of protectiveness rose in him at the thought of Fanal denigrating Claire's work.

"Ms. Logan has some rough edges," Fanal said.

Careful, Michael thought. "She's the most talented associate down there."

"I agree," Fanal said unexpectedly. "I know you're protective of that bunch of associates of yours, so don't get your nose out of joint. All I was going to say was, I wasn't crazy about Ms. Logan taking me down a peg or two that day we, ah, discussed the Hathaway case being overruled. But I've had time to think about it. The woman has guts. And guts and heart go a long way in making a good trial lawyer. I figure, if you look at a lawyer like you assess good horseflesh, you can't go wrong. Logan has the kind of will that'll take her across the finish line. I'm not so old and pompous that I can't see that."

Michael's body relaxed.

"Put her on the partner track, Michael," Fanal said. "Give her some tougher cases. Spend more time with her."

"I'm going with her to see the judge in the Persecki case, one of our *pro bono* cases, this afternoon."

"Good. As I say, spend a lot of time with her, work with her. File those edges, help her acquire some political skills. In a few years, I'd like to be offering Claire Logan a partnership, if you can bring her along."

A few minutes later, Michael got back on the elevator. He held his sculpture, and figuratively, his partnership, close to his chest. Spend time with Claire Logan, George had ordered. He resisted the urge to laugh at the irony, the fine satire of that order. His life was on track. His partnership was coming. And now he was ordered to spend time with the one woman who always seemed to upset his plans.

ANGELA HURRIED out of lit class. All she wanted in the world was to go to her locker, get that copy of the physics test and hand it over to Sabrina so that she was off the hook.

Head down, she rounded the corner, trying not to run.

"In a hurry, Angela?" It was her headmaster who spoke, and when she looked up, she saw that he and Dr. Samuelson were standing right in front of her locker, blocking her way.

Angela stopped dead. Her palms were suddenly damp, and she had to grip her books hard. Those books felt as if they were fifty pounds heavier.

A small crowd had begun to gather. Out of the corner of her eye, Angela saw Sabrina on the edge of the group, her face white and scared. Angela forced herself to take the last few steps toward the two adults.

The headmaster said, "Please hand over your books and notebooks to Dr. Samuelson. And I think we need to have a look in your locker. Would you open it for us, please."

Angela fought not to cry, not here, with all the kids watching.

"You don't need to open it," she said, her voice cracking. "You already know what's in there."

"Oh, Angela, I'm so disappointed in you," Dr. Samuelson said, distress in her voice, and in her faded blue eyes. "I had so hoped I was wrong."

CHAPTER ELEVEN

"DO YOU MIND coming along?" Michael asked Claire. He had just clicked off his car phone, where he had taken the puzzling message that Angela was all right but that Dr. Greene, the headmaster of Baldwin Academy, had to see him right away. "I could drop you off at the firm, but we're a long way out, and the school says it's urgent."

"No problem," Claire assured him, and she felt some of his own anxiety. "What do you suppose the problem is?"

Michael shook his head, and increased his speed. "Trouble in school, was all they said."

Michael and Claire had just met with the judge on the Persecki case, and the judge had accepted the arrangements worked out with the prosecutor. He had also seemed receptive to Michael and Claire's idea that they design the community service especially for Nick. All they had to do was come up with something that would truly help Nick. Claire had been excited about how the case was shaping up, but now she felt a letdown as she worried about Angela.

"She's seemed preoccupied lately, don't you think?"

Michael shot her a quick glance. "So, you noticed as well. Why didn't you say something to me? If I'd known you'd picked up on it, I would have tried to talk to Angela."

"It's just a feeling I had. Nothing specific enough to mention to you."

He didn't say anything to that, instead simply concentrated on driving.

At Baldwin, Claire followed him down the hallway to the headmaster's office, where she took a seat in the outer office. The place was eerily quiet with the students gone for the day. She settled down to wait.

She didn't have to wait long. Not fifteen minutes later, the inner door opened and Angela came out. Two bright spots of color lit the girl's cheekbones, and her head was held unnaturally high. Just behind her was Michael, his own expression dark and grim.

"Angela," Claire started, half rising.

"Claire's here, too?" Angela interrupted, her voice high and strained. "Oh, no." She took one more look at Claire and burst into tears.

"Angela, what's wrong?" Claire was out of her seat and going to her, but Michael held up his hand.

She stopped short. Michael was silent for a long moment.

"Tell her, Dad. Go ahead, just tell her," Angela said, sobbing.

Michael said in a low voice, "Angela has just been accused of cheating on a physics test."

Claire was aghast. "There must be a mistake. Angela would never cheat."

Michael's jaw was set, rigid. "That's what I thought, too. Until she admitted it was true."

Claire stared at Angela. Angela said, "Don't look at me like that."

"But why?" Claire asked softly.

"What difference does it make?" It was Michael who answered, his voice tight with suppressed anger. "There's no excuse for cheating." He strode forward, Angela and Claire trailing in his wake.

At the car, Angela got quickly into the back seat, where Claire had intended to sit. Michael stopped Claire as she was about to get into the passenger side. "Look, before you say anything, I'll handle this, Claire. She's my daughter."

Claire knew that. She didn't really intend to interfere, just be there if Michael needed her. But Michael was shutting her out again. Despite all they'd shared, and even though he knew she cared for Angela, he was shutting Claire out. An arc of hurt curved through her midsection. His words were only one more reminder that Michael had no intention of letting her be part of his life. Trying to put aside her feelings, she lightly touched his arm. "Michael, I know you're upset—"

"Damn right I'm upset." His face was shadowed in pain and anger. "I've tried with Angela. For two years I've been her only parent. I've tried to understand her and her moods. She's thirteen, you said. Give her freedom, you said. So I did. I gave her freedom. I let her choose her own clothes. I let her make her own decisions. And this is what she chooses to do."

Claire could have told him that letting his daughter pick out a few sweaters hardly meant he'd given her a license to cheat at school. But Michael was so angry, and she knew that angry people were not rational. Claire also knew that Angela needed her. Maybe, despite himself, Michael needed her. So, quietly, she got into the passenger seat of the car.

It was a bleak ride home. Angela was silent in the back seat. Michael didn't say a word. Finally, Claire asked, "Is Angela expelled?"

"Baldwin wants Angela to own up to her responsibility, and the headmaster wants to get to the bottom of the cheating. Angela won't be expelled if she names the people she was doing the cheating for."

"I wasn't cheating for anybody," Angela said from the back seat.

Michael ignored her denial. "She couldn't be doing this for herself. I've seen her study. She doesn't need to cheat. It's that Sabrina Simmons. She's been a bad influence all along." He rounded a corner, heading toward Lincoln Park, where Claire lived. "Dr. Greene is as convinced as I am that Angela was doing this for someone else, and he suspects, as I do, that Sabrina is behind it. Dr. Samuelson, of all people, actually defended Angela, advocated for her to stay at Baldwin, said she's a bright, interested student." He shook his head. "So far, she refuses to turn in the names of the others involved, and I feel doubly disappointed in her for that."

Claire felt a chill go up her spine. An angry Michael was a formidable man. Although he had yet to raise his voice, the weight of his disapproval would be hard for Angela to bear. Although Claire had no doubt Angela and Michael loved each other, she could feel the breach building between the two. She longed to try and talk to Angela. But Claire had no right to, not without Michael's permission.

That right had belonged to the girl's mother. Mary Jo.

Claire fought a sudden, hot prick of tears behind her eyelids.

"Even if there were other students involved, I couldn't tell you, Dad." When she finally acknowledged her father's suspicions, a nervous defiance filled Angela's voice.

Michael didn't answer; he was preoccupied with pulling into a space near Claire's apartment building. "Under the circumstances, I hope you don't mind if I don't walk you to your door."

"Actually, I'd prefer it if you did." Claire could certainly get to her own door by herself, but she wanted a few moments alone with Michael.

He looked startled, but moved to comply. When they were at Claire's door, he waited impatiently for her to fit her key in the lock.

Now that she had her chance to speak with him, Claire was at a loss as to how to begin. "Don't be too hard on her, Michael, until you've listened to her," she finally said.

"What could she possibly say that would make this right?" Michael raked a hand through his hair. "God, just last week I was telling myself what a good kid she was, being grateful she would never be another Nick Persecki."

"Michael, she will never be another Nick. She's only thirteen—"

"And old enough to know better!"

"Yes, she is," Claire agreed.

Her agreement seemed to make him pause. Claire pressed her advantage. "She was very wrong, but she's your daughter, Michael. Just love her."

"I'll handle this, Claire." Michael's face was stony, but the pain that underlined his words couldn't be missed. "As you just said, she's *my* daughter. She's *my* responsibility, and I'll handle it."

There was no way Claire was going to get through his anger. With a sense of failure, and an undefinable sense of loss, Claire opened her door and left Michael standing in the hall.

IN BED THAT NIGHT, Michael tossed and turned, twisting the sheets under him. He didn't know what to do, didn't know what was right anymore.

Angela was defying him. He'd demanded an explanation, and she'd refused to give him one. He'd asked that she turn in the names of the kids involved, and she'd flatly refused.

Love her, Claire had said. Listen to her.

He loved his daughter, but he couldn't let her get away with this. He was her parent. She had to name the other kids who'd cheated, or she'd be expelled.

The easiest course would be to let her leave Baldwin. She was only thirteen; she could put this behind her . . .

Wasn't that how it had begun for Nick Persecki, with his mother and his brother making excuses for him and bailing him out of trouble?

Angela was not Nick. Claire had said that, too, and he knew it, intellectually. But he just couldn't get the comparison out of his mind. And he was still shell-shocked, disbelieving. He and Mary Jo had tried so hard to teach Angela what was right.

Mary Jo. That was what was keeping him awake more than anything tonight. Hours ago, he'd tried to talk to Angela. Finally in frustration, he'd simply ordered her to give him the names.

And Angela had stood there and stared at him, and refused again, so he'd told her to go to her room and think about what she'd done.

And then, in a whisper that only conveyed her vehemence, Angela had said, "I want my mother. Not you, Dad. I want my mother."

Michael rolled over. He had no idea what to do.

A long time later, there was a soft knock on his bedroom door, and Angela put her head in. In a hesitant voice she said, "Dad? Can you come out? Claire's here."

Michael glanced at his bedside clock—2:00 a.m. "Claire's here? Now?"

The hallway light was on. In her oversize Hard Rock Café nightshirt his daughter looked very young. "I called her and asked her to come over."

Michael sat up in bed, running a quick hand through his rumpled hair, and pulled on a T-shirt over his sweats. Barefoot, he came down the hall, following Angela.

Claire was here. He'd told her not to interfere again, but Claire did what she wanted to do. She pushed and pushed, insinuated herself into his life...

And tonight he was very glad to see her.

She stood in the little entryway of his condo, wearing a pair of jeans and a faded sweatshirt with that Shakespeare quote that said, The first thing we do, let's kill all the lawyers. Only on Claire's shirt, the word *kill* had been crossed out, replaced with the embroidered word, *KISS*. She looked mussed; obviously Angela had got her, too, out of bed, and she held her jacket stiffly, as though she wasn't sure what her reception would be.

"Hi," he said softly. There was a reason he was so glad to see her, why his heart leaped at the mere sight of her, he told himself. It was because her presence possibly meant he was going to get through to Angela.

"Hi," she said, and her reserved smile looked wonderful to Michael.

He could have stood looking at her all night, and for a moment he indulged himself. In her fleecy sweatshirt, she looked soft, touchable, warm. With reluctance, Michael pulled his gaze from hers and focused on Angela. "Okay, Angela. We're both here. Come on in, Claire."

When they were settled in the living room, Claire in an armchair, Michael on the sofa, Angela perched stiffly on her favorite ottoman, Claire spoke. "Angela called me, Michael. And she told me a lot of things I thought she should be telling you. When I suggested she try talking with you instead, she asked me to come over." There was a steely determination in her gaze. "I know you don't want my help, Michael, but I'm here for Angela. She's a friend of mine and she asked me—"

"It's okay, Claire." From his seat on the sofa, Michael straightened. "I get it. I'm such a hard guy, you have to apologize for doing a favor for my family, and my own daughter feels she needs someone to run interference. Fine. I get it."

"Well, you are hardest on yourself," Claire added helpfully.

Michael sighed. "Okay, Angela. Let's try this one more time."

Angela fidgeted on the ottoman, shot a look at Claire, who nodded encouragingly. Finally, she spoke. "I'm not going to tell you any names, Dad," she warned.

"For now, just tell me what's on your mind."

That must have been the right thing to say, because Angela started talking, going faster and faster as the story developed. She spoke about not fitting in, and wanting to be accepted by some group of kids, and went on and on about some boy. He could understand some of what she was saying; he'd been a kid, too. But he still could find no justification for what she'd done.

Finally, when she seemed to be winding down, he interrupted. "So, it wasn't just this one cheating incident? It's been going on for some time?"

His daughter swallowed, nodded, looked away.

"My God, Angela, why didn't you tell me all this long ago?"

There was a little sob in her voice. "I knew you'd be mad."

She knew he'd be angry, Michael repeated to himself. Yes, of course he would have been angry. He was angry now. But for his daughter to have carried this secret, one that obviously had caused her pain, for so long and not to tell him . . . He wondered if, despite all those Sundays together, despite all his efforts to be a good father, he really understood his daughter at all.

"Okay, Angel." He made sure his voice was soft. "Let me make sure I understand. You claim you did all this to be popular?"

Claire spoke. "I think it's for this part that I'm here, Michael." She left the armchair and joined him on the sofa. Although she didn't touch him, her scent wafted toward him—her tangy scent that had become so familiar. "Angela is thirteen. I don't know what life is like for thirteen-year-old boys, but for girls it can be pretty rough. I know. I spent most of my teenage years feeling very different from other kids, and wishing I was popular." Her voice was low, intense. "I mean it. I can understand exactly what Angela has been feeling."

Michael was surprised. Claire had previously mentioned something about her teenage years being difficult, but that long-ago girl seemed incongruous with the woman she was today.

Lightly, she touched his hand. "I know you want to be everything for Angela. But there are some things a woman understands better about another woman."

Okay, he could accept that. If Mary Jo were alive, there were a lot of things he would have expected Angela and her mother to share. She did need a woman, a younger woman than her grandmother, and it seemed she had chosen Claire. Michael felt he had to respect that choice.

"Angela, I—" He stopped, started again. "Look, I don't want you to get the wrong idea about what I'm going to say." Michael could feel Claire next to him, tensing, and he knew, too, that what he was about to say was important to his future with Angela.

"I'm still very angry, and disappointed in you, and I still expect you to turn in those names. But I'll allow you to think things over, and decide on your own what's right." He could feel Claire relax slightly, and took it as a sign that he was going in the right direction. He took a deep breath. "I don't understand why you did this, and maybe I never will, but I—I love you, no matter what."

Angela came to him, then, and hugged him, and he held her, fiercely.

Finally, Angela settled on the floor in front of him, her head on his knee. "Um, Dad? There's more."

He shot a quick glance at Claire, who shook her head to indicate that she had not heard anything more.

"Okay," he said carefully.

"Well," Angela said, not looking at him, "there's this girl whose father hits her, if she gets a B instead of an A, and so I cheated for her, too."

Michael froze.

Claire leaned forward. "Hits her? What do you mean?"

"I don't know. I know she's real scared of him, though."

"We have to do something about that. There's no option, here." Michael tried to tamp the rage rising in him, not wanting to upset his daughter.

"I didn't want to tell you because I was afraid that's what you'd say."

"Angela, the man hits his teenage daughter. I can't let that pass."

She sighed. "I know, Dad. But can you not tell about the cheating, at least?"

The cheating seemed suddenly much less important to Michael than it had a few minutes ago. "Yes. I'll let you decide about naming the kids involved. But I need to know who the girl is, the one whose father abuses her. Is it Sabrina?"

"No, not Sabrina." She hesitated. "Actually, you know the man. The girl's Jenny Franklin. Her dad's that lawyer who works in the bank."

Michael's gut tightened. Cal Franklin was a big man, and Michael felt a little ill at the images that came to mind. But he wasn't surprised. After his years in the public defender's office, nothing would really surprise him about the things adults did to kids. "I'll call one of the people I know in Social Services, first thing in the morning. They'll handle it, they'll make sure she's safe, and they won't tell Jenny—or her father, that you're the one who told."

Angela turned, wrapping her arms around his calves, her chin on his knee. "I thought I shouldn't tell anybody." But she looked relieved.

"You can tell me anything, Angel, anytime," he said, and at that simple statement, Claire's smile turned radiant.

Warmth shot through him. Suddenly, he realized he felt good. Better than good—euphoric, almost.

Angela stirred. "I'm hungry."

Michael straightened. "Me, too. I guess neither of us felt much like eating dinner last night. How about an early breakfast?"

Claire stood up. "I'll be going, then."

The least he could do was make her breakfast. "Stay," he said, reaching out to emphasize his point. His hand landed on her forearm, on the worn, soft material of her sweatshirt. *Let's KISS all the lawyers...* It was all Michael could do not to take her into his arms.

"I don't want to interfere—"

"Since when?" he interrupted with a grin.

She gave him a rueful smile. "Okay, I'm starved," she admitted.

They were merry as Michael got out the fixings for breakfast. There was a kind of relief in that merriment, as though all of them realized they had faced something that could have driven them apart but instead had brought them together.

"I can't make eggs," Michael warned. "Bacon, toast, OJ I can do, but I've never got the hang of eggs."

It was there again, Claire realized. The subtle reminder of Mary Jo. No doubt she'd been the one to make breakfast. Claire braced herself for the hint of sadness always present in Michael's voice when he was thinking of Mary Jo.

But... It wasn't there. It wasn't there!

Did that mean...? She was almost afraid to voice the thought, even to herself. "I can make eggs," she said, hoping she didn't sound breathless.

"You could, if we had any." Michael pulled a skillet down from the rack above the stove. "Sit with Angela, and I'll make breakfast." He hummed to himself as he fried bacon—no tune, but a few husky notes, here and there.

Claire sat with Angela, while the girl ate Cheerios. When Michael brought Claire's plate to the table, she found she was ravenous. Michael also polished off a huge breakfast.

Afterward, he walked her to her car. "Do you want me to follow you to your apartment?" he asked as they entered the deserted lobby of his building.

"I'll be fine, Michael."

"Call me when you get home."

"I will," she promised.

"You know, Claire, I—" He stopped, his golden eyes dark, and swallowed. There was no hint of the teasing or humor he'd displayed at breakfast only a few minutes ago. "I just wanted to tell you how grateful I am you helped me with Angela. I'd like to think she and I would have found our way back to each other, but God knows how long it would have taken, and how much I might have hurt her."

"You're welcome, Michael." Claire found her throat unexpectedly tight.

There was a pause while they gazed at each other. Then he reached out and lightly touched her cheek. "You're so beautiful. Inside and out."

Tears pricked her eyes.

"Come here," he beckoned in a husky whisper, and he gathered her against him. He held her there, her cheek to his chest, where under the thin cotton of his T-shirt she could hear the steady thump of his heart.

His fingers threaded, over and over again, through the thick, straight locks of her hair. Claire closed her eyes and gave herself up to the pleasure of being held by Michael. He was aroused; that was evident, but there was none of the fierce passion that had marked their previous encounters, a fierceness that told her she had pushed him beyond his ability to endure. Instead, there was comfort, caring.

When, long moments later, he spoke again, it was in that same deep whisper. "Ah, Claire, I don't deserve you."

She could have challenged him. She had challenged him, many times. But she said nothing, just held him tighter, trying to tell him with her embrace how wrong she thought he was.

He kissed the top of her head, where her hair was parted. He nudged her face toward his, then planted the softest of kisses, just mere touches of lip to skin, on her forehead, her eyelids, the tip of her nose.

Finally, he put her from him. "We need to get you home."

"All right," she whispered, feeling dazed and weak and warm and in love. With fingers that trembled, she buttoned her coat and pulled on her gloves.

Michael said nothing as she pushed through the heavy glass doors into the gray Chicago dawn. As she pulled away from the curb, she could see him still standing behind the glass.

"WOULD YOU WAIT in the car a minute, Claire?" Michael asked as he got out at his parents' house. "I want to get my mother, and show her her gift."

It was the night of Sophie's after-Christmas party, and the little porch was strung with colored lights. As she watched Michael at the door, Claire could also see a brilliantly lit Christmas tree in the bay window. The lacy curtains covering the window lent the illusion of snow on the branches.

Michael had been very mysterious on the way over, as befitted Christmas, Claire thought, with its presents just waiting to be opened. Claire loved Christmas. She'd had a wonderful time in Nebraska, and a heart-to-heart talk with her sister about Michael that had resulted in a new resolve. It was time for her to take more initiative in her relationship with him, take a chance that she would be rejected, but take a chance. That resolve scared her to death, but she also felt anticipation, and somehow that seemed part of the season, too.

In her mind, nothing could be better than two Christmases, one in Nebraska and one in Chicago, and the chance to share the holiday with the man she loved, whether or not he loved her in return.

Michael helped his mother down the walk. Claire got out of the car and scrambled into the back seat.

"Thank you, Claire, and Merry Christmas," Sophie said as she settled into the car.

"Merry Christmas," Claire replied. As Michael pulled away from the curb, she asked, "Where's Angela?"

"Inside with Dad, waiting for the guests to arrive."

Sophie added, "That girl was a real help, getting ready for the party. These last days she's seemed more grown-up, don't you think, Mikush?" Without waiting for a reply, Sophie continued, "And I was thinking, why don't you let me keep her overnight tonight? It would be good if she spent some time with her *dzia dzia* before he has to go back to the nursing home."

After Michael agreed to let Angela stay, Sophie turned her head slightly, addressing Claire in the back seat. "I suppose you already know what Michael has picked out, Claire. I swear, I've never been driven to my Christmas present in my entire life."

Really, Claire had no idea what the gift was, and telling Michael's mother of her ignorance seemed to add to Sophie's excitement. The older woman woman acted like a young girl, and Claire felt she'd found a kindred spirit in her love of the season.

After they'd gone a mile or two out of the old neighborhood, Claire began to have an inkling of where they were going, and what Michael had in mind. A flicker of anxiety flashed through her. What if Michael was being high-handed again? What if Sophie didn't like her gift? She glanced at the back of Michael's head, at his shoulders as he drove. Even from the back, Michael projected a kind of confident maleness. He seemed very sure of himself, even joking a bit with his mother.

Finally, they were there. The old house he'd looked at for his mother was ablaze with lights, and there was a wreath on the door.

"What on earth . . ." Sophie was murmuring as she got out on the walkway. "We don't know anyone who lives here."

"You might," Michael said cryptically as he led her up the walk and unlocked the door.

As Claire stepped into the living room, she could not believe her eyes. The walls gleamed with a new coat of ivory paint, and the floor was polished to a high sheen. There was no furniture, but standing in the bay window was a Christmas tree, with little white lights and candy canes hung on it. There wasn't a dust mote in sight.

"Pretty room, Mom?" Michael was asking his mother gently.

"Well, yes. It looks like our place, Michael."

Michael nodded in supreme satisfaction. "It's a nice neighborhood. I thought you might like it."

"Well, it's . . . it's beautiful," Sophie said, sounding puzzled as she circled the room slowly.

"Is it the kind of house you'd like to live in?"

"Well, yes, of course it is. If the kitchen is cozy and the rest of the house looks like this."

"It's been for sale. The neighborhood is very safe, Mom, and you're close enough to the old neighborhood to attend church in your old parish, if you want. I already talked it over with Father John."

Sophie was nodding as he spoke. "I couldn't get myself interested in looking for anything." She smiled. "But I guess you couldn't wait for me, Mikush. And you're right about the old neighborhood—it's not safe." There was a pause. "This house is perfect, and even a stubborn seventy-year-old woman has to admit that. If the rest of it looks good, will you handle things with the real estate person? Make sure we get the best price? Dad and I have a bit of money saved, and if it's not too expensive—"

She fell silent when Michael handed her a small box he'd taken from under the tree. "You forgot it's Christmas, and that I was taking you out to give you your gift."

"Well, yes, but..." Seeming utterly confused, she opened the box, and when she found only a sheaf of paper, she looked up questioningly.

"It's a deed. To this house." He came to stand next to her. "See? In your name and Dad's."

"You bought this house? And a...a house like this? Not some ugly modern condominium?" Sophie asked incredulously. Claire held her breath, silently begging Sophie to accept her son's gift. Sophie's expression warred between delight and alarm. "But it must have cost so much money. I told you, Mikush, we don't expect you to be buying us a place."

"It's a Christmas gift. And good manners, according to everything you've taught me, requires that the recipient of a gift accept it with a polite thank-you."

"Mikush, I—" Sophie took one more look at him and burst into tears. But she was smiling.

Claire, too, felt the hot prick of tears behind her eyelids, and smiled a smile that held more than a tinge of relief.

She hung back a little as Michael put his arm around his mother's shoulders and showed her the rest of the house.

"Everything is in pretty bad shape," Michael admitted. "But we're working on it. Unfortunately, the living room is the only room we've had time to get ready. But that's good in a way, Mom, because I know you'll want to pick things out."

"We?" Claire whispered in an aside to Michael as his mother was inspecting the inside of a built-in cupboard in the dining room. "Who's the 'we,' you and Angela?"

"I decided to give Nick Persecki a job. The kid isn't half-bad with a floor buffer, if you keep on him all the time."

Claire's mouth fell open.

"I figured I'd work with him some while I'm on vacation over the holidays, then when I go back to work, I'll have the contractor take him on as a helper. If Nick does a good job, there'll be a reference in it for him, for his next job."

"You have been busy since I left for Nebraska, haven't you?"

"I've been feeling energized, Claire," he told her. "Like I've been treading water, swimming in circles, but now my life is changing. For the better. And I figured it was time to put some of my plans into action." He paused for a moment, then said, "I also called a guy I met, a state representative named Gordon Lyle. Lyle knows all sorts of people who've been affected by drunk driving, and he's suggested that Nick spend his community service hours in a hospital that has a program for kids who have a problem with alcohol. I'll give you the particulars back at the office, see if you agree. I think we could sell the plan to the judge, especially if Lyle writes a letter of recommendation.''

''Oh,'' was all Claire could manage.

Sophie came back into he living room. ''I can't wait to show this house to Mike. I managed to get a peek at the backyard, and there's a nice shade tree for Dad to sit under, come summer.''

They looked at each other and smiled again, together in the new-old house, with its bay window and twinkling lights and spicy fragrance of Christmas greens.

CHAPTER TWELVE

IT WAS LATER, when the party was in full swing at Sophie's old house, that Sophie cornered Michael. She brought two cups of eggnog to where he and Claire were standing, near the foot of the stairs.

"That was quite a stunt you pulled, young man, buying me a house for Christmas. But just what would you have done if I'd said I didn't like it?"

Sophie's tone had been tart, bantering, but Michael answered her seriously. "I figured it would be a good investment, regardless. If you'd hated it, I would have fixed it up and sold it. But then I would have dragged you all over the city, until you found something."

"Hmmph," Sophie said, smiling at Claire. "What did I tell you, Claire. The Chalinski men are full of themselves." With a laugh, she was off, walking with only a slight limp.

He and Claire were alone again.

Michael couldn't seem to take his eyes from Claire. All night he'd watched her—covertly, he hoped—as she filled drinks, shook hands and passed plates of sliced kielbasa. Purposely, he'd rationed his time with her.

She was beautiful, even though he could have done without the string of jingle bells she had hanging from her ponytail. But he liked the little crystal snowflake that hung from a black cord around her neck and caught flashes of light as she moved. And he definitely approved of those black velvet pants that hugged every luscious curve of her. The brilliant white of her satin tunic was a startling, and erotic, contrast to her dark hair. Black and white, he thought. Day and night. Ice and velvet... Yin and yang...

Man and woman.

God, he thought, he was losing it. Since when did his mind, the mind he'd trained to focus on facts, go off into flights of fancy like that?

Since that long-ago day in the law library of Haynes, Haynes, Collingwood and Crofts, he thought. That was when he first realized he desired Claire Logan with a pure physical intensity that he'd never before experienced.

He'd fought the desire, sought to disavow it, and when that hadn't worked, he'd sought to tame it. But it had always simmered just beneath the surface, always threatening to break through his control. Just now he had the strongest urge to stroke his hand over the heavy sleekness of white satin, and expose the tender skin beneath ...

Fortunately for Michael, John Persecki chose that moment to join them. "This was a nice idea, this after-Christmas party," he told them both.

John's attention turned to Claire. "I've been meaning to stop by the office and thank you for helping Nick."

Claire smiled. "No thanks needed. And, John, it seems you're doing pretty good with Nick, yourself. That haircut makes him look downright clean-cut."

John looked fondly over at Nick, who was standing by the tree, a soft drink in his hand. "Good-looking kid, now. But I can't take credit. Michael convinced him to cut all that hair."

Claire gave Michael a look that was at once surprised and pleased. He wished she wouldn't look at him that way. Claire would be lousy at poker; every expression showed on her face. And sometimes she gave him a certain look, a look that seemed to say he'd engineered every good thing in the universe. That look made him feel proud. It also scared the hell out of him.

Angela relied on him—that was as it should be; she was his daughter, and she had been brought into the world for him to nurture and love. But Claire? After he had failed Mary Jo, Michael was afraid to accept the responsibility for another adult's happiness.

"It wasn't that big a deal," Michael said. "I offered him a job, then told him the block patrol in my parents' neighborhood would go berserk if he showed up for work looking like he did. Not only that, but he's going before a judge soon, for sentencing. He balked, so I put him in the car and took him to the barber." In truth, it had been more trouble than Michael was telling, but in the end he had succeeded.

The three of them watched Nick for a moment. The kid's habitual slouched posture had not changed. Though obviously bored, the fact that he was at the party, instead of out looking for trouble, was a positive sign.

Claire picked up a tray of Christmas cookies that was on a table next to the stairway. "I'm just going to see if your dad needs anything. I promised your mom I'd keep checking on him, so she could enjoy the party."

His father's wheelchair stood in the doorway to the dining room, close enough for Mike to see everything, but out of the crush of the small room.

It seemed to Michael that his father was more alert tonight, although he hadn't moved his useless side at all. When Michael had taken time from the guests to spend a few quiet moments with Mike, telling the older man about the new house and his mother's happiness, he thought he had seen something—a little spark, or something, to his father's features.

But maybe it was just the Christmas holidays, Michael thought. Christmas and wishful thinking. Maybe there really wasn't any change in his father.

He watched Claire as she bent to his father, speaking softly to him, he was sure. When she'd met Mike Chalinski earlier that evening, she had taken his hand and shaken it, and treated him with respect.

Michael took a sip of eggnog, wishing that Claire could have known his father in days gone by.

Later, after the party broke up, Michael, his parents, Angela and Claire settled around the tree. Sophie had bought a gift for Claire. Then Claire pulled out a big shopping bag and started passing around the presents she had brought.

There was a silk scarf for Sophie and a gift subscription to the *Wall Street Journal* for Michael's father, and she had given Angela a book. Angela squealed when she saw it. "Oh, Claire, D. H. Lawrence. How did you know?"

"I liked him when I was your age," Claire said. "I still do, as a matter of fact, but back then, nobody I knew was reading stuff like that."

Angela nodded seriously, then clasped the book to her chest. "He is sooo romantic. I mean, there's so much agony in there, don't you think?"

Michael shook his head. He'd just about decided that he'd never understand his daughter.

"Open your gift, Michael," Claire was urging him, and he looked down at the box on his lap. When he'd given Claire her basket of chocolates at the office Christmas party, she'd given him nothing in return, although he'd got the usual assortment of wine, fruitcake and potted poinsettias from the rest of the associates. He'd told himself that was fine, that was great. Nobody needed another fruitcake.

When he opened the box, he saw a gift that only Claire would have chosen. The blue broadcloth shirt was expertly stitched, finely made, so he supposed the tie and suspenders must be silk, good silk. But... The tie was all color, wild swirls of red and violet, primrose and silvery-blue, like a Van Gogh painting, and the suspenders matched. He couldn't help it; he hated them both.

Sophie exclaimed over the colors, and Michael looked up to find Claire watching him expectantly. Her dark eyes seemed more glittering than the crystal snowflake around her neck.

"I thought I'd get you something to wear to work. You're always there," she explained.

"Yes, that's true," he said. "Thank you, Claire." He started to put the lid on the box. He could never wear this, never in a million years.

But—well, it was Christmas...

"Why don't I try the tie on?" he heard himself say. With the ease of long practice, he threaded the ends of the silk through his collar and his fingers flipped them into a perfect Windsor knot.

"I knew it!" Claire said promptly. "It'll go just right with your charcoal suit."

Michael opened his mouth to reply. But into the little silence came another voice. "Son."

Now the silence was complete, as all heads swiveled, staring at his father.

Over a wild rise of elation, Michael tried to calm himself. His father had not spoken a single coherent word in six months. He probably never would, the doctors said. This one syllable could be gibberish.

One side of his father's face worked hard. His hazel eyes were fierce as he concentrated . . . and they waited.

Finally, Michael said, "Dad? Did you say something?"

"Son." Again the word, clearer than before. Then: "L . . . ook . . . sss . . . g . . . oo . . . d."

"Dad—"

"Dzia dzia—"

"Mike—"

Sophie got there first. "Oh, Mike," she exclaimed. "I understood you. I understood you! You think Mikush's tie looks good!" She threw her arms around him, wheelchair and all.

HOURS LATER, Claire was in one of the darkened bedrooms, taking her coat from the bed. It was time to go home. Sophie and Mike, exhausted from the celebratory mayhem that had followed Michael's father's speech, were in the kitchen sharing one last eggnog. In the living room, Angela had fallen asleep on the floor with her head on one of the decorations, a stuffed snowman.

"Claire?" It was Michael, silhouetted by the light from the doorway.

"I'm coming." She turned, her coat over her arm.

He held a wrapped package. "In all the excitement, I didn't get a chance to give you your present."

"You got me that basket of chocolates."

He made a dismissive gesture with his hand. In truth, Claire had hated those chocolates, that clear statement that she meant nothing more to him than Stuart Tyler or Amanda Richmond or any of the other people he supervised.

He handed her the big box. "I knew what I wanted to get you all along. Then I waited so long to buy it, I thought it might be gone. But it wasn't."

Claire put down her coat, then leaned over to turn on the bedside light. It cast a little circle of light in the dark room. With fingers that shook a little, she pulled off the wrapping paper. She had been nervous all evening, and now that the evening was about to be over, and Michael would be taking her home, she felt more shaky than ever.

The jasmine scent from the lavender tissue paper wafted up, then, as she parted the paper, she let out a small gasp. "The sweater."

The red sweater, with that artless appliqué of a Scottish terrier, lay in the box. "You remembered." Claire was astonished, pleased beyond measure. Did it mean...? Claire caught herself. The gift might mean nothing more than that the sweater was the one thing Michael remembered her saying she liked. In that sense, it was a safe gift.

"Well, I knew you liked those whiskers and that button thing for an eye," he said in an offhand way, a way that belied the expression on his shadowed face.

"I love it," she said, and she couldn't keep a little catch from her voice. She leaned up toward him, the sweater over one arm, to plant a small kiss on his cheek. "Thank you, Michael."

Unexpectedly, he gathered her into his arms, the sweater a whispery tickle of wool between them. "Thank you, Claire. This night has been..." He hesitated, as if regretting that he had spoken. She waited. Finally he continued, a kind of astonishment in his voice. "Magic. As if anything could happen."

Magic. He made the word sound husky and male, and the sound thrummed through her.

"I could try on my new sweater. You could tell me if it fits."

He stiffened slightly, his breath catching almost imperceptibly. Claire had the sensation that he was sexually aroused, although he held her loosely, his embrace conveying affection rather than lust. Was this the right time to ask . . .

Gently, he released her. "I'll give you some privacy, to try it on. Then I think I'd better get you home."

It was now or never, she thought. Claire swallowed. "I could try it on at my apartment." Now that she'd made the decision, Claire couldn't quite manage the direct approach she'd planned. Guts in the courtroom didn't equate with boldness in seduction. "Since Angela's staying over with her grandmother, you could come up when you take me home."

He went still. "That's not a good idea, Claire."

"Why not?"

"You know why not. Every time we're alone, well, the last time I was alone with you, we nearly made love. If I come up to your apartment, there will be no block patrol at the door." He paused. "If you touch me, I'll end up staying. All night."

Claire's cheeks felt very hot. "I want you to stay. All night."

He groaned and crushed her to him, and this time she did feel his arousal, heavy and unmistakable, pressing into her. "I want to, Claire. Believe me, I want to. But I can't make promises. Not anymore. Maybe never again."

Claire was shaking inside, but her voice was surprisingly steady. "I'm not asking for promises."

He cupped her cheeks in his rough palms, looking down at her, his hazel eyes dark with suppressed passion. "Listen to me, Claire. You have a right to expect promises.

You're not the kind of woman who has a man over for a casual—"

"I'll decide what kind of woman I am."

There was a breathless pause, and Claire, her stomach fluttering, waited for him to respond. Emotions crossed Michael's face in quick succession—doubt, passion, hesitation, wanting. Then he pressed a kiss against her throat that felt hot enough to blister her skin. "God help me, Claire," he muttered. "I've wanted you so long, and I can't resist you. Not tonight."

He took the sweater from her, and helped her into her coat. Shrugging into his own, he caught her hand and led her to the door. Now that the time had finally arrived, Claire recognized Michael's intensity of purpose. She felt a shiver of anticipation.

She had not asked for promises. She knew Michael wasn't ready to give them. But she knew this for sure: no matter what he'd implied, sex with Michael would not be casual.

They practically sneaked out the front door. There was a Christmas carol playing on the radio in the kitchen. Claire planned to at least thank Sophie, but almost before she knew it, she was out on the cold walkway and Michael had opened her car door. When she settled herself, he reached in, buckled her seat belt, bent for a searing kiss.

He drove quietly. Finally, he said, "I think we'd better see if there's a drugstore open this late."

"That's all right, Michael. I took care of it."

He shot an astonished look at her. "You took care of it?"

"Yes. You weren't the only one making plans these last few days."

He said nothing after that, and Claire was suddenly more unsure than ever. She was nervous—yes, of course, but that felt right, this first time with Michael. What didn't feel right at all was the thought that just occurred to her. Did Michael find her securing protection unattractive? Had it marked her as brazen?

Her second thought was even worse. Mary Jo, the woman Michael had loved, would most certainly never have asked a man to sleep over, much less have purchased a package of condoms.

She tamped down her insecurities, determined to let nothing ruin this night, when Michael was about to become her lover.

When they were finally in the little foyer of her apartment, Claire tried to think of something to say. Somehow, in her planning, she had not accounted for these moments of awkwardness. As she slipped off her coat, she said, "Um, would you like some coffee or something?"

He shook his head. "No. All I want—" desire sent his voice a few notes lower "—is you."

With that, he took her into his arms, kissing her with alternating tenderness and demand. He stroked her breast, and her satin tunic was a slippery glide against the weave of his black wool sweater. He sifted his fingers through her hair, and the bells that held her ponytail fell to the floor with a jangle.

When he lifted the satin from her and deftly unhooked her bra, she pressed herself to him. He moved her across his chest, and the roughness of his sweater stimulated her breasts, until her nipples were hard and exquisitely sensitive. And when he took a breast in each hand, and bent to take a nipple in his mouth and suckle, she slid her fingers into the layers of his hair and moaned her pleasure.

She heard herself make sounds, little murmurs of joy and wanting as she held him.

He didn't speak, but his heavy breathing sounded loud in the quiet night.

He undressed her, stopping at intervals to kiss and lick at the skin he had exposed—her shoulder, the swell of her breast, the tender inside of her elbow and wrist—until she was trembling. When he seemed to have forgotten the crystal pendant she wore, she moved to undo the black cord herself. Michael spoke then, three whispered words. "Leave it on."

He removed his own clothing with quick, decisive movements. Now it was Claire's turn to explore, and she accepted the opportunity with a welling eagerness. The column of his neck was warm and strong, the skin over his chest a thin veneer over taut muscle. His chest hair caught the low light and shone a hundred shades of gold. As she leaned in to circle a flat nipple with her tongue, Michael smoothed her hair with a hand that shook.

They clung to each other for one charged moment. Then Michael lifted her, and carried her to her bedroom. He didn't pause to turn on a light, but instead placed her on the bed. In the half-light that came through her partially closed blinds, he loomed above her, her starkly golden lover.

Then he was beside her, pressing his warm, naked skin to her own flesh, with a sliding friction that inflamed her. Their breathing quickened, mingled. He touched her everywhere, as if he couldn't get enough of her body, stroking her breasts and belly, her thighs. He reached between her legs, and Claire moaned. His eyes met hers for a brief, timeless moment of sharing, and his fingers moved in a soft, sure rhythm. His touch said all the things he hadn't whispered, words of passion, and yes, words of love.

There was power behind his every caress, a quivering anticipation. That sense of power, of great desire greatly checked, excited Claire. Her own desire was a shimmering pool of color within her, deepest blue and glowing red, that grew hotter and hotter.

He was almost panting; his arousal pressed against her every time he moved. Boldly, she touched him, and he groaned. When she caressed him, the breath hissed from him as he thrust into her palm. Finally, he gently pushed her hand away, and, still without a word, reached for the package of condoms she had left on the bedside table.

This was Michael, the man she loved, the man she longed to feel deep inside her body. Claire held out her arms in welcome, and he settled himself between her thighs. For a moment, he was still, poised above her, as she lay, her heart thudding with want. Then he reached out, and his fingers touched the crystal snowflake she wore, and his expression held a kind of... wonder.

She kept her eyes wide open, searching his face, as he entered her, filled her. "Claire," he whispered then, his own gaze fierce and hot and locked with hers. "Oh, Claire."

She thrilled to the husky, incredibly intimate sound of Michael whispering her name. The shimmering pool within Claire shifted, glittered with pure gold, washed over its banks, bathing her in scalding heat. He thrust gently, then not so gently, and as they climaxed together, her name was a litany on Michael's lips.

MICHAEL WOKE to find Claire nuzzling his neck. Instantly aware of where he was, powerfully reminded of their lovemaking, he pulled her onto his chest.

"Oh, so you're finally awake," she teased, her eyes seeming darker and shinier than ever in the gray light of predawn. The ends of her hair and the tips of her breasts brushed his skin, and he felt himself hardening. "You were sleeping so soundly I thought maybe once was enough for an old guy like you."

"Right. Sure." He rolled with her until they were on their sides, facing each other. Once? he thought. He'd never get enough of her wonderful body, never get enough of her ready laugh.

"But I thought I could...persuade you." She touched him intimately, just enough to keep the excitement building.

He nipped at the skin of her neck, tickled her a little under the arms, listened to her breathless giggle. Last night had been powerful, profound. This morning, Claire was making him feel playful, of all things. Loose. That feeling was more exhilarating than ten glasses of champagne.

"Hang on," he said suddenly, sitting up, then heading for the hallway.

Michael found their clothes where they had left them the night before, in a jumble on the entryway floor. The sweater he'd given Claire was a puddle of red. As he lifted it, her jingle bells fell out of one of the folds, and the noise made him chuckle.

When he came back with the sweater in his hands, she said, "What's that?"

"What's that?" he repeated, feigning disbelief. "A man gives a woman something that represents his every fantasy, and she asks, what's that?" He put the red wool in her arms, unfolding it so that in the dim light she could see what he'd brought.

She looked doubtfully down at the sweater, then at him.

"It's a terrific sweater, Michael, but hardly *Playboy* material. It has a turtleneck collar, for Pete's sake."

"And whiskers," he added helpfully. "Try it on." She looked willing enough, but still a little puzzled, so he said, "You promised to try it on, last night. Now, I'm holding you to your promise. Only, the deal is, you've got to stay naked underneath it."

Her breath caught, and she looked at him with a shy smile, her lashes half-lowered.

That shyness was somehow...cute, in a woman who usually seemed so confident. And, okay, it was odd to keep fantasizing about a woman in a thick wool sweater, but... He helped her pull the garment on over her head. And discovered his fantasies were right on target—this half-dressed woman was the most erotic sight in the world.

He tugged gently so that she ended up on top of him, then pushed her back slightly so that, reaching under the sweater, he could touch her breasts. With a swift movement of her own, she straddled him more fully, and took him into her. He clenched his teeth at the unexpected rush of sensation. "Oh, Claire, you're beautiful in whiskers."

She was trembling, excited, smiling.

He was smiling, too, even as the pressure began to build relentlessly, and he grasped her hips as she moved on him.

LATER THAT MORNING, Claire found him in the kitchen, making breakfast. "Don't tell me. You don't do eggs."

"No kidding." Michael turned, skillet in hand, and smiled ruefully down at the overcooked mass of scrambled eggs in the pan. "I didn't think you'd mind my starting breakfast, but I didn't plan for you to wake up to the smell of burning eggs."

"That's not what woke me." What had awakened her was the unfamiliar, but very pleasant, sound of a man puttering in her kitchen. Michael was only half-dressed, and with his chest bare, he looked rumpled and sleepy-eyed gorgeous.

"I've got great toast," he said, putting a plate with about ten slices of toasted and buttered bread on the table.

"Are you always this hungry after making love?" She was teasing, but as he sat down across from her at the tiny table, she noticed a flicker of uncertainty cross his face.

"I guess. I've never thought about it. How about you?"

Claire looked at the floor, a little sorry she had spoken. "It doesn't happen often enough for me to have a habit," she confessed.

"Oh."

Lord, she thought, they weren't going to be embarrassed now, were they, after being as intimate as two people could be? Claire grabbed a piece of toast. "This was a good idea, making breakfast. I mean, naturally, I'm hungry. It is morning, after all—"

"Claire." Michael reached across the table, staying her hand. "You have no reason to feel awkward. Last night was fantastic. This morning was fun. Somehow, I'd never thought of sex as fun." He sighed. "But that first time... I was so nervous," he said unexpectedly.

"It didn't show. But I was really nervous, too." She paused. "What were you nervous about?"

He smiled with a tinge of self-consciousness. "That I wouldn't please you."

"You'll always please me, Michael," she said softly. "Always. And I was nervous because I worried you wouldn't think I was sexy enough."

He let go of her hand, then raked his hand through his hair. "Woman, if you were any sexier, I wouldn't have had enough energy to make scrambled eggs this morning."

There was a twinkle in his eye, a warm lightness to his manner. Claire took a bite of toast. It was delicious. Everything about this morning was delicious. Impulsively, she got up and went to Michael, standing behind him and looping her arms around his bare shoulders, clasping her hands. He raised his own hands to cover hers and tilted his head back, to look up at her.

"So, Michael, just how do you go about acquiring that great technique of yours?"

The man was blushing, she realized. It was so endearing, somehow, that the man she'd once thought so closed-off and distant could respond to her teasing with a blush like that. "Sheesh, Claire, come off it. All I did were some of the things Mary Jo liked—"

He froze. She had been looking at his mouth, that funny, upside-down smile, and she saw his lips thin and tighten.

And suddenly, there were three of them in the kitchen. Michael, Claire and Mary Jo. Claire snatched her hands from his and turned away.

"Claire," he said quickly. "I didn't mean— Oh, hell."

"Never mind," she managed to say. If she just didn't look at him, didn't have to see him bare-chested at her breakfast table, she could retain some vestige of dignity.

Behind her, he stood. She moved then, trying to put some distance between them, and came up against the countertop. Her kitchen was so tiny, and the room seemed smaller still with Michael in it.

He put his hand on her arm; she shook it off. But there was no escape. She was trapped between him and the counter, where a skillet of rubbery eggs lay right before her eyes.

Claire focused on those eggs. "Were you thinking about her?" she asked, her voice barely above a whisper. Now that her fears were out in the open, she felt a need to hear the worst. "When you were...doing those things she liked, were you thinking about her...pretending it was her?"

"Claire, look at me." Gently, then not so gently, he tried to turn her to face him. "Before we made love, I used to imagine how it would be between us. But it was better than anything I could have ever imagined. And when I was with you, all I could think about was you, the way you smelled, the way you looked with all that shiny black hair so smooth and free, the way your breath felt on my neck."

She turned, then. "If that's true, why is she here? Why is her name coming up?"

"I don't know." His face held guilt, confusion, sadness. "I guess because she's the only woman, other than you, that I ever went to bed with. I guess because for so long she was a part of my life, and in some ways, she always will be. But I know I never should have said what I did."

"But you thought it. What difference does it make whether you said it? If you could have her, you'd still be with perfect Mary Jo." Claire heard the bitterness in her voice and hated herself for it.

He didn't deny what she'd said. Slowly, his hand dropped from her arm and fell to his side. He looked away. So that was it then. Resolutely, Claire turned again to the counter, picked up the pan of eggs and carried it to the sink. Using the spatula from the pan, she started to stuff the food down the garbage disposal.

When she was finished, she turned from the sink to find him watching her, waiting for her.

He drew a determined breath. "You keep using that word *perfect,* and I don't understand—"

"*Perfect,* Michael," Claire cut him off. "It's a word you should understand. It's the word you always use to describe her." Suddenly, she was so angry. "But *perfect* is a word you'd never use to describe me, is it, Michael? I'm just this tall, mouthy woman who has a thing for you, and so I keep pushing until I finally get up the nerve to invite you to share my bed, and you're too much of a gentleman to refuse—"

"Claire—"

"And you're right. I'm not perfect. I'm a flesh-and-blood woman, one who talks too much and expects too much. Mary Jo is dead, and all the promises and the wishing in the world won't bring her back. And I think it's easy for you to say she was perfect, to idealize her. How can she say the wrong thing? How can she have an off day? She's gone."

Claire registered the stricken look on his face, but she hurt too much to respond to it. "You know what, Michael? You feel guilty about Mary Jo, about that damn promise you couldn't keep. But that promise says a lot more about your ego than it does about your love for Mary Jo."

He had straightened, and now he made no move to touch her. "Are you finished?" he finally asked, the mildness of his tone deceptive. His eyes flashed with anger, and two spots of color darkened the area under his cheekbones.

"Yes, I'm finished." And she was. She felt a little sick, a little numb.

"I should go. I have to pick up Angela from her grandmother's," he said, still with that mild voice, as if they were at work and he was merely explaining a complicated trial schedule. "Mom will have her hands full today, with Dad."

Claire began clearing the table. Her hands were quivering. "Go, then," she said quietly. "Just—go."

CHAPTER THIRTEEN

CLAIRE WAS MISERABLE. Even her body ached. She'd been unable to stop replaying the scene in her kitchen. Finally, she'd decided she needed to get out of her apartment. She'd spent the day shopping. But there didn't seem to be anything interesting to look at in all of Chicago. So she settled on a bottle of overpriced wine and a tin of even more overpriced gourmet popcorn and took a bus home.

She had her head down, and he was sitting on the stoop, low to the ground, so she didn't see him at first.

"Hi," Michael said softly.

The wine started to slip from her grasp; she made a grab for it. "Hi." She had known she would see him again at work. And she'd only begun to plan what to say—some nice, civilized words that would allow them to go back, finally and irrevocably, to senior and associate. But, today? Now? It was too soon, her sense of loss too immediate.

Michael's knees were drawn up, his arms wrapped around them; his face and hands were reddened. Here on the stoop, against the building, he was out of the worst of the wind, but the day was freezing. "Aren't you cold?" she asked. Stupid question. Of course he was cold; this was Chicago in winter. The real question was, what did he want?

"I'm freezing. I've been here a couple of hours."

"A couple of hours? Why didn't you wait in your car?" His Jag, she noticed belatedly, was parked in the small parking lot.

He shrugged, looking up at her. "I didn't want to take a chance on missing you. We need to talk."

She took a deep breath. "I already talked too much today, Michael. And I said some hurtful things. I've been feeling terrible about them, all day."

He shook his head. "You said what you thought, the way you always do. It hurt to hear, but maybe I needed to hear it. Sit with me a minute?" He reached out a hand toward her.

"Yes. Okay." She sat down next to him on the icy concrete steps, putting her bags aside. "Michael," she said as gently as she could. "I should invite you up, where it's at least warm. But ...but I'm not ready for that." She didn't think she could bear to see him in her small apartment, not after that beautiful night and her ugly words this morning.

"Just sit with me," he said. "This time I've got some things to say." He stopped, stared down at his wind-reddened knuckles as if for inspiration.

"First, there's no denying it—you're very different from Mary Jo. Now, don't go stiff on me," he said quickly. "Hear me out. Different is not bad, Claire. Different is just ... different."

She gave a small, bitter laugh. "Different. I've heard that all my life."

He covered her gloved hand with his bare one and gave it a squeeze. "Okay, you also know I loved Mary Jo. If we look at it like lawyers, these are facts we can agree on. Right?" Without waiting for an answer, he went on. "I don't blame you for thinking that you aren't as ...

appealing to me as she was, because for a long time, I kept asking myself why I wanted you, liked you, when you were so different from her. I thought there was something wrong in that. Somehow I was betraying Mary Jo. Perhaps I was caught up in some male fantasy, brought on by abstinence.''

She didn't believe it.

"Don't look at me that way," he said. He raised his hand and cupped her chin. "One thing I know I've told you is that I desire you." His hand dropped, and he looked away. "Hell, even that seemed wrong to me, that I wanted you so much. I've just never... felt like that.''

Under her coat, she shivered. From the cold, she told herself, although she felt a tiny tingle of warmth begin deep inside her. He was being honest. He deserved honesty in return. "You know, Michael, you weren't the only one who was thinking today. I know I have some insecurities. I should have been able to accept that you talk about Mary Jo once in a while, without feeling that you think less of me. Your timing was lousy, but I can see how you brought her name up. I really can."

He smiled at her gently. "I never meant to hurt you, Claire."

"I know. I'm sorry I hurt you, too." They were polite words, nothing more, Claire cautioned herself. But that tiny warmth within her seemed to be growing of its own accord.

"Apology accepted. Now, I've still got more to say, and I want you to hear it all. You're right about me idealizing Mary Jo, because I felt so bad about not being able to fix things after she died. Our marriage was good, but it wasn't perfect. How could it be? She was married to me, after all." He smiled, a faint, self-deprecating smile that came and went in a heartbeat.

"And you were also right about the promise, about my ego being all wrapped up in the promise." He was restless now, and shifted a bit on the stoop. "Still, it will never sit right with me, that I couldn't get my wife justice. And if I ever get the chance to nail the guy who hit her, believe me, I'll take it." A sudden fierceness lit his eyes, then his voice dropped. "But I've got to move beyond that. I've got to realize that Mary Jo is gone, and give myself permission to live my own life."

Something very tight inside Claire loosened. She could be generous, she realized. As long as Michael was able to move on, so could she. It really was all right if he remembered Mary Jo as a good part of his past.

"So, anyway, that's what I came to tell you." He stood.

Claire stood, too. In his whole speech, there had been no words about where they went from here. Whether Michael had room in his life for her, whether he even wanted to stay today. "Well, you must be cold." She forced herself to speak lightly. "Do you want a cup of coffee or hot chocolate or something?" She gestured to one of the bags on the stoop. "Or I have wine."

"I'd like to take you to dinner, if you're really speaking to me."

She smiled. "I'm very definitely speaking to you. Since when do I not talk?"

"Good, because I have something else to say, and I had to make sure we had everything straight between us before I said it." He took her hands in his, then hesitated. "I'm very afraid to say it." His eyes were shadowed and serious. A gust of wind ruffled his hair, blew strands of it over his forehead, and that movement served to highlight the utter stillness of his body. "What I wanted to say is— I love you, Claire."

Happiness welled in her; tears pricked the corners of her eyes, and felt scalding hot as they met the chill air. "I love you, too, Michael." What a giddy relief to say it at last, to believe that Michael wanted to hear it at last. "You're strong and loyal—"

"You're vivid and open—"

"Oh, Michael."

His arms went around her, and she buried her face in his neck, and smelled soap and suede, and felt hot and cold and elated.

"I'm not going to be the easiest man in the world to love."

She smiled, a wide, happy smile. "I know, Michael. But I think I'm up to the task."

His arms tightened. "I mean it about being afraid, Claire." His lips touched her hair, and he whispered his next words, "I know a lot about loss. And if, somehow, I were to lose you, I don't think I could bear it."

"You'll never lose me, Michael. I promise. You'll never lose me."

THOSE FEW DAYS before the New Year were the happiest Michael had known in years. He and Angela had a serious talk late one night, and she'd told him she was considering naming the other teenagers who had cheated on the test. She had a certain resolve about her that made her seem more mature, and Michael had begun to wonder if the whole incident, though difficult for them both, hadn't been a good learning experience for his daughter. Without a doubt, it had brought them closer together.

Claire was over most of the time during the day, and the two of them did quiet, family things—reading, cooking, watching movies with Angela.

One night Claire dressed up in a sophisticated sheath of black sequins, complete with an outlandish feather boa, and, after they'd gone out on the town, they'd ended up at a jazz club. The sultry beat had throbbed against Michael's skin, and the footlights had made Claire's dress look as though it were on fire. When he took her home to her apartment, they made love on the colorful rug on her living-room floor, most of their clothes still on, too excited to get as far as the bedroom.

Now they were in his kitchen, making dinner. "Hey, done with that cheese dip yet?" he asked, a bowl of nacho chips in hand as he came up behind Claire and nuzzled her neck. "I'm starved."

"Careful," she warned, pulling a casserole dish from the microwave. "I wouldn't want to spill this and burn you somewhere... ah, essential."

He laughed. He had laughed, it seemed, more this last week than in the whole thirty-five years that had gone before. Sometimes he wondered if he was still the same person he had been. But Claire was right about the hot dish, and so he resisted the urge to pull her against him. It was a good thing, too, because Angela chose that moment to appear in the doorway, holding a couple of videotapes.

"Okay," Angela said. "The video store is closed, so we have to watch something from my stash. What do you want, *Top Gun* or *Four Weddings and a Funeral?*"

"*Four Weddings,* definitely," Claire said.

"That's what I really wanted, too," Angela agreed. "Hugh Grant is not as cool as Tom Cruise, but he's still pretty cool. I'll cue up the movie and wait for you guys."

As Angela left the kitchen, Michael whispered to Claire, "So, which is your ideal man, Tom or Hugh?"

"I think I like the strong silent type better, one of those guys who plays a lawyer with such sophistication. You know, maybe Gregory Peck, a guy who knows how to pick a good tailor and has the shoulders to do the suit justice." She laughed lightly. "Maybe somebody more like the man in my real life."

Michael liked the sound of that. On occasion, he thought he sometimes still sensed insecurity in Claire, as if she was watching him, not quite sure that he really wanted to spend time with her. But today had been perfect. "So, I'm not really competing with the latest teenage heartthrob—"

The phone rang. Michael went to answer it as Claire got a couple of bottles of beer from the refrigerator.

It was Gordon Lyle, the state representative who was helping him with Nick. "Michael, how are you? Christmas okay? Not too much plum pudding and yuletide cheer?"

"Christmas was good, Gordon. The best. And yours?"

"Good, too. Spent some time with my kids and managed to get over to that hospital program I was thinking about for that boy of yours. Whatshisname."

"Nick."

"Yeah, Nick, and I got it all set up, and, since you did me a favor that time, I'll even come down personally and explain it to the judge." His voice got suddenly serious. "It's a good program, Michael. Nick will be dealing with people who've been injured by drunk drivers, assisting with therapy, things like that. It's sometimes painful for the kids doing community service, but it's something they seem to learn a lot from."

"I'll be there for Nick, afterward," Michael said.

"Sure." There was a pause. "By the way, I met an old friend of yours. Chester Marlowe. Said you'd remember him."

Michael remembered him, all right. Chester had been a good guy to have around, and a brilliant fellow law student at Yale. "How'd you run into Chester? I thought he was living in Maryland."

"Not anymore. He had a bunch of raw young law students from the university with him, and they were touring the program at the hospital. He's setting up a trial-practice clinic at the law school, where the students represent real clients under the supervision of a lawyer, get a dry run at learning to practice law before they graduate."

Michael nodded to himself. He was familiar with such clinics.

"Anyway, we got to talking shop, and your name came up. He's going to be calling you, says he needs somebody who knows trial work to head up one of those clinics." He gave a chuckle. "Need a job, buddy?"

What surprised Michael most was how tempting the offer sounded, just for a moment. To spend all his time with students, teaching them the nuances of trial practice, the strategies for winning over a jury...

"I've already got a job." His position was one any lawyer would kill for, and he was about to be set for life at Haynes, Haynes, Collingwood and Crofts.

"Yes, I told Marlowe that next to me, you're the most ambitious guy I know. But when you tell old Chester no go, tell him I said hello again, okay? The guy lives in my district."

"No problem," Michael said, wrapping up the conversation and hanging up the phone. He shot a glance at Claire. She was humming to herself, some pert sixties tune he couldn't quite place, and trying to fit all the food they'd prepared on one tray.

Soon he would tell Claire he'd be making partner at the firm. He suppressed the thought that she'd probably tell him to take the job at the law school clinic. If nothing else, she'd be happy for him when he got his partnership, because his dream was coming true.

The doorbell rang. Michael left Claire in the kitchen and answered the door.

In the doorway was Nick Persecki, in a worn-looking leather jacket. "I came for my money," he said, without bothering with a greeting.

"Oh, sure, come on in." Michael had forgotten he'd told Nick to stop over for his paycheck. He stood aside for Nick to enter, then went to the hall table and picked up his checkbook.

"Hi, Nick." Claire had come into the foyer. "We were just going to have some nachos and watch *Four Weddings and a Funeral.* Want to stay and watch with us?"

Nick was silent for a moment, looking around in both awe and discomfort, his gaze lingering on the huge living-room window with its wide-open view of downtown. "That mushy Hugh Grant thing? Forget it."

Michael finished writing the check and handed it to Nick. "Here."

Nick looked at the amount for a long moment, as if savoring the sight. "How soon can we get started on the next one?"

"As soon as the contractor has an opening." Michael explained to Claire, "When I was looking at places for my mom, I found a couple of houses that weren't suitable for her, but I thought they could be fixed up and sold at a profit. Nick and my contractor are going to tackle another house soon."

"That's wonderful, Nick." Although she spoke to Nick, Claire's bright-eyed gaze was focused on Michael.

He gave her a little shrug, but he felt good. Very good. Nick's work habits were steadily improving. The kid had needed a real chance, that was all.

"So, what're you planning to do with your first big check, Nick?" Claire asked. "A down payment on a new car?"

"Naw." Nick stuffed Michael's check into the front pocket of his jeans. He wouldn't quite meet Michael's eyes. "I figured I'd fix up the old wreck one more time."

"And with the rest of your money...?" Michael asked.

"Well, I—" Nick stopped, his hand in his pocket as if still fingering his check. "I'll tell you, but I don't want you to make a big deal out of it, okay? Not like my mom and John did. I'm going to take a few classes at the community college, air-conditioning and house-wiring and stuff, and this check'll start to cover the cost."

Beside him, Claire sucked in her breath, and Michael shot her a warning glance.

"Good idea," he said casually. "There's money to be made, so why not get your share?"

"Yeah, that's what I figured. Anyway, I gotta go. I told Mom I'd get a pizza on the way home."

As soon as the door had closed behind Nick, Claire threw her arms around Michael. "Oh, Michael, I'm so glad about Nick."

"Yeah," Michael whispered, mimicking Nick, his own arms circling her waist. "It *is* a big deal, okay?"

"Okay."

"Okay." He smiled at her, serious again. "I've always had a knack for picking a sound investment."

AFTER THE HOLIDAYS, Michael didn't return to work right away. Instead, he did something he hadn't done in ten years—he took a few days' personal leave. That was significant, Claire thought as she stood in the hallway of the firm, looking over a brief she'd just received. He was checking out therapy options for his father. He loved his parents; he would have bought them anything they asked. And he was giving them something even more precious—his time.

Her secretary interrupted her thoughts, telling her George Fanal wanted to see her right away.

As she headed for the elevator, Claire felt the flicker of uneasiness that meeting with one of the partners always caused. Some of the associates would have been out and out scared by the summons—it could mean anything from a favor being asked, to a raise, or to the word that you were fired.

"Ms. Logan, come in," George Fanal said cordially as his secretary showed her in. Conventional wisdom around the office held that the more polite the partners were, the more likely you were to be out looking for another job.

"Mr. Fanal, how was your holiday?" As she was exchanging pleasantries, she noticed another person in the room. As he stood, she guessed he was in his early sixties, his gray hair styled carefully, his jacket well-cut and his features as bland as milk.

Fanal was indicating the stranger. "Senator, I'd like you to meet the woman we were talking about. Ms. Logan, State Senator Beske. He's looking for a new lawyer, and he specifically requested you." Fanal looked very pleased about that.

Claire was more than pleased. She was delighted. Nothing was better for her reputation in the firm than bringing in a new client, especially an important one. "I'll have to thank whoever recommended me," she said, shaking hands with the senator. She was trying to play it cool, but that was hard when she felt like putting a thumb in the air and yelling, "Yesss!"

"Edward Halmeyer is a friend of mine. He says you're not afraid of a challenge, that you didn't mind taking on the Chicago housing bureaucracy for him. Also, I play golf with Judge Kurtz, and he said when you worked for him you were smart as a whip."

Claire flushed with pleasure. "So, what can I do for you?" she asked as they were seated. She put her legal pad in her lap as Fanal ordered the coffee brought in. Fanal sat back to listen. Claire realized he didn't trust her to handle her first important client totally on her own. Well, so be it.

Senator Beske dropped a cube of sugar in his coffee and stirred slowly. "I fired my attorney this morning. I'm in a bit of trouble, and he and I don't see eye to eye." He spoke without a trace of nervousness. He sat back, his coffee cup in his hand. "You see, Ms. Logan, I've been accused of driving under the influence of alcohol. I'm completely innocent of the charge, but my attorney—my former attorney—wants me to plead to a lesser offense." He leaned forward, more sharpness etched into his features now. "Can you imagine what that charge would do to my career? To be convicted of drunk driving on the evening of a day the legislature had been in session? I have to go to trial. What a flaming wuss my lawyer was. And he was from what is supposedly one of the best firms in the city." He made a sound of disgust.

Claire shot a look at Fanal. Thanks to her work on the Persecki case, she could shine with a DUI case. Michael had taught her everything she needed to know about such cases. "Was there an accident?" she asked.

"No, I was just picked up. I was tired, coming home from Springfield one night, and I lost control of my car. I went into a ditch, and because it was a clear night and the pavement was dry, a couple of hotshot cops got a little... concerned."

"Had you fallen asleep at the wheel?"

"No, of course not." His voice, carefully modulated, went crisp.

Well, that was a bit odd, Claire thought. He denied drinking, he denied falling asleep. If he had health problems, or some sort of mechanical failure with his car, he surely would have said. She asked the questions anyway, and he said no to each one.

"It's unusual for someone to lose control of a car, with no explanation," she said carefully.

Fanal sat up straight. "If the senator says he lost control, then he lost control."

She looked Beske in the eye. "You're the client, Senator. I accept your story. What I'm trying to say is, when we take this to trial, a jury would prefer a reasonable explanation for why you ended up in a ditch that night."

He looked a little sheepish. "Of course," he murmured. "Actually, I was tired—I told you that."

"Yes." Claire wrote "ashamed to admit he fell asleep?" in the margin and said, "I assume you tested all right on the breath test?"

There was silence. Belatedly, she looked up.

"Well, that's the rub, Ms. Logan. Claire. May I call you Claire?"

"Of course," Fanal answered for her.

"Of course," Claire said.

Beske took a delicate sip of coffee. "I tested at over point two on the breath test, which is quite intoxicated, I know. But—and it's a big but—that breath test wasn't administered until four hours after the police stopped me.''

Claire tried to cover her astonishment. ''How did that happen?''

''Well, they forgot to test me at the scene. So, I went home, and I was shook up. I had a few drinks. Then, hours later, these same two cops show up at my door, and demand I take the test. What could I do? I'd been drinking at that point. I told them that. So, bingo, I come out drunk. And they charged me. Can you believe it?''

''It's pretty hard to believe.''

''Well, can you get the breath test thrown out of court?''

Don't make extravagant promises to clients; you never know how a case will turn out. Claire could almost hear Michael coaching his associates. How thrilled he'd be for her, to land a client like Senator Beske. Claire couldn't wait to tell him.

''I think we've got an excellent chance. Now, I'll need to know about witnesses, all kinds of things.''

''Sure, Claire.'' Beske glanced at Fanal. ''I think she'll do just fine. That idiot I first hired didn't want me to second-guess the police, kept telling me I had some problems with the case. I want someone who tells me I've got an excellent chance.'' He stood, put his cup back on the tray. ''I'll tell you everything I know. But the case is set for trial in three weeks, and my attorney—my former attorney, I mean—has already tried the court's patience with continuances. Can you be ready?''

It wasn't much time. ''Certainly,'' Claire said, standing and tucking her legal pad under her arm.

Fanal spoke. ''Claire, tell Michael I said if you need help, you're to get it. He can reassign some of your cases, if necessary.''

"I'll manage." She smiled at Beske. "I'm very happy to be your attorney."

He shook hands gravely. "And I'm happy to get an attorney who isn't a quitter."

As soon as Claire got back to her own floor, she asked one of the firm's paralegals to pull the police records on any former convictions for the senator. Then she headed down to the police station to interview the police officers who had stopped Senator Beske.

A short time later, she decided the case was getting more unusual by the minute. The two officers gave conflicting reports.

"He was drunk," Officer Kyle stated flatly. "He wasn't falling-down drunk, but he was definitely drunk. I started to give him a standard roadside sobriety test, and he couldn't touch his fingertips to his nose while his eyes were closed."

"Is it possible he'd fallen asleep, and was just a little bleary?" Claire asked.

"Not in my opinion."

"Yes, he could have been sleepy," Officer Landford cut in. "That's a perfectly reasonable explanation."

Claire wrote. "All right. Now, how about when you asked him to walk the line?"

"He wasn't given that part of the test."

Curious. "Why not?"

Kyle shot a disgusted look at Landford. "Officer Landford was in the squad car running the license plates. He came out and said we would not be proceeding with the test."

"Why not?"

"He was not drunk. In my opinion." Landford was firm.

"And the detective in charge told Landford we didn't need to do any more," Kyle added, his distaste evident.

"I see," Claire said, although she wasn't quite sure just what she did see. Shoddy police work, or some kind of cover-up? Or maybe just an overworked man who'd fallen asleep at the wheel. And the police, for the sake of his career, didn't want to make an issue of it when there had been no accident.

"But you later gave him the breath test."

"Yes." Landford nodded. "Kyle here didn't like how it was left, and he called the prosecutor on duty. The prosecutor said we should administer the test, even though it was late. So we did. It didn't prove anything except that he'd been drinking over the last few hours."

"So, his story is plausible."

"Yes," both officers agreed, Landford eagerly, Kyle reluctantly.

But they did agree. The breath test, normally the most important piece of evidence in a DUI case, was highly questionable.

CLAIRE HAD TO CUT the interview with the officers short, because Mr. Fanal had specifically requested she attend the case conference scheduled for that afternoon. In Michael's absence, Fanal intended to chair it.

A few minutes later, she understood exactly why she'd been summoned to attend. Fanal was regaling the assembled associates with Claire's coup in landing an important client.

"Good legal work is essential, that goes without saying," Fanal was holding forth from his place at the head of the table. "At this stage of your careers, that's enough, but at some point, you need to bring clients into the firm. And Claire, here, has done that."

Fanal smiled at her, and Claire didn't miss his use of her first name. The other associates were staring at her, their expressions a mixture of congratulations and envy. Farther down the row, Stuart Tyler was beaming at her, and Amanda Richmond gave her a little thumbs-up sign.

Thank you, Stuart and Amanda, Claire thought gratefully, *for being so genuinely happy for me.* She hadn't done much work yet on a very complicated case. It felt odd to be singled out at this stage of the case. She looked down at her notes.

"Hello, everyone," Michael said from the doorway.

He wasn't supposed to be here, but Claire was delighted to see him. He looked good, refreshed, dressed in a pair of gray cords and a matching sweater.

"I just came in to pick up my mail, and see how hard a time you were giving George," Michael said easily. "I hope you're not holding back, that it's argument as usual." He sank into a chair next to Fanal, and they exchanged a few low-pitched words. Something had changed in that relationship, Claire noted. Fanal and Michael seemed to be on particularly good terms. More casual, or something.

"I'm glad you're here, Michael," Fanal said finally. "We're having a little celebration. Claire was about to tell us about a new case of hers. She pulled in her first big client this morning."

"That's terrific." Michael spoke with so much warmth, for a moment Claire was nonplussed. They had not yet discussed how to handle the gossip that would inevitably arise when people in the firm realized she and Michael were seeing each other. "Tell us about it, Claire."

"It's a driving-under-the-influence, a DUI." Her gaze shifted to include all the associates. "Michael and I have been doing a *pro bono* case involving drunk driving, so I feel good about handling this one. There are some interesting evidentiary issues surrounding the breath test. And it's definitely going to be a full-scale trial. Senator Beske assured me he won't consider—''

''What?'' Michael had been lounging in the leather chair next to Fanal, but now he was sitting up straight. His face had gone white.

Claire was as startled as everyone else in the room. ''I said, Senator Beske wants a trial. He says he's innocent—''

''He is not innocent.'' Michael's voice was curiously flat and as cold as ice.

Claire stopped. Everyone else was still for a long moment. Finally, Michael got to his feet. She tried to catch his eye. Something was terribly wrong. He headed for the doorway. Once there, he said, ''Excuse me,'' almost as an afterthought. Then he turned and left the room.

Fanal cleared his throat. ''Well, perhaps we'll just go on with the meeting.''

''I think, Mr. Fanal, that I'd better be excused, too,'' Claire said, rising. She tried to think of a plausible reason for Michael's behavior. ''Perhaps Michael is ill. Or something has happened to his father. I'll go make sure everything is all right.''

Fanal didn't question her departure.

Claire decided to check Michael's office first. He was there behind his desk. But he simply sat, making no move to touch any of the papers or books on the desk.

''Michael, what's wrong?'' She started to go to him.

He held up a hand. ''That's far enough, Claire.''

She stopped, halted more by the hard, bleak tone of his voice than by his command. Now that she was nearer to him, she could see that his expression was closed, the angles of his face starkly drawn.

"I've always known you have plenty of nerve," Michael said. "What I never realized was that you were even more ambitious than me." He pushed his chair back, cocking his head, assessing her as if she were a stranger. "Or, did you rationalize it to yourself, think that since it was a completely different case, it was all right to represent the man who murdered my wife?"

The man who murdered his... "Senator Beske is the man who hit your wife?" Her voice rose with shock and disbelief.

He stood. "Cut it out, Claire. We've talked about this—I've told you what happened. Dammit, I trusted you."

"Michael, please." Despite his warning to her to stay away, she went to him anyway. She took his hands, and they were dead weights in her own. "Listen to me. You never told me his name. You never told me he was a senator, or even a politician. I didn't know. Do you hear me? I—did—not—know."

He stared at her for a long moment, and then abruptly took her into his arms. "Oh, God, Claire," he said, his voice shaky. "I really thought—"

"I never would have accepted him as a client if I'd had the slightest idea."

"I should have known that," he said, holding her in a crushing grip. "I'm so sorry I doubted you, even for a moment."

Claire held him too, relieved he believed her. Her hands made soothing circles at the small of his back, desperate to offer him comfort. This was so unfair, that Michael should have to deal with this man now, after he'd resolved to put his sorrow behind him.

"Michael," she whispered, "believe me, I'd get off the case now, if I could."

He pulled back from her, looking down at her in renewed shock. "You mean you're actually going to keep representing this bastard?"

"How can I not?"

They were both silent for a moment. Michael held her loosely. He was frowning. This was hard, Claire thought, brutally hard, a difficult test of their new love. But that love wasn't fragile. She was strong, he was strong, and he was the most loyal person on earth. And both of them, she was certain, were remembering the ethics of their profession. She had no choice. Now that she had accepted Beske as a client, she was his attorney until Beske himself or a judge dismissed her.

Finally, Michael released her and went to the window. For a long moment, he stood, staring out. Claire waited. She longed to go to him, but she felt he deserved a moment to himself.

"You can tell him you can't represent him in good faith," Michael said finally.

Claire began to feel a little ill. She expected resistance from Michael. She understood his pain, and she was willing to give him all the time he needed to adjust to the idea of her representing the senator. Could she make him understand her point of view? "The problem is, I *can* represent him in good faith, Michael," she said softly. "We know what he did to Mary Jo, and someday maybe a jury will get a chance to review that case. But this is a new case, and I'm not certain about his guilt or innocence in this matter."

He made a sound of disbelief.

"There are evidentiary issues," she insisted, trying to sound professional, explain herself without dissolving into tears.

"Claire, I..." He hesitated, then turned to look at her. "I love you. I think I could handle anything you wanted to do, support you in any venture. Anything but this."

Claire stood very still. "I love you, too, Michael. Please, don't let this come between us."

"I never thought I'd get a chance to nail Beske, but I never really gave up." He jabbed a finger at the folded newspaper on the credenza. "Do you know my advertisement still runs in the paper, looking for witnesses to the accident that killed Mary Jo?"

Claire started to tremble. "This is not the same case. There was no accident this time."

"Think, Claire!" His voice, carefully controlled until now, started to rise. "Okay, so this time he didn't kill a mother. But he could have. He could have! Have you looked at his police record?"

"I haven't had a chance—"

"I have. I've looked at that police record a hundred times. He has two prior offenses, a failure to control, a safe-driving violation—both euphemisms for drinking and driving. All he needs is a conviction for actual DUI, and his driver's license will be pulled, and maybe he'll even spend some time in jail." He raked a hand through his hair. "Okay, so this isn't Mary Jo's case. But you have to let him hang, so he can't destroy somebody else's family next time."

Claire thought hard. She was a lawyer, and this was about law, nothing else. Michael was right, as far as it went. Beske might very well deserve to go to jail, and he surely shouldn't be driving, if he was guilty. But he was still her client. She'd made a professional commitment, and she had no choice but to honor it.

"I think we should talk about this after we've had some time to think," she said. Putting off a discussion was out of character for Claire. But, much as she wanted to be re-assured of Michael's love, she knew he needed time to adjust to the news. Surely once he'd had time to think—

Michael came toward her, his eyes alight with a fierce glow. "I don't have to think, Claire. There's a way out of this. Look, every lawyer knows there are clients you do a fantastic job for, give their cases your all. And then there are clients that you just—" He stopped.

Claire felt truly sick now. "You want me to deliberately lose the case?" she asked incredulously.

He advanced another step, his gaze intent and a little wild. "No, not deliberately lose. Never that. But there are evidentiary issues, you said. If you didn't fight so hard on those issues—after all, the man is guilty. Do your job, just don't fight tooth and nail on the legal technicalities. Let the jury see all the evidence."

"Sell out, you mean. Michael, listen to yourself," she said, feeling desperate and trapped. "This isn't you. You believe in the system."

Another step, and he was very close to her now. "You know as well as I do that the real world isn't neat and pretty. When I was in the public defender's office, there were plenty of guys who did exactly what I'm suggesting, and no one questioned their ethics."

"Did you do that?"

A flicker of uncertainty crossed his features. But even as she watched, his jaw hardened. "No. But this discussion is about my wife and the man who killed her."

Claire hurt all over, and she knew Michael was deeply shaken. She would do almost anything to reassure him. Surely she could make him understand. He might think of himself as cynical, but underneath he was as idealistic as she.

"All my life," she started slowly, feeling for the right words, pulling them from the depths of her being, "I've struggled to be understood and appreciated for who I really am. Who I am is a strong, smart woman who has trained for years to be a good lawyer. When I passed the bar, I took an oath to represent clients to the best of my ability. I like to think of myself as honest, a person with self-respect, and..."

For a moment, she faltered, then went on. "And I don't believe for a minute you want me to do as you're suggesting. If I really believed you want me to deliberately do less than my best, then..." She swallowed hard, trying to get her voice to come up above a whisper. "Then you're not the man I thought you were."

His body was terribly still. There was a kind of agony in that stance that was more powerful than a raging tirade. "You're saying you're going to represent Beske, and you're going to do everything you possibly can to win your case."

Claire took a deep breath. The room suddenly felt as if there wasn't enough air in it. Her next words were the hardest she had ever said. "Yes, that's what I'm saying."

"Then, I think you'd better ask Russ Mallory to supervise you on this case." Although he hadn't raised his voice, his anger was so real Claire imagined she could feel it on her skin. "Now, one other thing, and then you're free to go. I want you to keep your distance." His voice went a note or two lower, and Claire had no doubt he meant every word he said. "Unless it's necessary for firm business, I don't want to see you anymore. Ever. I don't want you near my parents, and, most of all, I want you to stay away from my daughter."

CONTROL, Michael thought. Stay in control.

He was quivering, hurt and anger so entwined that he

couldn't separate the emotions. Since Claire had left his office a few minutes ago, he'd been striving for control.

She had been crying when she left, and a small part of Michael ached with self-blame, an urge to comfort and even a certain understanding of her point of view. But there was too much anger in him to allow those emotions to the forefront. He had made her cry. But he hadn't made her change her mind.

He didn't know if he was right or wrong, but he knew he could not accept Claire's choice. And he'd meant his last words. He could not stand to see her anymore. She had no place in his life.

Michael had promised Mary Jo, his dying wife, to bring Beske to justice.

Claire had promised Michael would never lose her.

Promises . . . an agony of promises.

He was alone. In the end, he was always alone. How many times could a man have his world shattered and be expected to come up fighting?

Yes, he was alone again. And in dark, alone times, his work became his lifeline. He forced himself to think like the lawyer he was.

He pressed his intercom button. His first priority must be to make sure Beske was convicted, and the only way he knew to help insure that conviction was to see that Claire was as preoccupied as possible in the days leading up to the trial.

He wouldn't allow himself to think about Claire, about what he was about to do to her. This was a task, a strategy.

"Eileen, please take a look at the cases coming up on the associates' calendars. Choose four or five of the more complicated ones, and make sure to pick at least two that are set for trial in the near future, okay?"

"Sure, Michael," she said, and even over the intercom Michael could sense her puzzlement. "I'll check, and make a list."

"Good." He spoke crisply, as if there was nothing on his mind but business. "Then, reassign every one of those cases to Claire Logan."

CHAPTER FOURTEEN

"TELL MICHAEL I've got to cancel again." Claire tossed the words over her shoulder at Eileen as she raced down the hall with her file, late for a meeting with a client.

For two weeks, her caseload had been staggering, worse than it had ever been before. In a way, that was good. She got to bed long past midnight these days, but her body was so exhausted that she was able to fall into a restless sleep.

She was coping, hanging on by her fingernails, but coping. She refused to bow under the pressure Michael had placed on her. All she had to do, she knew, was make one call to George Fanal's secretary, and her new caseload would disappear like magic. But she didn't make that call.

Her moods shifted these days, from sympathy toward Michael, to anger at what he was doing to her. But mostly, she ached, a dull, miserable pain that throbbed behind her eyelids and weighted her steps and took every last bit of color from her life until everything seemed faded and static and uninteresting. Even Lake Michigan, which she'd always loved to look at on her walks, seemed lifeless, the waves a flat slate-gray. She'd believed that beneath the hard, distant exterior Michael displayed to the world, was a caring, loyal man, capable of loving her as much as she loved him. Yes, she had gambled—risked her heart. Unstintingly, she'd offered Michael everything she had to give.

It was a gamble she'd lost. And even knowing she had done the right thing was small comfort.

She never saw Michael these days. For one thing, she always seemed to be in court. And Michael remained in his office, his door closed. He'd always made a point of leaving his door open. And he'd often been in the hallway or coffee area, anywhere the associates were likely to be talking shop, anywhere he could dole out his unique combination of advice and camaraderie.

Claire sighed and rubbed the bridge of her nose. She and Michael had had one tense, miserable case conference since their confrontation over Beske. After that, she'd canceled the others, saying she was too busy. It was the truth. And Michael must have been relieved, because he never pressed.

Back at her office, Claire dealt with her client. Then, as she did every time she had a spare moment, she pulled her notes on the Beske case toward her.

The case was going well. Almost too well, although she'd had a temporary setback when the judge would not throw out the evidence of the senator's breath test. But she still felt she would have a good chance with the jury, when the case went to trial. What was odd was how united everyone seemed to be on the subject of the senator's drinking.

She had found a witness, a bartender who had served coffee to Beske a half hour before he was picked up by the police. It didn't really prove anything, other than Beske had ordered coffee on that particular occasion. But the jury would want to hear the evidence and it went nicely with the theory she was building, that the senator had fallen asleep at the wheel.

She had interviewed everyone who worked in Beske's office. No one denied that he drank socially, but everyone denied that he was ever intoxicated.

"Ms. LOGAN, would you call the defense's next witness?"

"Ron Randall, Your Honor."

Claire stood as Randall was sworn in.

Over at the prosecution table, Rex Caspar frowned at his own witness list. Caspar had taken a strong interest in the case. He'd done a good job yesterday, managing to make Officer Kyle look like the more credible of the two officers. Kyle had assured the jury with calm professionalism that he believed Beske was intoxicated on the night the senator was picked up. Claire hadn't been able to shake his story.

Now she came around from the counsel table, standing where the jury could see her clearly, trying not to be conscious of the packed visitors' gallery. Yesterday, George Fanal had stopped in. Today, there was a contingent from the law school and several of her colleagues from the firm. Michael, of course, had not been among them.

Michael... For a moment, her heart gave a sad lurch. Michael... She would not think about Michael.

She focused on her witness. "Mr. Randall, where are you employed?"

"I own a little grill on the South Side, Randall's Ready Draft."

"Do you serve liquor in that establishment?"

"Well, yes, but it's a sort of neighborhood place, a pub kind of thing. Where people come in to talk and share news."

In other words, a bar, Claire thought. But Randall had explained things in a way that gave no negative connotations. "Do you know Senator Beske?" she asked, careful to use her client's title at every opportunity.

"Sure, he's a regular. He comes in for an hour or two most nights, has a burger and talks to folks about what's going on in his district."

"Does he ever drink alcohol?"

"One only. Never more than one. He has a vodka with tonic and lime, then just coffee."

"Objection." A bit late on the beat, Rex Caspar was on his feet. "What's the relevance of this testimony, Your Honor? There's no allegation the defendant was at the Ready Draft on the night he was picked up by the police."

The judge looked inquiringly at Claire.

"We're establishing a pattern of conduct, Your Honor."

"All right, then, overruled. You may continue, Ms. Logan."

Casper didn't try to hide his disgust. And really, Claire thought, it was amazing what she was getting away with, at this trial. The judge was clearly friendly toward her client, giving her wide latitude. And Claire was using that latitude. A good lawyer used everything available, she told herself.

There was only one problem, Claire thought as she asked her witness a few more questions, then sat back as the judge took care of some routine matters for the jury: Beske was guilty.

Over the last day, she'd become convinced of it. Trials were never this neat. People forgot things, got dates and times mixed up. But all of Beske's witnesses were so sure of everything. What and where he drank, and exactly how much. It was almost as if they had planned what to say.

Officer Kyle had been a compelling witness. Claire believed him and trusted his opinion.

And really, how likely was it that Beske—stone-cold sober—had put his car in a ditch on a dry road with a broad shoulder on a well-lit highway?

And then how likely was it that this supposedly stone-cold sober man had gone home and immediately had enough drinks to become intoxicated? Especially a man who allegedly was so careful to have only one vodka-and-tonic at a time.

There were those two prior convictions, which, thanks to Claire's skill with the rules of evidence, the jury would never know about.

And then, of course, there was Mary Jo...

"Ms. Logan, you may call your next witness."

Claire stood and prepared to do her job.

AT THE BREAK, the senator brought her a cup of coffee. "The trial's going so well, Claire." His bland face had taken on a little color; he was beaming at her. A gold cuff link at his wrist glinted as he handed her the disposable cup.

"Yes, it is, isn't it?" Claire should be happy about that, she knew. Mr. Fanal had called her at home last night, asking for a progress report. She was getting the attention of the partners. She'd learned a lot, working in Litigation, and her skill was apparent; her hard work had paid off. And she knew that real lawyers believed in the system and could represent clients they knew were guilty relatively easily.

Well, maybe she wasn't a "real" lawyer, because Senator Beske suddenly made her sick.

"I understand you were never charged with anything when Mary Jo Chalinski was killed," she said abruptly.

The smile on Beske's face vanished. "There was no reason to be charged. What happened was unfortunate, but it was an accident, pure and simple. My insurance took care of everything." He took a slow sip of coffee, the expression on his face regretful, distantly regretful, and as though he might actually believe what he'd just said.

"Your insurance didn't bring back a wife and mother, Senator. Did you know Mrs. Chalinski was pregnant when she was killed?"

Something flickered in his eyes; perhaps a genuine sadness, even guilt. It was gone very fast. "I didn't know at the time, of course, but I found out later." The senator took another careful sip from his cup. "What's your point, Ms. Logan?"

"If you don't see the point, Senator, then maybe this conversation doesn't have a point."

The door to the courtroom opened, and the bailiff stepped out. "The judge is retaking the bench. Break time's over, people."

Claire turned to go.

Unexpectedly, the senator gripped her arm, hard. "You're doing fine so far, Ms. Logan, and I look forward to our long association." His eyes narrowed. "Don't disappoint me."

Claire met his gaze. "I won't, Senator. That's just the damn sorry thing about this whole situation. I intend to do my best to make sure that jury comes back with a not-guilty verdict."

Russ Mallory, Michael's counterpart in the other half of Litigation, caught up with Michael as he was leaving the conference room. They'd both been part of a meeting about office procedures that had just broken up.

"You didn't have much to say at the meeting, Michael. How're you doing, anyway? Haven't seen much of you these past few days."

Come on, Michael thought. Did Russ need to ask how he was doing, with the Beske trial going on? But Russ was the last person Michael would ever share his feelings with. "Fine," he said shortly, heading for the elevators.

"Going back to your office, or home?" Russ persisted.

"Office."

"Me, too." The elevator doors opened, and Russ followed him on. Great. Michael stabbed at the button for their floor.

"You know, Claire is doing very well on the Beske trial."

Michael said nothing. He'd told Claire to have Russ supervise her just so he wouldn't have to hear exactly how well she was doing.

"Yep," Russ continued, fiddling with some change in his pocket. "You taught her well, pal. I understand she's great at DUI because you did a case together. She'll get her client off."

Michael shot a glance at the other man, wondering if he knew who Beske was. Claire wouldn't have told him, he was sure of that, but the gossip mill was probably in overdrive with the news. Russ was smirking.

"How Claire does on this trial is no business of mine."

"Oh, really." Russ feigned surprise. "Fanal has been stopping in to watch the trial. You know, I always thought our beautiful Miss Logan had a big mouth. I guess she still does, but she's a star. She'll be on the fast track to partner when she wins this case."

His hands clenched into fists, Michael watched the overhead lights, which signaled the floors as the elevator rose. They were nearing his floor, and escape.

Russ chuckled. "Wouldn't it just be a kick in the pants if Claire pulled off a partnership before either of us? She's getting noticed, man. She's getting noticed."

The elevator doors opened. Michael headed to his office without a backward glance. Mallory was taunting him; Michael knew that. But Russ had known where to hit, and the hit had been hard. He'd known Claire would do well with the case. He'd feared it enough to give her all that extra work. And if someday she got a partnership at the firm, that was her business. What Claire Logan did or did not do no longer concerned him. She had betrayed him.

But for this case—*this* case—to be the one that made Claire's career, for her to use this case—

Yes. A kick in the pants about summed up the way he felt.

EARLY THAT EVENING, Claire was in her office going over the case. Final arguments were scheduled in the morning, then the jury would deliberate. The senator's fate would probably be settled by noon.

She rubbed her eyes. She was exhausted. A lawyer had to be so cautious of every move she made, so conscious of how the jury would react.

Under normal circumstances, she'd be working strategy with Michael. She'd have a war story or two by now, a tale to tell of one of the quirkier things that had happened at the trial. For just a moment, she imagined herself stringing out that tale, going for drama, watching for that moment when Michael caught on, and his eyes lit with appreciation . . .

But that part of her life was over.

She didn't even know if anyone had told him how the trial was progressing. Did he want to know? A clip from her direct examination of the senator had been on the ten o'clock news last night. Had Michael been watching? Or had he switched off his TV, folded his newspaper carefully, to conceal the pages containing the legal news, and gone to bed early?

Her intercom buzzed. Wearily, Claire pushed the button.

"Angela Chalinski is on line two," her secretary said.

"For me? Where's Michael? He must be around here somewhere." It wasn't that late, she knew, not considering the hours Michael kept.

"I didn't check. Angela specifically asked for you, Claire."

Claire hesitated. It hurt to know she wouldn't see the girl anymore. But she planned to honor Michael's wish that she keep her distance. It was the least she could do.

"She sounded upset," her secretary said.

That decided the issue for Claire. "I'll take the call."

"Claire?" Angela's voice was breathless.

"I'm here, Angela. Is everything all right?"

"Well, sort of. I mean, not really. I mean, I knew what to expect, but—" Her voice faltered. "It's just that I didn't think it would hurt, and it does. Is that right, Claire? Is it supposed to hurt?"

Claire was alarmed, although she had no idea what on earth Angela was talking about. "Is what supposed to hurt, honey?"

"My . . . period. I got my period." Distress was evident in the girl's voice. "I got home from school, and everything was fine, then I noticed I got my period."

"Your first?" Claire asked quietly. Surely Michael must have anticipated this, and prepared for it.

"Yes. And now I have these really weird cramps."

"That's normal, Angela." Claire tried to sound matter-of-fact and reassuring. "Do you have sanitary napkins?"

"I've got all that, I just . . . I didn't know who to call, then I thought of you. I know it's dumb, but I'm really sort of scared."

"We should probably find your dad—"

"No!" Angela cut in. "I'd be so embarrassed."

Claire made a quick decision. "I'll be right there."

"You don't have to come." But Angela managed to make the words sound like a plea.

Michael lived relatively close to the Loop; in a few minutes Claire was knocking on the door of his condominium. Angela must have been waiting right by the door because she let Claire in immediately.

"Is everything okay? Are you feeling a little better?" Claire asked quietly as she took off her coat.

"Yeah, I checked everything about five times, and it seems okay. It was dumb of me to call you."

Impulsively, Claire put an arm around the girl's shoulders. "It wasn't dumb at all. This is very private and very important, and every woman needs another woman to talk to sometimes."

Angela smiled gratefully.

Claire handed her the paper sack she carried. "I know you said you had some pads, but I brought my brand, in case yours aren't comfortable."

Angela looked in the bag and gave an embarrassed sigh. "Oh, I've got those kind, and everything else. Come look."

She led Claire down the hall. The linen-closet door was open, and Claire's jaw dropped. The closet looked like the feminine-hygiene aisle in the supermarket. Two shelves were crammed with every brand of sanitary napkin and tampon available. Sitting next to the packages were three books, and two videos— *You're a Woman Now,* and *Facts about Menstruation for Preteens.*

Angela was standing beside her. "Dad got all this a year ago. I think he didn't know what kind of stuff to buy, or something. And he made me watch those ugly video-tapes, and he said if I had any questions, I should ask him." She giggled again, nervously. "But his face was all red, and he was so stiff, so how could I ever ask him anything about it? It'd be so embarrassing, I'd want to die."

Claire imagined Michael in a store, buying a hundred dollars' worth of paraphernalia, then coming home and dutifully promising to answer his daughter's questions. But she had to give the man points for effort. And for caring.

"And I figured *Busia* would have forgotten how it felt by now."

"Well, I doubt she's forgotten, Angela, but it was fine that you called me. Now, do you want to have something to drink, maybe, and talk a while?"

"Sure." Sounding much more confident now, Angela led the way down the hall. "I've got coffee. Dad didn't drink the whole pot this morning, and I could reheat it in the microwave."

"Sounds yummy," Claire said dryly.

Angela carefully poured the leftover coffee into a mug and set it in the microwave to heat. "Was it really okay to call you, Claire? You haven't been around."

"I'm glad you thought of me." A wave of loneliness swept over Claire. "I wanted to see you, but your father and I—well, things just didn't work out between us."

Angela's back was to her. "Yeah," she said finally. "Those are about the exact words Dad used, too. And he said that you wouldn't be coming over anymore, but that it wasn't my fault."

"It isn't. Believe me, if I could have, I would have called—" She stopped, not wanting to blame Michael and hurt his relationship with his daughter.

Angela set a steaming mug in front of Claire. "It's all right. Dad said he'd asked you not to call me or anything. But, I still hoped you'd come around, sometimes."

"Oh, Angela, I'm sorry." Claire reached out and gave the girl's hand a squeeze.

"I know." She went to the refrigerator and poured herself a glass of diet cola. "But it's really hard to know what the right thing is, and then to do it."

Michael's daughter sounded so grown-up. Claire realized she had gone beyond mere friendship with Angela—she loved the girl. And her loss of Michael was thereby doubled.

Angela sat down next to her, and sipped her cola. "I decided to do the right thing, myself. I turned in the names, you know, at school. I told the headmaster who cheated."

"Really? I'm glad."

"I thought their parents should know, because they weren't studying or learning anything, and Dad said it meant they weren't really getting an education. And I kind of wanted to tell, and then forget it ever happened. Actually, there's this girl, Rachel Kellermann, who's going to a new school, and Dad says we should maybe check it out." She sighed. "Since I told, I've been feeling kind of alone. Sabrina isn't my friend anymore."

"She couldn't have really been your friend," Claire said gently.

"Yeah, but it still hurts, you know?"

Claire knew. She laid her hand over Angela's and they sat together in silence.

And that was how Michael found them when he opened the door to the kitchen a few moments later. He hadn't seen Claire in nearly two weeks. He couldn't bear to look at her and remember all the things they had shared. Now her head was bent, her glistening ponytail half-undone, strands of her hair almost mingling with Angela's blond curls. Her hand was covering his daughter's. Seeing her there, in his kitchen, knowing she'd been at the Beske trial all day—

"Michael." She looked up, her face going pale. "I didn't hear you come in."

He didn't seem able to move. "What are you doing here, Claire?" He steeled his heart against her obvious distress.

"I thought I'd stop over and see Angela." She rose quickly. "But I'll be going now." She took a step toward him. "Excuse me, Michael. You're blocking the door-way."

"You just decided to stop over and see Angela?" He couldn't believe even Claire would do such a thing. His voice rose. "After I specifically asked you not to—"

"Dad, please."

He glanced at his daughter; there were tears in her eyes. "I'll walk you to the elevator, Claire. There are some things I need to say to you in private. Things you obviously didn't understand the first time."

"Wait, Dad. Wait!" Now Angela stood, too.

Damn Claire for creating a scene in front of his daughter.

He made sure his voice was soft. "Angela, this is between Claire and me."

"You don't understand." She was still standing by the table, and there was a deep blush on her cheeks. "Look, I got my—" She looked away, then said, "I got my period today, and I didn't know who to call, and I was scared, and Claire said it was okay to want to talk to another woman about it, and I didn't want anybody but Claire—"

"Oh, Angel." All the anger seeped out of him, and with the passing of that anger, he seemed to find his legs again. He went to his daughter, and put his arm around her shoulders. "Why didn't you tell me, Claire?"

"I thought she deserved some privacy," Claire said simply.

He smoothed a strand of his daughter's hair. "You could have called me, Angel. I would have come home, no matter what."

"I know that." She gave a little sniff, half embarrassed, half disdainful. "But you can't do it all, Dad. You're a guy, and everything."

He sighed. "That's true," he said softly. Then he turned to Claire. "Come on, I'll walk you out." He held her coat for her and as she shrugged into the sleeves, he caught the scent of her. Maybe more than anything else, that scent reminded him of all he'd lost, the citrus-and-flowers perfume sending commingled regret and longing flowing through him.

In the hallway, they waited for the elevator in silence. Finally, Michael spoke. "Thank you for being there for Angela."

"That's all right. I love Angela, you know."

He cleared his throat. It felt suddenly so thick and tight. "I thought you might."

"And I love you, too, Michael. Even after you dumped all those cases on me."

He rubbed the back of his neck. "God, I'm so sorry about those cases. I just—hurt so bad." She nodded and he wanted more than anything to take her in his arms and soothe away the pain he saw her trying to hide. But he couldn't. She had chosen Beske and her career over him.

He'd thought things over since his angry words of three weeks ago. "Look, I can understand—" He broke off and shut his eyes briefly, unable to bear the flare of hope in hers, then opened them and said, "You're doing what you thought you had to do. A part of me will always admire you. But I can't accept your choices."

The elevator came, the doors opening with a whoosh. The doors closed again a moment later, when nobody got on.

The hope he'd seen in her expression died. Michael suddenly felt infinitely weary. He had been angry for so long. He was tired of always being angry. "We can't fix this, Claire, no matter how hard we try. I owe something to Mary Jo, and to every mother or child who might be in the path of your client."

She touched his arm, lightly. "The senator is guilty. I believe that. And if it's any consolation, I hope he's convicted."

He nodded. "Thank you for that."

Claire pushed the elevator button, and the doors opened. She got on. "Well, Michael," she said quietly, "I'll say goodbye, then."

The doors closed, and she was gone, just like that. He was momentarily amazed that it was over, their last personal conversation. Subconsciously, he guessed he'd expected her to keep pushing, insisting that he talk, argue her point of view, because that was Claire. Her quiet, pain-filled acceptance seemed out of character. And maybe because it was so unlike her, it also seemed so very final.

But that was the way he wanted it, he told himself, wondering why he suddenly had the urge to put his fist through the wall.

CHAPTER FIFTEEN

IT HAD BEEN one of the worst days of Michael's life. After being tormented by Mallory, Michael had spent hours thinking about the trial and imagining Claire furthering her career by helping his old enemy go free. And then he'd come home to find Claire in his kitchen, holding his daughter's hand, as if she belonged there. He tossed in bed later that night, trying without success to get to sleep.

He rolled over and turned his pillow, so the cool side was against his cheek.

His bedside telephone rang. "Yes?" he said into the receiver.

"Mr. Chalinski?"

"Yes."

"My name is Deborah Stern. I work for Senator Beske."

Abruptly, Michael sat up. His stomach clenched. The caller didn't speak again, and for a dreadful moment, Michael was afraid she was going to hang up. "Ms. Stern, how can I help you?"

She hesitated. Then she said, "I'm the witness you've been looking for. I know something about your wife's death."

For a moment, the whole word seemed to tilt. His throat closed. He fought to push the words out. "What do you know about my wife's death?"

"I know the senator was drinking on the day she died." Her voice dropped even lower. "You see, I was there. In the car with Senator Beske."

Michael could not speak.

"Now, with this trial going on . . . I need to talk to you. Can I come over?"

Michael finally found his voice. He gave his address and added, "Come now. Please, come now."

HE OPENED the door a half hour later to find a tall, striking blonde standing before him. "Come in, Ms. Stern," he invited, trying to sound low-key. His heart was hammering in his chest. He took her coat, and offered coffee, which she declined.

"I'd just spill it," she said with a nervous attempt at a laugh.

Michael led her to a chair in the living room. He took the sofa across from her, and leaned forward only slightly, feigning a pose of professional interest. He was screaming inside with a million questions, but he'd had enough courtroom training to know when a witness was about to bolt. "So," he started, "you work for Senator Beske."

"Yes, I have for four years." She waited until he nodded, then continued, "What you've got to know is, the senator is real good to me. I'm his assistant. Basically, I keep his life on track, and I have great organizational skills. If the senator is re-elected, he'll take me as his aide." She paused and took a deep breath before adding, "Everybody thinks we sleep together. But we don't."

Michael nodded again. "That must make things difficult for you." Come on, he thought. What do you know about Mary Jo?

"People talk, you know? And I've got a few political ambitions of my own." She studied her clasped hands for a moment, then looked around the room, looked everywhere but at him.

Michael waited, resisting the urge to fill the uncomfortable silence.

Finally, she spoke, "As I told you, when your wife was killed, I was in the car with the senator."

Michael leaned forward, his pose forgotten, his whole being focused on the woman sitting in front of him.

"Yes, I know you didn't realize there was somebody with him. No one did." She met his eyes for a split second, then stared at the wall of bookshelves to his right. "I knew he was drunk and shouldn't have been driving. But the senator can get...insistent about things when he's had a few." She licked her lips. "Anyway, after the accident...I didn't know what to do for your wife, Mr. Chalinski." Her words slowed. "I could tell she was in...bad shape. Believe me, if there was something I could have done..." Deborah took a ragged breath, her eyes still fixed on the books.

Her words brought everything back to Michael; the telephone call that had got him out of a court hearing, the short, shell-shocked ride to the hospital, Mary Jo, hooked onto every machine imaginable, Michael holding her hand, even as he'd lost her...then having to tell Angela her mother was never coming home. "Go on," he whispered, his voice low and hoarse.

"I'm the one who called 9-1-1, from a pay phone, anonymously so no one would ever know it was me. Then...I couldn't go back to the scene of the accident." Tears flowed down her cheeks. "It was the middle of the day, and we weren't at the staff meeting where we were supposed to be. We'd taken a long lunch—too long, and I knew how it would look. The senator's married, Mr. Chalinski. So, after I called for rescue, I took a bus home.

I was just . . . so scared, and all I could think about was getting away from there."

She finally turned to look at him. "And for more than a year and a half, I've seen your advertisement in the *Tribune,* looking for witnesses to the accident. I try not to look at that part of the paper, but somehow it seems like I have to." Her voice caught on a sob, then gained strength. "I can't put this behind me, get on with my life, because that . . . damn . . . ad keeps running, and it won't let me forget that Mary Jo Chalinski had a husband and a child who miss her."

Abruptly, Michael stood. He couldn't sit still any longer. Going to the large window, he looked out. When he felt he had command of his emotions, he said, "So, are you ready to go to the police with your story?"

"Yes." Her voice was resigned.

He couldn't help asking. "Why now, after almost two years?"

"Because he's on trial again. I can never get any peace, with his trial going on now."

So, Claire's trial had finally brought forward the witness he'd been waiting for all this time. How ironic. God, how very ironic that was.

"I can't get it off my mind because I know something about this trial, too."

Michael whirled from the window.

"I was there, before he put his car in the ditch that night."

"In the car?" He was incredulous.

"No, of course not in the car. But I was with him for several hours before, and he was definitely drinking. I work for him, remember? I'm like his right hand. The night the senator landed in the ditch, we'd had a rough legislative session. I was in the office late, looking things up for his speech in the morning. A few of the senator's constituents stopped in, and they had liquor. I poured some of it.'' Deborah paused. ''You know, I really think I could use that coffee, after all, Mr. Chalinski.''

''Sure.'' Michael left her sitting in the living room. His thoughts were racing. At last he had an eyewitness to Mary Jo's accident. Surely this would be enough to get Beske prosecuted—even after all this time.

Automatically, Michael poured coffee into the filter, set the filter in the coffee machine and plugged it in. An idea began to form. Maybe he didn't need to wait for justice. There was a trial going on. Even if a conviction for drunk driving didn't land Beske the lengthy jail sentence a vehicular homicide would, there was a perfect opportunity to help in his conviction. Deborah Stern could testify that Beske had been drinking on the night in question, the night he'd put his car in a ditch.

How would Claire feel about a surprise witness?

Michael was suddenly aware of how much he'd changed. His only goal for almost two years had been bringing the senator to justice. Nothing was allowed to stand in the way of that goal, not even his personal happiness. Yet, tonight he was thinking of Claire, about how this witness would affect her.

She had said she hoped Beske would be convicted, and she had meant it, he knew. Claire said a lot of things, but she never said anything she didn't mean.

Michael went to the Rolodex that stood by the telephone.

Claire wanted a conviction. But George Fanal wanted to win. George would be furious when he found out Michael was handing a star witness to the prosecution, but Michael didn't intend to hide that fact. And certainly, what he was about to do would end forever his opportunity to make partner at Haynes, Haynes, Collingwood and Crofts. The partnership offer was due in less than a month, and when it came, he would be set for life.

Michael didn't hesitate. As he dialed Rex Caspar's number, he felt nothing but relief.

THAT RELIEF STAYED with Michael after Deborah Stern had talked to Rex Caspar and gone home.

Hours later, he sat on the sofa in his darkened living room, his stocking feet propped on the coffee table, his fingers wrapped around a full mug of cold coffee. He gazed out through the window, beyond his snow-dusted balcony, out over the glittering lights of Chicago. It was a three-quarter-million-dollar view, and once, he'd thought having it was the epitome of success.

Now he knew he had to make one more telephone call in the morning. He'd talk to Chester Marlowe and accept the post of head of the law school trial clinic. Michael realized he was looking forward to the university job more than he had looked forward to anything in a very long time. Deciding to leave the firm had brought . . . relief.

Was relief all he was supposed to feel tonight?

He'd always expected to experience a sense of euphoria when he finally fulfilled his promise to Mary Jo. The lifting of his ever-present frustration felt good, as did the thought that he was back in full control of his life again. He was relieved.

But where was the excitement, the high, the exhilaration?

He'd felt those things before, he realized, and not so very long ago. He'd felt the excitement when he was arguing cases with Claire in his office, and when store windows seemed filled with glowing color, just because he was with her . . .

He'd felt the exhilaration when . . . she said she loved him.

And he loved Claire in return, completely and utterly, from the bottom of his soul. He respected her strength and courage and honesty.

He wasn't the same person he'd been two years ago.

For a moment, his thoughts were still as he sent a silent message of gratitude and goodbye to Mary Jo. His old life was over, and Michael felt complete acceptance. He didn't want his old life anymore.

He wanted Claire, for the rest of his life.

"WHAT DO YOU THINK the outcome will be, Claire?"

It was at least the fourth time Senator Beske had asked her a variation on the same question. The jury had been deliberating for over four hours, an extraordinarily long time for a simple DUI case. Conventional wisdom held that the longer a jury was out, the more likely it was that the defendant would go free. Claire was scared to death at the thought she might win the case.

Things had been going very well for the defense until the prosecution had managed to persuade the judge to allow a surprise witness. Deborah Stern had been good, her story delivered in a highly emotional but sincere way. Now it was simply a question of whether the jury found her and Officer Kyle the more credible of the witnesses.

"Come on, Claire, tell me. What do you think?"

I think the jury should find you guilty, Senator. I think, at the very least, you should give me the pleasure of a few minutes minus your company.

"What I think," Claire said, "is that it's all up to the jury now, so you should have another cup of coffee."

"I guess you're right." With that, Senator Beske got up and went to the small concession stand set up in the open area by the stairs. Claire watched as he greeted a couple of the courthouse personnel as if they were old friends, then she leaned back and closed her eyes. Waiting was grueling, even without her client's hovering. The prosecutor had long since gone upstairs to his office, leaving instructions with the bailiff to call him when the jury came back with a verdict.

Claire wished she had the same luxury, but protocol dictated that she wait with her client.

"Hello," a voice said softly.

Claire's eyes flew open. Michael! He stood before her, dressed in jeans and a sweatshirt.

"Michael." She scrambled to her feet. "What are you doing here? And...dressed like that? How come you're not at work?"

He shrugged, smiling. Smiling—as if the Beske trial was not about to be decided. "I had some calls to make. First, a job offer to accept. Then, I was planning a special dinner for two, and I had to line up a caterer, roses, champagne, that sort of thing."

Claire shook her head to clear it. What he'd just said made no sense. And his smile wasn't just pleasant, it was downright incandescent.

"But," he continued, "I couldn't wait." His smile faded; his eyes grew serious. "I've waited so long, you see. And I had this thought that you might appreciate what I had to say more if I got to you before the jury came back with a verdict." He took her hand. "Walk with me?"

Momentarily speechless, she nodded. Michael held her hand close to his side as they went down the marble steps to the floor below, and then down one of the lesser-used hallways of the courthouse. The sun, streaming through a stained-glass window depicting the scales of justice, cast jewel tones on the hallway floor. Their footsteps echoed; they were alone.

He stopped her in a pool of pink light. He took her other hand, and held them both in his, facing her. "I love you, Claire," he said simply.

She replied just as simply. "I love you."

The warm light played over his features, highlighting his cheekbones.

"I'd be lying if I said I didn't care what the verdict is," he continued. "But for us, it doesn't matter. Because I love you, whether Beske goes to jail or remains free. I love you unconditionally. And, I'll love you for life, because for me, you're the perfect woman, beautiful, smart and strong, with the courage to follow your own path."

"Oh, Michael," she whispered, going into his arms as shifting patterns of rose and purple light played over their bodies.

He cupped her cheeks, looking into her eyes. "Do you want me to propose now, or wait for those flowers and champagne?"

"Now." Her voice rose with certainty. "Now, Michael. Right now. Immediately."

He chuckled. "I get it, Claire. So, will you marry me?"

"Yes. Definitely, yes."

He sighed in pleasure, and started to hug her even tighter, then loosened his grip as they heard footsteps. It was the judge's bailiff, and he was puffing with exertion. "Ms. Logan, we need you upstairs. The jury's back."

Michael put his arm around her as they went up the stairs. When she met Beske just outside the courtroom, the senator did a double take as he recognized Michael. Michael just stared back, a long, steady look that finally caused the senator to drop his eyes.

Senator Beske was uncharacteristically silent as he and Claire took their places at the defense table. Over at the prosecution table, Rex Caspar nervously straightened his tie.

"All rise."

Automatically, Claire rose with the rest as the judge took his place. He directed everyone but the defendant to be seated. Claire remained standing next to her client. As the judge went through the ritual of taking the slip of paper from the bailiff, and asking the foreman whether the jury had reached a verdict, Claire tried to focus on the faces of the individual jurors. Michael always contended you could tell a lot from the expressions of the jurors in those moments before the foreman read the verdict.

But she was conscious only of Michael, in the back of the courtroom, conscious only of his unconditional acceptance and love.

Now the foreman was reading the verdict. "On count one of the indictment, we the jury find the defendant guilty as charged."

Noise erupted. The judge banged his gavel. Next to her, Beske cursed and muttered something about wanting an immediate appeal.

And Claire had never been happier in all her life as, without a word, she headed through the wooden gate separating the courtroom from the visitors' gallery, and straight into Michael's waiting arms.

EPILOGUE

"YOU KNOW, you've turned into a beautiful girl." Claire's eyes felt moist at the praise from her father. They waited in the vestibule of Saint Stephen's. Outside, a light spring rain was falling in the cool night air.

Inside Claire's mother had already been seated, and the first solo had been sung. The air was mellow with the smell of incense and candle wax and flowers.

Sophie and Claire's mother had helped plan the wedding, down to the last, traditional detail. Once her mother had got over the disappointment of Claire's announcement that she wanted to be married in Chicago, she had joined in the planning with gusto. She had even used Claire's tiny oven to make the wedding cake, a confection of frosting ruffles, complete with spun-sugar bells, that Angela had declared awesome.

Angela had enjoyed picking out her maid-of-honor gown, a lavender sheath that was slightly off the shoulder, and having her hair professionally styled into a French twist. She was radiantly pretty, and looked grown-up and happy. She'd transferred from Baldwin in late winter, and now Rachel Kellerman was as close a friend as Sabrina had once been. It was a friendship of equals, one where Angela could be herself. Jenny Franklin had been over a couple of times recently, too. The prosecutor had decided not to charge Cal Franklin with abuse. In the end, Jenny's father had been almost relieved that social services had intervened, and was willing to enter therapy. Claire was pleased that things seemed to be working out for Jenny.

Taking a chance on being seen by the wedding guests, Claire left her father to go to the doorway of the sanctuary.

Sophie sat in one of the front pews. She and Mike had moved into their new home and had made friends in the neighborhood. They seemed content. Claire smiled as she looked at Mike who was decked out in a tuxedo for the occasion, his wheelchair tied with lavender streamers. He would probably never walk again, but Claire knew that when the ceremony was over, his baritone voice would boom with congratulations.

Also on the groom's side were all sorts of young faces. Michael's students. And on her side were Amanda Richmond and Stuart Tyler, and all the associates from Litigation. Even George Fanal and his wife had come, the latter resplendent in a haute-couture dinner suit.

Claire smiled. Mr. Fanal was getting used to her style at work. Though disappointed with the loss of the Beske case, he'd watched enough of the trial to be impressed with her performance, and he'd told her so. She might even make partner in a few years. And when she did, the firm was going to put more emphasis on family and a lot less on killer hours and billing percentages.

On cue, Michael came out a side door, standing to the side of the altar. It was hard to tell his expression from this far away, but he stood straight and tall and gorgeous in his black-and-white tuxedo.

Next to him was his best man, Nick Persecki. John had probably wanted to do the honors, but Michael and Nick had become close in recent months. The transformation in Nick was amazing. His slouch was gone, and he stood almost as straight as Michael.

The music changed; it was Angela's cue.

"Go for it," Claire whispered, as, smiling nervously, Angela stepped into the aisle.

Claire went back to her father, who handed her her bouquet. As she reached out to take it, the large, square-cut ruby of her engagement ring caught the light.

"Ready?" her father asked, tucking her arm in his.

Claire nodded.

He sighed, looking down at her. "I mean it about your being beautiful. But, really, that gown—you've always been headstrong, I guess. I never could change your mind about anything, even all those years ago, and God knows I tried. I guess I should be grateful you're finally getting married."

"I would never change my mind about wearing this." Her dress was the one detail of her wedding she had chosen without advice from anyone, and she loved it. And some things about her father she simply had to accept, she realized. There was no way she would allow him to dim her happiness this day.

"And you're sure Michael will like it?" her father asked.

"I'm sure," she said, and she was. She had been sure ever since the night Michael had slipped that ruby on her finger and kissed her, and whispered, "No cool, insipid diamond for my bride."

The trumpeter had joined the organist. It was Claire's cue. She smiled, stepped into the aisle, and the lights came up more brightly.

The congregation stood, turned . . .

And gasped . . .

Because from the tip of her scooped neckline to the V of fabric at her wrists, to the end of the six-foot train of her traditionally cut gown, the bride wore purple.

Claire looked only at Michael. His smile of appreciation and love was dazzling.

The collection of the year!
NEW YORK TIMES BESTSELLING AUTHORS

Linda Lael Miller
Wild About Harry

Janet Dailey
Sweet Promise

Elizabeth Lowell
Reckless Love

Penny Jordan
Love's Choices

and featuring
Nora Roberts
The Calhoun Women

This special trade-size edition features four of the wildly popular titles in the Calhoun miniseries together in one volume—a true collector's item!

Pick up these great authors and a chance to win a weekend for two in New York City at the Marriott Marquis Hotel on Broadway! We'll pay for your flight, your hotel—even a Broadway show!

Available in December at your favorite retail outlet.

NEW YORK
Marriott®
MARQUIS

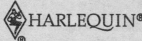

HARLEQUIN®

Silhouette®

NYT1296-R

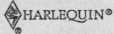

HARLEQUIN ®

Scandals

A passionate story of romance, where bold, daring characters set out to defy their world of propriety and strict social codes.

"*Scandals*—a story that will make your heart race and your pulse pound. Spectacular!"   —Suzanne Forster

"Devon is daring, dangerous and altogether delicious."
                                                        —Amanda Quick

Don't miss this wonderful full-length novel from Regency favorite Georgina Devon.

Available in December, wherever Harlequin books are sold.

Merry Christmas, Baby!

A romantic collection filled with the magic
of Christmas and the joy of children.

SUSAN WIGGS, Karen Young and
Bobby Hutchinson bring you Christmas wishes,
weddings and romance, in a charming
trio of stories that will warm up your
holiday season.

MERRY CHRISTMAS, BABY! also contains
Harlequin's special gift to you—a set of
FREE GIFT TAGS included in every book.

Brighten up your holiday season with
MERRY CHRISTMAS, BABY!

Available in November at
your favorite retail store.

HARLEQUIN ®